"Isn't that the letter *U*?" Finn asked. Maybe he was just fooling himself, because he'd been talking about letters on a Pez.

Emma hopped over the lever to Finn's side. She dumped more baking soda beside Finn's area, and swiped her own paintbrush across that zone.

The letters *S* and *E* appeared beside the *U*.

"Use," Finn read. "It's the word 'use.'"

Emma threw her arms around Finn's shoulders.

"Finn! You're amazing! Thank you for making us check for fingerprints! You've found another code!"

ALSO BY
MARGARET PETERSON HADDIX

REMARKABLES

THE GREYSTONE SECRETS SERIES
THE STRANGERS

GREYSTONE SECRETS

THE DECEIVERS

MARGARET
PETERSON HADDIX

ART BY ANNE LAMBELET

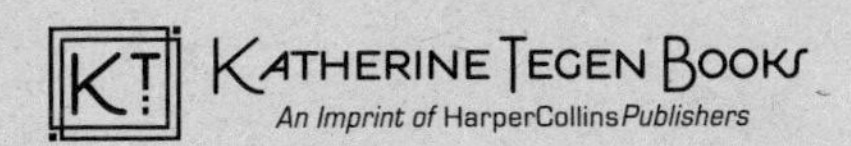

Katherine Tegen Books is an imprint of HarperCollins Publishers.

Greystone Secrets #2: The Deceivers

For information address HarperCollins Children's Books, a division of HarperCollins Publishers, 195 Broadway, New York, NY 10007.
www.harpercollinschildrens.com

Library of Congress Cataloging-in-Publication Data

Names: Haddix, Margaret Peterson, author.
Title: The deceivers / Margaret Peterson Haddix.
Description: First edition. | New York: Katherine Tegen Books, an imprint of HarperCollins Publishers, [2020] | Series: Greystone secrets ; #2 | Audience: Ages 8–12. | Audience: Grades 4–6. | Summary: Told from separate viewpoints, as Finn, Emma, and Chess Greystone and Natalie Mayhew, ages eight to thirteen, continue their quest to rescue their mothers they must return to the alternate dimension where truth is illegal.
Identifiers: LCCN 2019026615 | ISBN 9780062838414 (pbk.)
Subjects: CYAC: Missing persons—Fiction. | Brothers and sisters—Fiction. | Family life—Fiction. | Honesty—Fiction. | Supernatural—Fiction.
Classification: LCCPZ7.H1164 Dec 2020 | DDC [Fic]—dc23
LC record available at https://lccn.loc.gov/2019026615

Typography by Aurora Parlagreco
21 22 23 24 25 PC/BRR 10 9 8 7 6 5 4 3 2 1

First paperback edition, 2021

For truth seekers everywhere

PART ONE

ONE

FINN

Every day after school now, Finn Greystone played pitch-and-catch with another kid's dad.

Ever since he'd been old enough to pick up a baseball, Finn had loved the game. He loved the arc of the white ball against the blue sky and the thud of the ball in his glove. Now he also loved the way Natalie Mayhew's father called out, "What an arm for an eight-year-old!" even when the ball wobbled overhead and dropped down in the wrong place, out of reach.

The truth was, Finn loved most games.

But ever since his mother had disappeared two weeks

ago, everything had a double meaning. Pitch-and-catch wasn't just a game anymore.

It was Finn's job.

Finn was supposed to keep Mr. Mayhew busy. Or "distracted and unsuspecting," as Finn's sister, Emma, put it when they were divvying up assignments.

"You're the only one who can still act happy," Finn's brother, Chess, had said. Chess had a knack for making Finn feel better about what he could and couldn't do. Emma, at ten, was probably a genius, and she was the best at solving codes. Chess, at twelve, remembered the most about what had happened when they were all really little and their father was still alive—it was like Chess had a brain full of clues. And then there was thirteen-year-old Natalie, Mr. Mayhew's daughter, who wasn't related to Finn but had forced her father to take in the three Greystone kids when they had nowhere else to go. She was really good with computers and cell phones and, well, secrets. She was the best at keeping secrets.

But Chess made it sound like Finn being happy was the best skill of all.

The funny thing was, Mr. Mayhew probably thought *he* was distracting *Finn*. Mr. Mayhew didn't want any of the Greystone kids thinking too much about the fact that their mother was still missing, or that their backyard had blown up, or that the police couldn't find Natalie's mother, either.

And Mr. Mayhew didn't even know the half of what had really happened. He didn't know anything about the secret code the kids still needed to solve to get their mothers back. He didn't know that every afternoon while Finn played pitch-and-catch with Mr. Mayhew, the other kids were scrambling to find a way back into another world, a place of both known and unknown dangers.

At least Finn had gotten the big kids to promise that they wouldn't go back without him.

"Don't tell Natalie," Mr. Mayhew said as he released another pitch into the air, aimed for Finn's glove. "But this is exactly how I pictured being a dad before she was born. Playing games, carrying her around on my shoulders . . . All the stuff she's too old for now—or *says* she's too old for. I didn't even think about how being a dad also meant changing diapers and cleaning up vomit and wiping up pureed spinach, which, I'll tell you, I always thought was the nastiest of all the baby foods . . ."

Natalie was the prettiest girl Finn had ever seen. She had long dark hair that rippled down her back, and when Finn's class had read a story in school about an elegant queen, and Finn's friend Tyrell had poked him in the side and whispered, "What's 'elegant' mean?" Finn had whispered back, "You know. Like Natalie."

And Natalie was strong and tough and fierce, and she could type out a whole text message with her thumbs without even looking at her phone once, and she could do it faster than Finn could think. And when she wanted something, all she had to do was tilt her head to the side and raise one eyebrow, and her dad would say, "Oh, you're right! We *should* order pizza for dinner tonight!" Or whatever she was asking for.

Natalie was *powerful.* That was an even better word for her than "elegant."

So, yeah, Natalie probably would not want to hear that her dad was talking about changing her diapers and cleaning up her vomit when she was little.

The ball hit Finn's glove a little too high and rolled off the top. Finn had to dart over and scoop it up before it rolled down into the pond that lay in the middle of the park.

"You'd think it'd be a good thing, being the fun dad," Mr. Mayhew said while Finn jogged back into position. "You'd think that's what people would want."

A shadow crossed Mr. Mayhew's face, which was really tan from all the time he spent out on the golf course, selling people fancy sports cars. Finn had known Mr. Mayhew for only two weeks, and he still didn't understand what playing golf had to do with selling cars. But it seemed to work for Mr. Mayhew.

Finn did understand the shadow on Mr. Mayhew's

face, and the way Mr. Mayhew's shoulders slumped when he thought Finn wasn't looking. It meant Mr. Mayhew was going to start talking about Natalie's mother, Ms. Morales. Mr. Mayhew and Ms. Morales weren't married anymore, but it still seemed like he missed her a lot.

Or maybe he just missed arguing with her.

"Don't you think kids and parents should have fun together?" Mr. Mayhew asked. He clapped his hand over his mouth, as if he'd just remembered he was talking to Finn, whose mother was missing and whose father was dead. "I mean, kids and *grown-ups* should have fun together. Like we are now. You and me. Life should be fun."

Sometimes Finn wanted to hold up a scorecard for Mr. Mayhew, as if Mr. Mayhew were an Olympic athlete, and Finn could grade him on his recovery from saying the wrong thing. This was one of his better efforts.

It really wasn't Mr. Mayhew's fault that there were so many wrong things people could say to Finn, Emma, Chess, and Natalie right now.

"This is fun," Finn said, tossing the ball back to Mr. Mayhew. He felt the little twang of his arm muscles; he watched the ball soar through the sky. He forced himself to smile, and it almost felt real. For just that moment, he let himself forget that Emma, Chess, and Natalie hadn't made any progress at all figuring out how to rescue their mothers. For all the closer they'd gotten to finding a way back to the dangerous world—and finding their mothers—they might as well have spent every afternoon of the past two weeks doing nothing but playing pitch-and-catch alongside Finn and Mr. Mayhew.

"Now, that's what I'm talking about!" Mr. Mayhew said, which was an expression Mr. Mayhew used a lot. He smiled back at Finn, and with his light brown hair and his tan skin and his white teeth, he looked like someone in a toothpaste commercial.

Maybe Mr. Mayhew's smile was just as fake as Finn's. Finn glanced past Mr. Mayhew, and past the fence that separated the trees and grass and paved trails of the park from the trees and grass and paved trails of Mr. Mayhew's huge backyard. Finn gazed straight up, to the blinds covering the windows of Natalie's second-story bedroom in Mr. Mayhew's house. Finn had a deal with the other kids: They left the blinds down when they wanted to tell Finn, *Keep playing. We need Mr. Mayhew to stay away longer.* When they were ready to give up for the afternoon, they pulled the blinds all the way up.

Finn had to shade his eyes with his hand, because staring back at Mr. Mayhew's house also meant staring toward the sun. So for a moment, Finn couldn't quite believe what he was seeing.

The blinds were still down, but they weren't flat and motionless like they'd been most of the afternoon, and most of every afternoon, every day for the past two weeks. Instead, the blinds were flashing back and forth—open, shut, open, shut—in a way that made Finn think of butterflies flapping their wings. Or dozens of butterflies flapping their wings all at once, in unison.

This was a third code, one that Finn had seen only once before, when they were practicing.

This code meant, *Come back immediately! We found something!*

TWO

EMMA, MOMENTS EARLIER

The cop had rung the doorbell, stepped back, and then stood perfectly still, like a statue dropped from the sky onto Mr. Mayhew's doorstep. Emma let out a deep sigh as she watched through Mr. Mayhew's security system—which she'd called up on her laptop the instant she heard a car outside.

"Police, but . . . just one," she reported to Chess and Natalie beside her. "And he's so young I'm not even sure he shaves yet. His uniform looks like this is the first time he's wearing it. So . . . this is an Officer Nice Guy. Not anyone with actual news about Mom and Ms. Morales."

Emma could have gone on with the details that made her

sure this was just a rookie checking in, not a top detective who'd found an important clue. The cop kept his eyes trained directly ahead, not darting around watching for potential danger. His police car was neatly parked in the driveway, as if the cop had taken the time to aim for an invisible box with exact, ninety-degree angles. (Emma really would have preferred to see a cop car driven hastily over a curb, and abandoned in a rush.)

But most of all, she knew this cop didn't know anything because . . . he *couldn't.* All the cops thought the kids' missing mothers were somewhere on planet Earth, in the same dimension as the cops themselves. So that was the only place the cops knew to look.

If she'd been in a more playful mood, Emma might have enjoyed imagining the cops' reaction to the news that they needed to extend their missing persons search to an entirely different dimension.

But Emma hadn't been in a playful mood in two weeks. Not since she'd turned around in her own basement and seen a wall of broken shelves and dirt in place of the tunnel that, as far as Emma knew, might have been the only route between the two worlds.

What if the kids themselves had destroyed the only route for getting back into the other world to rescue their mothers?

Or, if another route existed, what if they never found it?

"It's . . . nice that the police want to make us feel better," Emma's older brother, Chess, said faintly, from his spot curled up with a different laptop in Mr. Mayhew's La-Z-Boy recliner. Chess had spent so much time lately cooped up inside staring at computers and codes that his skin had taken on the same pallor as a mushroom. Even his voice sounded slightly mushroomy.

At the other end of Emma's couch, Natalie only snorted.

"Finn's not here, you know?" Emma said. Usually Finn was the one they dispatched to speak to the cops, or grown-ups in general. As Mr. Mayhew put it, Finn "could charm paint from a wall."

"Fine," Natalie huffed. "*I'll* send the cop away."

Natalie unfurled herself from the couch. She'd been lying upside down, her neck bent back over the edge of the couch, her dark hair streaming down like a flag behind her, her own laptop held downside up at eye level.

"Um, Natalie?" Emma said, pantomiming smoothing down her hair, because Natalie's was flipped around so wildly.

"Yeah, yeah, whatever," Natalie muttered, though she did comb her fingers through her hair as she headed for the front door.

The day Emma first met Natalie, Chess had said she was a Lip Gloss Girl—one of those older girls who cared a lot about how she looked. The world really had gone crazy if *Emma* had to remind *Natalie* to pay attention to her appearance.

But as soon as Natalie pulled open the door, she transformed into Natalie the Imposing, Natalie in Charge. In spite of herself, Emma listened and watched carefully, as if she were observing a science experiment. Once they got their mothers back, Emma fully expected to go back to her original lifetime goal of making as many mathematical and scientific discoveries as possible, just for the fun of it. She didn't envy Natalie's very different talents. But Emma *was* curious—how exactly did Natalie do it?

"Oh, Officer . . . Dutton!" Natalie exclaimed, adding the name so quickly that the poor cop probably thought she remembered him, not that she'd looked at the name badge pinned to his uniform. "Do you have news for us? Did you find my mother? Or Mrs. Greystone?"

"N-N-No," the cop stammered, as if Natalie were his boss and he was terrified of being scolded. "We're trying, though. I promise, we're trying."

Emma felt kind of sorry for the cop. She knew what it was like to try your hardest and still fail.

"Oh," Natalie said, visibly deflating. Emma knew Natalie well enough now to see: This was Natalie being kind. What Natalie really wanted to do was stomp her feet and scream at the top of her lungs and demand her mother's return.

Emma knew, because that's what she wanted to do every time she talked to a cop about her own mother's disappearance.

The cops can't do anything, Emma reminded herself. *It's all up to Chess, Finn, Natalie, and me.*

"I'm sorry," the cop said. "I just came to bring you these." He held up two large white garbage bags, both full to the point of bulging. "I know you and your dad said to donate all the flowers to charity, but people keep leaving stuffed animals and toys at the explosion site, too. And, well, the guys down at the station thought the little kids might want to pick out a few things for themselves before we give the rest away . . . I can come back tomorrow for anything they don't want . . ."

He thinks I'm a little kid, Emma thought. *When he talks about "little kids," he means me and Finn.*

That made Emma want to stomp and scream, too.

She was not used to being angry all the time. Before her mother disappeared, Emma could have counted on one hand the number of times she'd been really mad. Now the fury popped up at the weirdest times.

Sometimes Emma even got mad at numbers. Twelve—that was how many days had passed since the last time Emma had seen her mother. Three hundred and seventy-two—that was the number of attempts Emma had made at solving the secret code her mother had left behind.

And . . . one. That, Emma was convinced, was the number of right answers waiting out there. One, out of an infinity of possibilities.

No wonder she was furious.

No wonder she was having trouble eating and sleeping and . . . even doing math.

Emma heard the front door shut, and she realized she'd zoned out and missed the rest of the conversation between Natalie and the cop.

"Okay," Natalie said, dropping the garbage bags to the foyer floor and starting to dig through them. "Humor break. One for you—" She tossed something yellow and orange toward Chess. "And one for you." Emma saw a blur of purple and pink headed her way.

Emma held up her hands to fend off whatever it was. Something bounced from her fingertips just as she saw Chess snatch a little toy tiger cub from the air.

"Oh, er, thanks," Chess said, blushing. He tucked the stuffed toy into the chair beside him as if he intended to treasure it forever.

Seriously? Emma thought. *Ohhh . . . because* Natalie *picked it out for him?*

Sometimes Chess could get a little weird around Natalie.

Sometimes Emma wanted to shake him by the shoulders and shout, *Snap out of it!*

And sometimes Emma wanted to shake Natalie, and boss her around: *Whatever you do, don't hurt my brother! Even if you don't have a crush on him like he does on you, be nice to him!*

Which was crazy, because Natalie was nice to all three of the Greystone kids. Now, anyway. She hadn't been like that when they first met.

"Emma, you haven't even looked at yours," Natalie complained, pretending to pout. "It's *so* sparkly—I know you'll love it!"

This was a joke. Emma looked down, ready to act disgusted. The object she'd knocked to the floor was a pink pillow covered in sequins. But . . . it was actually an *interesting* sequined pink pillow. The sequins were two-sided, and they were sewn on in a way that made them reversible. Emma had seen this kind of thing before: If she ran her hand across the pillow in one direction, the sequins would show an iridescent white heart. Running her hand in the other direction would flip the sequins to purple.

But when Emma knocked the pillow to the floor, it had landed oddly. Half the heart was white; half was purple.

And in the middle, on the jagged line that divided the white from the purple, one row of sequins stood straight up, as if they couldn't make up their minds which way to go. One or two of the sequins were even broken—bent or warped in a way that made it seem like they would never lay right again, in either direction. Emma squinted thoughtfully at the narrow, jagged line that was neither white nor purple, but clear, see-through.

And then Emma leaped up, snatched the pink pillow from the ground, and screamed, "That's it! This is the clue we needed! Now I know how to find Mom!"

THREE

CHESS

Clearly Emma had lost it.

"Um, Emma, just because that's a heart, it doesn't mean it's from Joe," Chess said. And though he tried to sound comforting and big-brother-ish and as if he could take care of everything, his voice came out sounding nothing but sad. He didn't know how to sound any other way lately.

For the umpteenth time in the past two weeks, he wished that their last moments with access to the other world had ended differently. What if Chess hadn't pulled the lever that shut the tunnel to the other world forever? What if he'd

shoved all the other kids—and Ms. Morales—
then marched back to confront the awful peop
them?

What if Chess had run even farther back once eve
one else was safe, and found Joe, the mysterious man who'd helped them escape and promised to rescue their mother, too?

Chess was sure Joe had failed. If there was any chance Mom and Joe had escaped from the other dimension, Mom would have come and found the three Greystone kids immediately.

"I *know* this isn't from Joe!" Emma said. She was practically jumping up and down, holding the pink sequined pillow in the air like a trophy. "The heart he showed us was red, and it was drawn by Finn. Joe was using it as a *symbol*. Nobody wanted *this* heart to mean anything except, I guess, 'Sorry you poor kids lost your moms.' They weren't trying to tell us anything else. But the sequins, the sequins—they helped me figure out everything!"

It hurt Chess's eyes to watch Emma move so quickly when he felt so sluggish. But finally her words sank in.

"Everything?" Chess whispered.

"Yes!" Emma spun around, as if the pillow were a dance partner. "See, I was all wrong in how I was thinking of the other world. I was thinking of it as being underground, and so we needed to find another tunnel. With another lever to open the tunnel, and another spinning room to burrow through."

"Isn't that what we need?" Natalie asked.

"*No*," Emma said. "I mean, I guess that would work, if we found it, but we've been trying for two weeks, and it's like looking for a needle in a haystack. Or a single basement tunnel on a planet with millions of basements. We don't even know if there *is* another tunnel. But we've already got what we need to get back to the other world. We had it all along. Like Dorothy had the ruby slippers that would get her back to Kansas practically the whole time she was in Oz."

Automatically, Chess glanced toward Emma's feet. She *was* wearing red sneakers, her favorites. But he didn't think that was what she meant.

"Look," Emma said, holding out the pillow. "Think of our world and the other world like this heart. Let's say we're purple, and they're white." She ran her hand back and forth over the sequins, flipping the colors, white to purple, purple to white. "The worlds are underneath each other, but they're also above and beside. Every molecule of their world is crammed in between every molecule of our world. Like the white side of the sequins are all in between the purple sides. Every sequin is both things at once. And it's clear in between. There's part of the sequin that touches both the white side and the purple. So *every* part of our world is connected to the other world!"

Sometimes Emma made Chess's brain hurt. He did perfectly well in math and science at school—his teachers always praised him as a good student. But he couldn't flip his brain inside out thinking wild thoughts as much as Emma could.

Looking at the pillow did kind of help. He understood two-sided sequins. He understood how the heart changed from one color to the other, and how every sequin had a middle that was neither white nor purple.

"Okay," he said slowly. "But what's that got to do with Mom and—"

"It means we can go back to the other world *anywhere*!" Emma said. "We can crawl through any sequin!"

Chess glanced toward Natalie, hoping she could read his mind: *Please don't tell Emma she's crazy. Please play along. Remember, she's only ten.* Natalie was squinting at the pillow just as intensely as Emma.

"I'm trying to understand," Natalie said. "Really I am. But this is like when Mom and I go back to Mexico and her relatives are all speaking Spanish a million miles a minute, and I can't keep up. Translate, por favor. The two sides of the sequins are the two worlds, and the way to 'crawl' from one side to the other is . . . is . . ."

Chess could tell that Emma was trying not to look

disappointed with him and Natalie.

"With the *lever*," Emma said. "The lever we tore off the wall when we closed the tunnel. It's the key, the connection between the two worlds, the thing that opens the route. The lever itself isn't broken—it's just that *location* that's off-limits now. Like this sequin." She tapped one of the ruined sequins, showing how it was too warped now to flip colors. "The lever is like a bridge through the middle, from one side to the other. And the lever will still work in other places besides our basement. I'm sure of it!"

Chess and Natalie both gaped at Emma for a long moment before Chess said gently, "Emma, we don't actually have that lever. It's still back at our house."

"Right," Emma replied. "So we have to get Natalie's dad to take us there." She dropped the heart pillow and started tugging on Natalie's arm, pulling the other girl toward the stairs. "Come on. Let's go signal Finn to bring your dad back!"

Chess watched the two girls run up the stairs. They didn't need his help with the blinds. But he sat up straight, feeling his first glimmer of hope in two weeks. He believed Emma's theory was . . . possible, at least. He picked up the pillow Emma had dropped and brushed his fingers back and forth against the sequins. The way they flipped from one color to another could stand for lots of things.

Purple, white . . . this world, that world . . . hope, fear . . .

Chess's stomach clenched. Last time they'd gone into the other world to rescue Mom, they'd only ended up losing Ms. Morales and Joe.

What if something even worse happened this time?

FOUR

FINN

"What's the plan?" Finn whispered to Natalie while Mr. Mayhew put the baseball gloves and ball away. "How are we going to ditch your dad? Or are we telling him everything and taking him with us?"

"We're not putting Dad in danger," Natalie said firmly. "And . . . we're not giving him a chance to be overprotective and refuse to let us go rescue our moms. We're keeping him in the dark."

"Okay . . . ," Finn said, waiting. Sometimes Natalie could be like a general giving orders to her troops. You didn't rush her.

Mr. Mayhew came back from the garage. Finn saw how Natalie, Chess, and Emma were lined up in the foyer. All three of them were bright-eyed and rosy-cheeked—totally transformed from the gloomy, droopy kids they'd been before.

Finn elbowed Natalie, and she had the sense to slump a little. Finn raced over to wrap his arms around Chess and Emma.

"I missed you!" he pretended to wail. "I'm glad the two of *you* didn't disappear like Mom!"

He took a quick peek over his shoulder. Mr. Mayhew was gulping and looking away. During one of their pitch-and-catch sessions, he'd told Finn he never knew what to do when anyone cried.

"Hey!" Mr. Mayhew said, too loudly. "Want to go out for dinner tonight? I'm thinking the Rusty Barrel would be fun. What do you think?"

Natalie looped her elbow through Mr. Mayhew's.

"That's a great idea!" she said. "But can we stop on the way? I have that science project on leaves due tomorrow, and we get extra credit for having certain ones. Chess and Emma told me about some weird trees by the pond near their house—maybe I can find the leaves I need there."

Finn let go of Emma and Chess just in time to see Mr. Mayhew frown.

"I'm not sure we should—" he began.

"Are you worried about us, Mr. Mayhew?" Emma said. "Chess, Finn, and me, we'll be fine. It won't bother us to be back in our old neighborhood. We can just wait in the car. No problem."

Emma was really, really good at about nine billion things, but acting wasn't one of them. Finn didn't know the plan yet, but he could tell that Emma had no intention of waiting in any car.

Fortunately, Natalie was maneuvering her dad toward the door, and he probably didn't notice.

"Let's go before it gets dark!" Natalie said.

Mr. Mayhew didn't have an SUV like Natalie's mom, or a station wagon like Mom. He had a little red sports car with barely any back seat. That meant that when Natalie sat in the front with her dad, the three Greystone kids had to fit themselves into an area that was probably not meant for anything bigger than a briefcase. Chess's legs were so long that his bent knees came up to Finn's ears; Emma solved the space problem by curling into a ball and wrapping her arms around Finn in the middle.

Finn actually loved riding in the back of Mr. Mayhew's car. He loved being squashed together with Emma and Chess. It made him feel like they were all puppies or kittens, jumbled together. Like they were still a family, even without Mom.

It also made whispering easier.

"We're all sneaking over to our house, right?" he whispered to Emma as she hugged him close, because there wasn't room not to. Her arms were like a second seat belt. "How—"

"Shh," Emma said, glancing worriedly toward the front seat. "Just Chess and me. You and Natalie stay by the pond with Mr. Mayhew and keep him distracted until we get back."

"I always have to do the distracting!" Finn protested. "You promised—" Finn couldn't help himself. His wail rose over the music Mr. Mayhew always kept pumped up in his car. Today it was about someone being wanted, dead or alive.

"Don't worry, Mr. Mayhew," Chess shouted toward the front seat. "Emma and I are taking care of Finn."

Mr. Mayhew nodded. But maybe he was just nodding along with the music.

"No one's going back to rescue Mom *yet*," Emma hissed into Finn's ear. "We're just picking up . . . supplies. The right tool."

Did Chess and Emma *know* the right tool for getting back to the other world and rescuing Mom? Had they figured out that much?

That was enough to make Finn beam at Emma. And

then he was the one who had to duck down and hide his smile.

But when they pulled up by the pond in their own neighborhood, Finn felt a weird little gurgle in his stomach. The last time they'd seen this pond, it had been the other world's version, and Finn, Emma, Chess, and Natalie had been running away from a big, scary place alongside three kids they'd rescued from being kidnapped.

There was a secret about those other kids that Finn didn't like thinking about. Those other kids, who were named Rocky, Emma, and Finn Gustano, had been kidnapped and taken to the other world because some bad guys thought they belonged to Mom. If the bad guys had really known what they were doing, they would have kidnapped Chess, Emma, and Finn Greystone instead.

The Gustanos' mom and Finn's mom were just the two different worlds' versions of the same person. And it was the Greystones, not the Gustanos, who actually belonged in the awful other world.

Finn tried not to think about any of that. All he wanted to think about was getting Mom back.

No—he only wanted to think about *having* Mom back. It would be okay with Finn if they all skipped ahead in time, past all the danger of going back to the other world and rescuing Mom. It'd be great if they could get the rescuing behind them, go back to their normal lives here in this world, and totally forget that the other world even existed.

Just like the Gustanos had been able to go back to their normal lives, reunited with their parents. *They* didn't have to think about the other world anymore.

Don't worry about the pond, Finn told himself. *It's just water. You're not afraid of water. You know how to swim!*

This pond was also pretty, with flowering bushes around it, and picnic tables and a swing set off to the side. The version of the pond they'd seen in the other world had looked dead and gloomy—maybe it was even poison, because nothing grew around it.

Finn's stomach wasn't gurgling because he was scared of this pond. It was because being near the pond reminded him how scared he was of the other world.

If a stupid old pond could scare him, he was kind of glad he didn't have to go back to their house with Chess and Emma.

But I'd do it if I had to, he told himself. *I'd do anything to get Mom back.*

Mr. Mayhew turned off the car, and Natalie whirled around to face Finn.

"Chess and Emma, we'll be quick, I promise," she said.

"Finn, you never like sitting still, do you? It would help if you come with Dad and me. Dad could hold you up to get leaves from the tallest trees. You wouldn't mind doing that, would you?"

"Sounds like fun!" Finn made himself exclaim.

Natalie helped pull him out of the back seat. He took a deep breath as soon as he had his feet firmly on the sidewalk. The air smelled like lilacs, nothing at all like the foul smell of the other world.

"I'm not sure how long it will take Chess and Emma," Natalie whispered, bending down to his level. "We may have to act really stupid about finding the right trees. You be the lookout—let me know when Chess and Emma are back in the car."

And then Mr. Mayhew was out of the car beside them, and Natalie switched to exclaiming, "How much do *you* know about trees, Dad? Can you tell which ones are unusual?"

As Natalie pulled her dad down toward the pond, Finn looked back over his shoulder. Chess and Emma were already out of the car, bent low and half tiptoeing, half sprinting down the sidewalk. Finn felt a little pang, even though he trusted his brother and sister one hundred percent. If they said they wouldn't go to the other world without him, they truly wouldn't. Not if they could help it.

But what if something happens, and they can't *help it?* he wondered. *What if they think they're just picking up whatever they need, but the tunnel opens again when they don't expect it, and they get sucked into the other world by mistake? And then they're trapped, too?*

Finn knew he should turn around and help Natalie keep her dad looking at trees and leaves. But he kept facing backward a moment longer.

That's how he came to see a dark car park far down the block. A man with close-cropped hair got out of the car and began doing elaborate stretches that involved propping first one foot, then the other, against the hood of his car, and bending down to touch his chin to his knees again and again.

It struck Finn that those exercises put the man in the perfect position to watch Mr. Mayhew's car and Chess and Emma as they sprinted away.

And it struck Finn that the man's exercise clothes were all navy blue and orange. All the mean people in the other world had worn navy blue and orange.

So what? Sometimes people in this world wear navy blue and orange, too, Finn told himself. *It could just be a—what's it called?—a coincidence.*

Still, Finn decided he needed to stay close to the street

and keep an eye on the man who seemed only to be pretending to exercise.

From down closer to the pond, he heard Natalie tell her dad, "No, I don't think that's just an ordinary willow tree. Hold that branch still so I can take a picture and do an image search on my phone. Finn? What are you doing? Can you come help us?"

"Just a minute," Finn said. "I'm . . . tying my shoe."

And then he really did dip down and pretend to fiddle with his shoelaces. It was a shame he couldn't shout back, *I'm doing something more important here! You have to handle your dad by yourself!*

When he stood back up, he glanced first toward Chess and Emma, who were two blocks away now, and moving fast. While Finn watched, they turned the corner, out of sight.

What if there was another guy in blue and orange just around the corner? What if it was another kidnapper? Finn wouldn't be able to stand it if anything happened to Chess and Emma.

He *really* wouldn't be able to stand it if something happened to Chess and Emma, and Finn could have stopped it—but didn't.

He glanced back toward the stretching man. Now

Exercise Guy was in a half crouch with one ankle braced against the other knee, as if he wanted to sit crisscross applesauce in midair.

Just an ordinary runner getting ready to jog, Finn told himself. *That's all. It's just a guy from this world, doing normal this-world stuff.*

The man finished his stretches and took off running toward Finn—and toward the street where Chess and Emma had turned.

I'll just watch until he goes past, Finn told himself. *Or until he's past that street, and he doesn't turn, so I know he's not following Chess and Emma.*

The man was getting closer and closer. Finn ducked down behind Mr. Mayhew's car, but he could still see the man through the car windows.

The man's face looked familiar: dark eyebrows, gray eyes, big nose, and a small mouth with deep frown lines around it.

Not a neighbor, Finn thought. *Not the dad of anyone I know at school. Not one of the cops . . .*

It was thinking of the cops that helped Finn figure out where he'd seen this man before. The man had been in a guard's uniform, standing on a stage. And he'd been announcing the start of a trial, saying Finn's mother was guilty.

This man was from the other world.

For a long moment, Finn stood frozen, too terrified to move. That gave the man time to put on a burst of speed, move far past Mr. Mayhew's car—and then turn at the same corner where Chess and Emma had turned.

Finn began to scream.

EMMA

Emma was having doubts.

Oh, she was plenty sure that she *could* be right about the two worlds fitting together like reversible sequins on a pillow. And she was plenty sure that there *could* be multiple entry points into the other world. But what if she was wrong about the torn-off lever from their basement being the key to everything? What if she'd gotten Chess, Finn, and Natalie all excited about nothing?

The scientific method—and allowing for lots of trial and error—was great when you just wanted to find out if a hypothesis worked. When you had all the time in the world, and could have fun figuring everything out.

It wasn't so great when your mother was in danger, and you already felt like time was running out.

"Chess . . . ," Emma began as they raced toward their own block.

Chess barely grunted a reply. Their own house had just come into sight. It still had crime scene tape around it, with the stark black letters on the yellow background spelling out POLICE LINE DO NOT CROSS again and again. Two new signs were posted on the front door: One said, "NO TRESPASSING," with a bunch of small print underneath; one said, "REWARD!" with two pictures underneath.

"Ooh," Emma moaned, realizing that the pictures were of her mom and Ms. Morales.

The police were offering a reward for information about the whereabouts of both women. Emma hadn't known that.

It made them seem like criminals. Or . . . like they were gone forever.

But we *know they're in the other world,* Emma reminded herself. *Mom has information that protects her there—that's why we rescued the Gustanos instead of her. Because the Gustanos* weren't *protected. And Ms. Morales . . . she's smart. She can take care of herself. So can Joe.*

Even if Emma had been absolutely certain that her mother, Ms. Morales, and Joe were safe, she still would have hated seeing her house this way. The police tape and the signs made it seem like the house belonged to somebody else entirely—total strangers, even.

It looked almost as foreign as the run-down, dilapidated version of their house she'd seen in the other world.

Somewhere far behind them, Emma heard someone scream. It was probably just kids playing—there were lots of kids in their neighborhood, and Finn's friends in particular screamed at the top of their lungs all the time. But today it sent chills down Emma's spine.

"I'm glad Finn didn't have to see this," she muttered to Chess, pointing toward the signs on the door.

"We'll go in through the garage," Chess muttered back. He held up the spare garage key, which Mom usually kept tucked in a flowerpot at the back of the house. Emma felt a little burst of love for Chess, that two weeks ago in the midst of shock and horror, he'd had the presence of mind to snag the spare key without the cops noticing. Chess was like that, quietly taking care of things.

Emma or Finn would have wanted to brag, *See how smart I was? See what I did?*

Chess and Emma reached the edge of their own yard, the patch where four-leaf clovers grew in the spring. A year ago, Emma had sectioned off quadrants and made a graph showing where the clovers grew the most, with theories about whether it was soil quality, sunshine, or rainfall that made the difference.

It felt like Emma had been a totally different person a year ago. Who cared about four-leaf clovers now?

"Wait," Chess murmured, putting his hand on Emma's arm.

They stood at the edge of the yard for a moment, Chess glancing all around. It was a quiet street, and no one was out, though Emma guessed someone *could* be crouched down out of sight, hiding behind one of the cars parked in driveways or along the street. Or not. This was the time of night when all the parents had come home and called kids in for dinner.

Doesn't that make it seem weird that I just heard a kid scream, playing a few streets over? Emma wondered.

She pushed that thought aside, and tugged Chess forward.

"Let's get this over with, so Natalie and Finn don't have to keep Mr. Mayhew distracted forever," Emma said.

They crept toward the door at the side of their house. It was their own sidewalk, their own driveway, their own grass, but both of them moved like intruders. Like they didn't belong.

Chess reached the door and glanced around once more before slipping the key into the lock.

"Chess, you're being paranoid!" Emma protested. "Hurry up!"

Chess turned the key, and Emma pushed her hand forward to turn the knob as fast as she could.

And then a man in dark clothes came out of nowhere and tackled them, knocking them both to the ground.

SIX

CHESS

"Get off me!" Chess screamed as Emma hollered, "Let go!"

Chess tried kicking and shoving the man away, and he was pretty sure Emma did, too. But the man seemed to know exactly how to keep both of them pinned to the ground, no matter what they did.

"Yeah, just found two kids trying to break into the house. . . ." The man seemed to be reporting into some walkie-talkie buried in a pocket, or maybe a microphone embedded in his clothes. Chess wiggled around enough to see the man's chin lowered toward his shirt collar, but the rest of the man's face wasn't visible.

"We're not breaking in!" Emma protested. "We *live* here! Or—we used to! We have a key!"

Chess shook his head silently against the ground.

Oh, Emma, he thought. *What if we don't want this man to know who we are?*

Then Chess heard a speeding car and screeching brakes and running feet.

"Hey, hey! Those are the Greystone kids! Let them go!"

It was Mr. Mayhew's voice.

And then Finn was screaming, "Stop hurting my brother and sister!" And Natalie was shouting, "Dad! Is that man a cop? Or, wait—does he work for you?"

Chess realized the man had let go. Still, Chess remained facedown on the ground for a moment, overcome. They hadn't even gotten back into the other world yet, and already Chess felt defeated and powerless.

Already, he'd failed to protect Emma. If Mr. Mayhew, Finn, and Natalie hadn't shown up—and Chess didn't quite understand how they'd *known* to show up—then this man could have done anything he wanted.

He could have kidnapped Chess and Emma.

He could have taken them back to the other world, and Finn and Natalie wouldn't have even known.

Finn started yanking on Chess's arm, trying to turn him over.

"Chess! Chess! Are you in there?"

That was the kind of thing Finn used to shout when the Greystone kids were playing make-believe—pretending to be in danger, pretending to need help, pretending to have barely survived some awful fight with pirates or bandits or other made-up bad guys.

Chess winced, because Finn was shouting this for real now. Finn really was wondering if Chess had survived.

Chess made himself roll over and stand up.

"I'm fine, buddy." Chess forced his mouth into a shape that he hoped looked like a smile. His legs felt shaky, but he locked his knees and stood firm. "I'm just . . . surprised. How'd you know to come rescue us?"

Finn darted his gaze toward Mr. Mayhew and shook his head warningly.

Okay, that's a secret, Chess thought. *Something else we can't talk about in front of Mr. Mayhew.*

Emma had already sprung up and was advancing on the man who'd tackled them. She had a finger poked against the man's chest.

"Do you just go around knocking people down for no reason all the time?" she challenged. "Don't you know people have *rights*?"

"It was a misunderstanding," the man said, peering toward Mr. Mayhew, as if he expected Natalie's dad to explain.

But Natalie's dad was too busy trying to fend off Natalie.

"Honey, *please*," he was saying. "I hired extra security to watch the Greystones' house to protect *everyone*. And maybe to solve the mystery. You know how your mother, well . . ."

"My mother *what*?" Natalie demanded, facing off against her dad like Emma stood against the tackling man.

"You know, some of the people she associated with, they had ties to . . . bad elements," Mr. Mayhew finished weakly.

"My mother helped women who were in danger!" Natalie exploded. "Women whose boyfriends and husbands were *evil*. That doesn't mean Mom associated with bad elements! It means she was a hero! She *is* a hero!"

She spoke so forcefully, the tackling man took a step back.

Chess looked around. It was a warm night, and Chess could see open windows in neighbors' houses. He could imagine people pausing over their dinners, peering out to see what the disturbance was.

What if it wasn't just neighbors who were listening, but . . . others? Spies from the other world?

"Could we maybe move this inside?" Chess asked quietly, taking Natalie's arm and tugging her toward the door into the garage.

"Good idea," the tackling man said, starting to herd the others into the garage, too.

Chess realized that the tackling man had a patch on his black shirt that said "Ace Private Security Experts." He also had bulging muscles that threatened to rip through his sleeves. Chess felt even more helpless—he and Emma could never have overpowered this man.

Emma at least had had the courage to berate him.

Chess turned on the garage light. The single bulb overhead was the energy-saver type that came on weakly at first, and needed a few seconds before it put out much of a glow. So everything in the garage looked shadowed and spooky.

Chess moved closer to Emma and Finn and put his arms around both of them. Finn sniffed, and rubbed dust off the window of Mom's station wagon.

"It's weird seeing Mom's car here," he said. "Without Mom."

Chess knew that Mom's car still being in the garage was one of the reasons the police didn't quite believe that she'd gone on a business trip before disappearing. Should Chess, Emma, and Finn maybe *not* have told them she usually drove her own car to the airport?

The day the police thought there'd been a natural gas explosion, Natalie had quietly counseled the three Greystone kids on the fine art of lying: *Only make up what you have to. Otherwise, tell as much truth as you can. That means you have fewer lies to keep track of, and you're not as likely to trip yourself up.*

It kind of bothered Chess that Natalie knew so much about lying.

"Dad, why didn't you tell me you'd hired a security guard to watch the Greystones' house?" Natalie was demanding.

"I didn't . . . want to worry you," Mr. Mayhew mumbled.

It almost sounded like he was the kid making excuses, and Natalie was the angry parent.

"Mr. Mayhew, sir, if these really are the Greystone children, and they have every right to be here, I should go and get back into stakeout position," the tackling man said, as though he didn't want to watch Natalie and her dad argue, either. "I would remind you, though, that the police still regard this as a potential crime scene, and anything that is removed should be catalogued."

"Yes, I know that!" Mr. Mayhew snapped.

The tackling man—or, security guard, rather—slipped out the garage door and eased it gently shut behind him.

"Well," Mr. Mayhew said weakly. He wiped sweat from his forehead with the back of his hand. "What do you say we just forget this and go have dinner?"

"Chess and Emma haven't had a chance to get the *toys* they came to pick up as a surprise for Finn," Natalie said.

Okay, got it, Chess wanted to tell her. *We can go with that cover story.*

"The surprise part is kind of ruined, but . . . you all stay right here," Emma said. "Chess and I will be right back."

She grabbed Chess's arm, pulling him past Mom's car and toward the door that led on into the house.

They raced toward the basement stairs without turning on any lights. It was like neither of them wanted to look too closely at their own house.

"You find some toy of Finn's we can show Mr. Mayhew," Chess told Emma as they clattered down the stairs. "I'll get the lever."

He'd have to figure out some way to hide it under his T-shirt. He tried to picture it in his mind—was it about the same length as his arm? Would it even fit under his shirt?

He jumped past the last three stairs and hit the basement light switch. He took a shaky breath. The basement still smelled vaguely like kitty litter and their cat, Rocket, even though Rocket had been with them at Mr. Mayhew's for the past two weeks.

The door to Mom's basement office—which the Greystone kids called the Boring Room—hung completely open, not shut and locked the way she always left it.

That's because we *left that door open two weeks ago,* Chess told himself. None of them had been thinking clearly after they'd escaped from the other world and shut off the tunnel that led out from the Boring Room. Plus, they'd had the Gustano kids with them, and the Gustanos had been desperate to get out. Being kidnapped had left them with a fear of basements.

I'm not feeling too great about basements myself right now, either, Chess thought.

He made himself take another breath, a deep one this time. He was both relieved and a little disappointed that he caught no hint of the foul odor from the other world. That had to mean the tunnel was still firmly shut, and Chess was in no danger if he walked through the Boring Room to pick up the broken lever.

But it also meant he still couldn't get back through that tunnel to rescue Mom.

He sped past Mom's desk in the Boring Room, then ducked around the bookcase at the back of the room that doubled as a secret door. It led into the hidden room that Chess, Emma, and Finn hadn't discovered until after their mother vanished.

Just pick up the broken lever and leave, Chess told himself. *That's all you have to do.*

But his hand shook as he reached for the light switch, and he had to grope around on the wall to find it. Even in the dark, he turned toward the place where he'd dropped the broken lever to the floor two weeks ago, after giving up on making it work again.

Finally his fingers found the light switch, and he flipped it on. The light flickered once, then came on in a solid glow.

Chess kept staring at the floor. He knew he was looking at the right spot.

But there was nothing there. Nothing—but a faint outline in dust of the missing lever.

SEVEN

FINN

Natalie and her dad were still arguing. Finn didn't think he could take one more second of standing in the garage with Mom's car, but without Mom.

"Since it's not a surprise anymore, I'll go see what Chess and Emma are getting," he announced.

Natalie turned as if she intended to follow him. But if she came, her dad would want to as well.

"Be right back!" Finn said, making shoving motions toward Natalie with his hand. He hoped Natalie could tell he meant, *Sorry! It's still your turn to keep distracting your dad!*

As soon as he got into the house, he saw that the basement

door was open and the lights were on downstairs.

And then he heard Chess scream, "Emma!"

Finn raced down the stairs.

"Chess? Emma? Are you okay?" he called.

At the bottom of the stairs, he saw Emma dropping handfuls of Hot Wheels cars and speeding toward the Boring Room door.

"Hot Wheels—really?" Finn called. "You were going to make me have to pretend to be thrilled about *those*? Or—are they really a clue to getting Mom back?"

"Decoys," Emma gasped as she ran. "Sorry."

"Emma, get in here!" Chess hollered again from the Boring Room. Or, more likely, from the secret room behind it.

Emma and Finn ran together. As soon as they ducked past the bookcase/secret door, they bumped into Chess. Finn threw his arms around his brother's waist.

"You're okay!" Finn exclaimed. "Nobody's hurt!"

Absentmindedly, Chess patted Finn's back.

"But the lever's missing," Chess said dejectedly, slumping down against Finn's head.

Emma slammed back against the wall as if she was upset, too.

"So what?" Finn said, peering back and forth between his siblings. "That lever was broken, remember? It doesn't work anymore!"

If Chess and Emma were going to get all panicked and sad about every little thing, it had to be Finn's job to cheer them up. And to keep them focused on getting Mom back.

Chess kept his arm around Finn's shoulders.

"Emma thinks the lever could still work somewhere else," Chess said gently. "She thinks it's only the tunnel leading out from this room that's ruined. Not the lever itself. *That's* what we were coming back for."

"Oh," Finn said.

Emma and Chess kept staring inconsolably at the floor. But Finn glanced around the whole space. The room still looked like a hoarder's pantry, with canned food, jars of applesauce, boxes of granola bars, and other similar items on every shelf. Their whole family could probably live in this room for a year and never go hungry.

Finn knew that all the packages of food—and the cash hidden in some of the shoeboxes—were actually items Mom had stashed to take into the other world, to help people there.

He tried not to look at the back wall of the pantry, where the shelves were cracked and dirt shoved through the broken wall. It reminded him too much of the moment when the tunnel closed—leaving Mom, Ms. Morales, and Joe trapped in the other world.

But Finn couldn't help seeing that somebody (probably the cops) had cleaned up the jars that had broken when they came crashing down from the collapsing shelves. All the toppled cans appeared to have been left in place, though.

Oh, because someone might get hurt on the broken glass, and the cans don't matter, Finn told himself. *And the food in the cans won't start rotting and stinking up the basement, like the food from the broken jars would.*

He liked that it made sense, what the cops had done.

Then he saw a rod made of metal—or maybe stone—propped against the broken shelves.

"Wait—isn't *that* the lever?" he asked Chess and Emma, pointing toward the back wall and the rod. "It's not missing. The cops just moved it! Maybe because they thought they needed to hold up the shelves?"

"You're right!" Emma hugged Finn, then raced toward the lever. She picked her way through the piles of upended cans as though they were an obstacle course in gym class. She grabbed the lever. Then, instantly, she dropped it back on the floor. She clutched her face in her hands.

"No, we're wrong!" she moaned. "That wasn't propping up anything, and the cops wouldn't have moved it. So why is it *here* instead of *there*?" She pointed to the outline in dust on the floor. "What if it was somebody who knows about the other world who moved it?"

The color drained from her face. She dropped to her knees in the mess of overturned cans. Finn hoped that whoever cleaned up the broken glass had done a really, really good job.

"Oh no, oh no," Emma groaned. "What if the person who moved it . . . was *from* the other world?"

EIGHT

EMMA

Sometimes ideas came to Emma so fast that they crashed into each other, like cars whose drivers weren't paying attention.

"We could have looked for fingerprints—or the cops could, if we wanted their help—but I probably just messed that up!" she wailed. "I touched it!"

Chess and Finn stared at her as if they couldn't catch up.

"*How* do you know it wasn't the cops who moved that?" Finn asked.

"Logic," Emma said. "Why would they pick up the lever but leave all the fallen cans in place? Remember how the security guard said they're treating this like a crime scene?

The cops didn't move anything they didn't have to move. And . . . you can tell the lever lay right there on the floor until just recently. Nobody moved that lever for at least a week. Because there's the outline of dust around the place where we left it."

"The dust could give us other clues," Chess said. "Whoever moved the lever might have left footprints. We should look for footprints."

But Chess, Finn, and Emma—mostly Emma—had already walked around too much in the secret room. If there'd been footprints left behind by whoever moved the lever, the kids had destroyed those, too.

"Hey, kids! Hurry up and let's go get dinner! Aren't you starving?" Emma heard Mr. Mayhew yell from above.

"Quick, Finn," Emma said, spinning back toward her little brother. "Take off your shirt."

"What?" Finn protested.

"So we have something to wrap the lever in, so we don't mess up any fingerprints that are still on it," Emma said. "And so Mr. Mayhew doesn't see what we carry out of here. We can say you got that shirt dirty, and you need another one from your room."

"Fine," Finn said. He yanked his shirt over his head and tossed it to Emma. Then he tugged Chess's arm. "Come on, Chess. Come with me to get a shirt upstairs."

You shouldn't need Chess's help getting a shirt from your own room, Emma wanted to complain to Finn. But she caught a glimpse of his pale, pinched face, the usual dimples in his cheeks totally gone. He *was* scared just of walking upstairs to his own room.

Finn and Chess ducked back through the secret door, Chess calling politely up the stairs to Mr. Mayhew, "We're almost ready! We just need one more thing. . . ."

And then Emma was alone. Alone in the secret room that had once been capable of turning into a secret tunnel—alone in the room where they'd lost Ms. Morales. Emma shivered.

"Stop that," she said aloud. "Focus."

She picked up Finn's bright yellow T-shirt from the pile of cans where it had landed. She shook out the wrinkles, and pulled the shirt over her hand like a glove. Then she picked up the lever. She started to fold Finn's shirt around the lever, but then she stopped.

What if I try the lever in a different room of our house? she wondered. *Not to actually go to the other world, not right now. But just to see if my theory's correct, to see if it can open anything in another place. . . .*

Carrying the partially wrapped lever in one hand, she ducked out of the secret room, then retreated from the Boring Room as well. She stepped over the pile of dropped Hot Wheels cars and came to a halt beside Rocket's kitty litter pan. No one had bothered cleaning the litter two weeks ago, the last time they were in the house, so it was still clumpy and nasty. Kitty litter was the most ordinary thing in the world; in a weird way, Emma felt safer standing next to Rocket's kitty litter than anywhere else in the basement.

I could try this wall, see if the lever can connect here and turn in either direction, Emma told herself. *Maybe this is far enough away from the ruined spot. If it works, I'd have such good news to tell the others. . . .*

Emma stood staring at the wall, gripping the lever. She thought about how scared she'd been, each trip she'd made from the secret room to the other world. She thought about how terrified she'd been just moments earlier, when the security guard slammed her and Chess to the ground.

Emma made no move to touch the lever to the wall. She couldn't. Not while she was alone.

I'm a coward, too, she thought sadly. *I'm just as frightened as Finn.*

NINE

CHESS

Dinner lasted forever. Chess tried to pay attention to Mr. Mayhew's fake happy chatter at the Rusty Barrel; he tried not to leave it entirely to Finn and Natalie to hold up the conversation. But the Rusty Barrel was one of those restaurants with loud music and flashing lights and people screaming constantly. Just about every time Chess tried to say something, his voice was drowned out by the roving band of waitstaff clapping and shouting in another part of the restaurant, "Happy, happy birthday! It's your special day. . . ."

Even when his life was normal, Chess had hated places like the Rusty Barrel.

Tonight was so much worse. Chess felt like he had to cover for Emma sitting in almost trance-like silence, her dark eyes unfocused, her jittery fingers tapping the table. For all Chess knew, she might be spelling Morse code versions of secrets she was figuring out—what was Morse code for *The sequined pillow revealed all*? But none of her brilliant deductions would do any good if Mr. Mayhew decided Emma was so far gone she needed medical attention and whisked her away.

So in addition to having to remember to eat his own chicken sandwich, carrots, and fruit, he had to keep nudging Emma to remind her to dip her spoon into her macaroni-and-cheese-and-broccoli mix and bring the spoon up to her mouth. Sometimes he even had to nudge her to remind her to chew and swallow.

But finally, after an eternity, dinner ended and Mr. Mayhew paid the bill and they all piled back into his car. Chess, Emma, and Finn had to keep their feet up off the floor of the car to avoid stepping on the lever wrapped in Finn's T-shirt. So on top of everything else, Chess's legs ached from being curled up like a pretzel all the way back.

But it will be worth it, if this helps us find Mom, Chess told himself.

As everyone walked back into Mr. Mayhew's house, Mr. Mayhew asked Natalie, "Sweetie, do you need me to write a note to your teacher, to explain why your leaf project is going to be a little late?"

"No, Dad," Natalie said in a cutting voice, as if Mr. Mayhew was being stupid. "I'll explain, and they'll believe me. Turns out, having a missing mom excuses *everything*."

"Um," Mr. Mayhew said, standing helplessly in his own foyer. Chess felt a little sorry for the man.

"Thank you for dinner," Chess said politely. "Thank you for everything you've done for us. I'm sure it won't be much longer before, uh . . ."

Mr. Mayhew held his hands up in the air, beseechingly. Chess pretended not to see that Mr. Mayhew's eyes had flooded with tears.

Natalie grabbed Chess's elbow.

"Come on," she said. "Help me get the little kids ready for bed."

They were halfway up the stairs before Chess realized that Natalie was practically shaking with rage.

"He's so ridiculous," she muttered. "Mom would have been *so* mad at us. She would have yelled at me for hours for letting you and Emma go back to that house by yourselves. *She* would have figured out I was lying about needing those leaves. She would have grounded me so fast. . . ."

"Wait a minute," Chess said, stopping on the stairs. "Are

you mad at your dad for *not* yelling at you? For not punishing you?"

Natalie glanced at him from beneath lowered lashes.

"I didn't say it made sense," she mumbled. Then she stopped on the stairs, too. "Except, it really does. When Mom yelled at me, I always knew she cared. And Dad . . . Dad just does what's easiest. He never wants anyone upset with him. Not even me. Like, does he think I won't love him anymore if he yelled at me?"

Chess didn't know what to say. Maybe he could have figured something out if he wasn't so busy noticing that Natalie's eyelashes were really, really long and pretty. And when she lifted her head and looked him full in the face . . .

"What is wrong with you two?" Emma called from the top of the stairs. "Hurry up!"

Chess and Natalie darted the rest of the way up the stairs.

All four kids convened in Natalie's room. Chess made himself leave Natalie's side to crouch beside Finn.

"Are you doing okay, buddy?" Chess asked, putting his arm around his little brother. "Now can you tell me how you, Natalie, and Mr. Mayhew knew to come find Emma and me? I mean, I think you saved us from being pulverized. Did you see the muscles on that guy?"

Chess was torn. Normally he would have played up how

much Finn had helped, to make Finn feel better. But was Natalie listening, too?

Chess didn't want to make himself sound too pitiful and weak around Natalie.

Even though he had been pitiful and weak.

"Natalie and me, we just told Mr. Mayhew I did a freak-out when I saw you and Emma weren't in the car," Finn said matter-of-factly. "But really . . . I saw a guy running after you, wearing navy blue and orange. And he looked like the guy up on the stage with Mom. You know, in the other world. But *he* wasn't the guy who tackled you. And Natalie said it was probably just *this* world's version of the guy on the stage that I saw. So everything's fine. Me being wrong just helped you." Finn leaned close to whisper, "I don't really think that muscle guy would have beaten you up. I think he was just acting tough."

Sometimes Chess wished he saw the world the way Finn did. Everything always worked out for Finn. And it wasn't just because Finn was eight and Chess was twelve that Finn was so much more happy-go-lucky, so much more carefree. Even when Chess was eight, he'd been a sad, quiet, too-grown-up child, still missing his dead father, still feeling like he needed to take care of his mom and Emma and Finn. Even if Chess went all the way back to when he was four and his dad was still alive . . . It was hard to remember, but even then, it seemed like Chess had known there were problems around him, things his parents whispered about when they thought Chess wasn't paying attention.

That's because there were *problems around us,* Chess thought. *I was just being . . . smart. Aware.*

When Chess was four and his father was still alive, the Greystones had still lived in the other world, and Chess's parents were risking their lives to try to make it a better place.

And that was why Chess's dad had died. And then Mom had brought the rest of the family to this world to keep them safe.

Emma clapped her hand against the wrapped-up lever to get everyone's attention.

"Okay, I'm not *exactly* sure how to do this, but if my theory is correct and we can get into the other world from anywhere, I *should* be able to fit this lever against the wall, and it'll just . . . nestle in somehow, and then we can turn it and see if a tunnel opens into the other world," she announced. "Is everybody ready?"

Chess gulped. Finn said, "Sure!" Natalie said, "Absolutely." When Chess added, "Go ahead," he hoped nobody else noticed how much his voice shook.

Emma kept the lever held high. She stepped over to a blank section of Natalie's wall, between the desk and the doorway to her huge walk-in closet. Emma unwrapped one end of the lever—the end that had once attached to the wall in the secret room back at the Greystones' house. She pressed that end of the lever against Natalie's wall.

Nothing happened.

"Maybe you should try an exterior wall?" Natalie suggested. "Maybe a tunnel can't form with the closet behind it?"

"That shouldn't matter, but . . . okay," Emma said.

She walked over to a space between Natalie's windows and slid the lever against the wall. Nothing happened this time either, except that some of the purple paint scraped off Natalie's wall.

"Maybe . . . maybe it's just not working because we're on the second floor?" Chess asked. "Maybe if we go down to the basement . . ."

Emma threw the lever to the floor.

"I told you—it's not about basements! I'm just *wrong*! This theory is wrong, too! We're never going to find Mom!"

And then Emma collapsed to the floor and began crying.

TEN

FINN

Finn, Chess, and Natalie all ran over to comfort Emma.

"We *will* figure it out!" Natalie said, smoothing Emma's hair. "We have to!"

"Don't worry. Eventually we'll think of something that works," Chess said, patting Emma's arm.

Finn settled for patting her back. He tried to think what else he could say to make her feel better. He finally came up with: "You're the smartest person I know! You've got this!"

Emma whirled on him. She had tears rolling down her cheeks, a little line of snot wiped to the side of her nose. Her eyes were just shadows. Emma always had such happy, *busy* eyes—Finn often felt like he could look into her eyes and see how fast the gears of her brain were moving.

But now her eyes looked empty and sad and still. And stuck. She looked like her brain gears were all jammed.

"What if I'm not smart *enough*?" she asked. "What if none of us are? This is the three hundred and seventy-third idea I've tried, and I've failed every time. And I thought this one was different. I was so sure the lever was important! I thought I had to be right this time!"

Chess and Natalie kept patting and smoothing, but Chess covered his face with his spare hand, and Natalie wiped her own eyes.

Chess and Natalie were crying, too, or close to it. Neither of them said anything. Maybe they didn't know what to say.

"Well . . . ," Finn began. "Maybe the lever *is* important, just not the way you thought. Why would someone have moved it from one place to another in the secret room if it *wasn't* important? Didn't you say we should look for fingerprints on the lever? Why don't we try that? If we try everything we can, *something* has to work. Right?"

"That's not . . ." Emma sniffed. "I don't think that's statistically sound reasoning."

Finn had no clue what that meant, so he just kept talking. "Somebody help me. How do we check for fingerprints?"

Natalie wiped the back of her hand across her face again, then pulled out her cell phone. She typed something quickly before handing Finn the phone.

She'd called up a website about dusting for fingerprints.

"Okay, this says we can use baking soda," Finn said, handing the phone back. "Natalie, your dad's got baking soda in the kitchen, right?"

"Probably," Natalie said, with a sniffle of her own. "But if you go down there, he'll want to talk to you, and—"

"I'll be sneaky!" Finn called back over his shoulder as he raced for the door.

Finn didn't really care much about fingerprinting the lever. He didn't know if it was important or not. But he couldn't stand seeing the others so frozen. At least if they tried to find fingerprints on the lever, they'd be doing *something.* Not just huddled in a heap, missing their mothers.

When Finn got to the staircase, he switched to tiptoeing. He shouldn't have worried about being quiet, because Mr. Mayhew had the TV downstairs cranked up loud, some sports announcer calling excitedly, "Did you see that? No one else has quite that approach. . . ."

Finn jumped past the last three stairs, hitting the floor with a thud.

"Natalie?" Mr. Mayhew called, spinning his chair to the side.

Oops.

"No, it's me," Finn said, holding up his hands as if to prove he was innocent. "I'm just, uh, going to the kitchen for a drink of water." Now, why wouldn't he get it from the bathroom upstairs? "I wanted ice."

"Okay," Mr. Mayhew said. But he didn't spin back to the game. "Is Natalie still . . . Oh, what am I saying? She lost her mother. Of course she's still upset. She's never going to get over that. And . . . neither am I."

He whispered the last part.

Don't think about Mom, Finn told himself. *Don't let yourself be sad like Mr. Mayhew.*

But he couldn't help feeling a little sad *for* Mr. Mayhew. It suddenly seemed awful that Mr. Mayhew was sitting in his huge living room all alone, watching the basketball game all by himself. At least Finn and the other kids had each other.

"If we Greystones weren't here," Finn began, "would Natalie be with you, cheering for, well, whoever you're cheering for?"

"Are you asking if she's a Cavs fan, too?" Mr. Mayhew said. He slid down in his chair. "Or are you asking if she'd be down here with me or upstairs texting in her room like she probably is right now?"

"Teenagers do that," Finn said, as though hanging out with Natalie made him an expert.

Mr. Mayhew gave a sad laugh. "Well then . . . how about *you* stay and watch the game with me?" He winked. "We'll pretend it isn't past your bedtime."

"Thanks, but . . . I'd fall asleep," Finn said. He faked a huge yawn. "Then you might have to miss a big play, carrying me up to bed."

"Yeah, I guess you're right," Mr. Mayhew said. He winked again. Or maybe he was blinking back tears. "Who's the grown-up here, and who's the kid?" He waved his hand in a way that was probably supposed to look cheerful. "Go on, get your drink of water. Then it's off to bed for you, young man!"

Finn kind of did want to stay with Mr. Mayhew now, to cheer him up.

But when we get Mom and Ms. Morales back, that will cheer up everybody, he told himself. *That will fix everything. So that's what we have to focus on.*

He watched Mr. Mayhew spin his chair back toward the TV. Then Finn sprinted for the kitchen, grabbed the baking soda, and raced back up the stairs.

The other three kids had unfrozen enough that they'd assembled paintbrushes, Scotch tape, and black construction paper.

"This says we sprinkle the baking soda on, brush it off as gently as possible, and if there are fingerprints, we'll see them outlined in white," Natalie explained, reading directions from her phone. "We put tape over each distinct fingerprint, pull the tape off, and then move the tape to the black paper. That preserves the image."

"And I say we start on this flat section in the middle," Emma said, pointing. "I'm pretty sure I only touched the edges, and Chess says he only touched the edges on one end when he pulled on the lever, opening and shutting the tunnel. . . ."

Finn saw how the edges of the lever were raised higher than the midsection.

"Hey, does anybody else think this looks like a big Pez?" he asked.

"A what?" Natalie said.

"A Pez—you know? The little white candy you get from a Pez dispenser?" Finn said. "The candy doesn't taste like much, but it's fun because the dispensers can be shaped like Darth Vader heads or frogs or Batman or . . . whatever . . . and so eating Pez is like eating Batman's tongue, or Darth Vader's, or . . . didn't they have Pez dispensers when you were my age, Natalie?"

"Finn, I'm only five years older than you!" Natalie protested. "Of course we had Pez and Pez dispensers when I was in second grade!"

But Finn saw he'd gotten Natalie to laugh. Finn counted that as a victory.

"Yeah, see, you just need to put the letters *P-E-Z* right there on that lever, and it'd be, like, Pez for giants!" Finn said.

He pointed, and Emma grabbed his hand.

"Don't touch!" she reminded him.

"Here," Chess said, opening the box of baking soda in Finn's other hand. "How about you start pouring this?"

Finn let the baking soda rain down onto the lever. His aim wasn't great—some heaped over the edge onto his old shirt, which the others had kept under the lever.

"It's snowing!" Finn called, because even if this didn't work, he was determined to cheer up the others by making this fun. He grabbed a paintbrush. "And now I'm painting with snow. . . ."

"Gently, remember?" Emma said.

Finn had just speared a particularly large clump of baking soda, and he'd been about to yell, *Hi-YAH!* He decided not to do that. For a moment, all four kids silently bent over the lever, brushing baking soda in from the edges, toward the hollowed-out part.

No matter how hard he tried, Finn just could not go as slowly as the others. His brush caught on something. He squinted down at the lever.

"I'm looking for lines, right?" he asked. "But little wavy ones, not thick ones?" He shoved his brush forward, and inched around to the lever's other side to squint again at what he'd found. Everyone else was staring down at their own space; nobody was looking at his area of the lever.

"What if someone had a tattoo on their fingertips?" Finn asked. "Like, of some word? Would that show up as letters instead of fingerprints?"

"What do you mean?" Emma asked, turning her head.

Finn pointed.

"Isn't that the letter *U*?" he asked. Maybe he was just fooling himself, because he'd been talking about letters on a Pez.

Emma hopped over the lever to Finn's side. She dumped more baking soda beside Finn's area, and swiped her own paintbrush across that zone.

The letters *S* and *E* appeared beside the *U*.

"Use," Finn read. "It's the word 'use.'"

Emma threw her arms around Finn's shoulders.

"Finn! You're amazing! Thank you for making us check for fingerprints! You've found another code!"

ELEVEN

EMMA

“I have?” Finn said blankly. “But ‘use’ is a real word. What if it’s not another code but—”

“Instructions!” Emma yelled. “You’re right! Maybe you’ve found instructions!”

She picked up the baking soda box again, then changed her mind.

“The letters are carved so lightly we can’t see them, so . . . I think this will go faster if we do something like a tombstone rubbing,” Emma said. “Natalie, now we need white paper and a pencil. Where’s . . .”

She didn’t wait for Natalie to answer. She just stood up,

walked over to Natalie's desk, and pulled out the supplies she needed.

"What's a tombstone rubbing?" Finn asked.

"Oh, I know what you mean, Emma," Natalie said. "Did you have Mrs. Creveau for third grade, too? Finn, maybe you'll do this next year. Tombstone rubbings are for when the letters have worn off a gravestone over centuries, so you can't read it anymore—sometimes, you can't even see that there are words there—so you use pencil and paper to . . . well, it's exactly what Emma's doing now."

Emma was glad Natalie had answered Finn. Emma was too busy shaking the baking soda away and then laying the paper down carefully over the middle section of the lever. She had to bend it a little, since there was such a gully in the lever. Then she pressed the pencil point sideways against the paper and began running it back and forth.

"I did that in third grade, too," Chess said. "But do you think this *lever* is hundreds of years old, like the tombstones?"

"I don't think the words on this lever wore away over time," Emma said. "I think this message was *designed* to be impossible to read unless you know it's there. Unless you know to do a tombstone rubbing and look for it."

"Okay," Natalie said. "What does—"

But Emma was already holding up the first sheet of paper:

USE IN A
EXISTS IN

Silently, Chess handed her a second sheet of paper.

Emma placed it on the next section of the lever and began rubbing the pencil back and forth again.

Then she dropped both sheets of paper to the floor, side by side.

USE IN A SPOT THAT
EXISTS IN BOTH (WORLDS)

"It *is* instructions!" Emma exulted. "And I *was* right about the lever all along! Just not totally, one hundred percent right!"

"Were you ninety-eight percent right?" Finn asked. "Ninety-five percent?"

"Oh, who cares about the numbers!" Emma said, grabbing her brother by the shoulders again and swinging him back and forth. "I was right enough that we can go rescue Mom!"

TWELVE

CHESS

Chess watched Finn, Emma, and Natalie hugging and congratulating each other. Then Finn switched to fist-bumping everyone.

"We're the best team ever!" he crowed. "We all worked together! Now let's go!"

"Go where?" Chess asked quietly.

"Somewhere we know exists in both worlds! That's where the lever will work!" Emma said. "That has to be what this means!"

"So you're saying . . . the only reason the lever didn't work here in my room is . . . doesn't this room exist in the other world?" Natalie asked. "Are you saying Dad's whole *house* might not exist in the other world?"

"I guess not!" Emma said, shrugging. "That'll teach me to consider all the possible variables the next time!"

Natalie scooted back against the wall. She drew her knees to her chest and wrapped her arms around her legs.

"Dad had this house custom-built after Mom said she wanted a divorce," Natalie said. "He said *he* wasn't going to be one of those sad-sack divorced dads living in an empty condo and getting all depressed about losing everything. He said . . . he said he'd show Mom he was fine without her." She tilted her head back to gaze toward the ceiling. A dreaminess settled over her face. "If this house doesn't exist in the other world, what does that mean?"

"It means we have to go somewhere else to use the lever and go back to the other world!" Finn said, as if that should be obvious to everyone.

Chess made himself stop gazing at Natalie.

"We shouldn't try our house either," Chess said. "Not just because the tunnel in the basement collapsed, and maybe that closes off the whole house as a place to travel from. But also . . . the authorities in the other world know where we were traveling back and forth before. Don't you think they're probably guarding the house on the other side?"

"So maybe we go to a neighbor's house?" Finn asked.

"Or . . . can we find somewhere to put the lever beside the pond back in our neighborhood? We know the pond exists in both worlds!"

"I don't think we should cross into the other world outdoors, where anyone could see us," Chess said. He tried not to let his voice tremble, so no one would hear how much that idea terrified him. "And what would we tell our neighbors about why we want to hang out in their house? How could we say, 'Oh, just leave us alone and don't worry if we disappear'?"

"Natalie's mother's house," Emma said firmly, as if she was settling an argument. "*That's* where we try the lever next. We skip school and do it first thing tomorrow morning."

"We don't know for sure that Mom's house exists in the other world, either," Natalie objected. "Not the same house in the same place. We never saw it when we were there before."

"But if it does—and if that's where you and your mom live in the other world—then it's the safest place to go back," Emma said. "A place where you, at least, would look like you belong, Natalie. So that's what we try first."

Slowly, Natalie nodded. Chess wanted more time to think through everything.

When they'd been in the other world the last time,

they'd seen the other-world version of Natalie's mom, but not Natalie or her dad. But they knew those other-world versions existed, and it had helped a lot to have Natalie pretend to be the other Natalie.

But what if it's extra dangerous to be in a place where this world's Natalie could easily run into that world's Natalie? Chess wondered. *At her mom's house, wouldn't it also be more likely that she'd run into the other world's version of her mom? And wouldn't the other world's version of Ms. Morales see right away that our Natalie is different from the Natalie there?*

Would the other world's Natalie *really* be that different from this world's? Or would she be someone else who could help them?

But what if the other world's Ms. Morales saw Finn, Emma, and me? Chess wondered, panic rising in his chest. *What if she figured out we're connected to Mom? That world's Ms. Morales was a judge! The judge who tried to make Mom seem guilty!*

Chess's brain hurt thinking of all the things that could go wrong. But he couldn't tell the others it was a terrible idea to cross over at Ms. Morales's house.

Because wasn't it actually just a terrible idea to cross over, period?

"Wait, go back a little," Finn said. "Did you really say, 'skip school'? We get to skip school?"

"Do you want to wait a moment longer than you have

to, to go rescue Mom?" Emma asked.

"No," Finn said, shaking his head so emphatically his hair flopped around. "So why don't we go *right now*?"

Chess thought about what it would be like to sneak out in the dark. He thought about arriving in the strange, awful other world at nighttime, when they couldn't even see the dangers around them.

"We need time to prepare," he said. To his surprise, his voice came out sounding firm and certain. "We need to take supplies—like, food, even—in case we have to hide out for a while. It wouldn't be a bad idea to have some of the tools and electronic gadgets Joe carried with him. Last time we went to the other world, we didn't know what we were getting into, and we were lucky we managed to escape. This time we need to be ready."

Emma and Natalie nodded, backing him up.

"And I want to solve the rest of Mom's coded message before we go," Emma said. "I'm sure it'll tell us more about what went wrong in the other world, and how it became such an awful place. Maybe if I stay up all night working on it, by morning I'll know . . ."

"That you're too tired to think straight?" Chess finished for her. "Emma, we've been working on that message for two weeks! An extra twelve hours isn't going to make a difference!"

"Nine hours," Natalie said, checking the time on her phone. "We leave in nine hours. We should leave when I'd normally catch the bus—I'll come up with some excuse for Dad about why you three have to leave with me."

Chess could tell Natalie was figuring out logistics. Emma stuck out her lower lip, like she was mad that Chess didn't think she could solve Mom's code in the next twelve hours. Or nine.

"Emma . . . ," Chess said.

"I know, I know—sleep is important!" Emma said. This was something their mother said all the time; hearing Emma say it made Chess's eyes tear up. He had to turn his head to the side so Emma and Finn wouldn't see. "But doesn't it seem dangerous to go back *without* knowing everything we possibly can?"

"Yeah," Chess muttered. "But what else can we do?"

The next few hours passed in a blur. Chess, Emma, and Natalie stayed up past midnight making lists and packing backpacks, then double-checking lists and backpacks and cramming in "just one more thing that could save our lives." Finn tried to stay up, too, but early on Chess turned to ask Finn a question and discovered his brother curled up and snoring on the floor beside the lever. Chess crouched down beside him, planning to pick him up and carry him to his own bed. Then he felt Natalie's hair tickle his arm. She leaned close.

"Would it be so terrible," she began, peering down at Finn, "if we left him here tomorrow morning? Just let him keep sleeping? *He'd* stay safe that way. And he could keep Dad company if . . . if . . . He could explain everything if . . ."

Chess knew exactly what Natalie wasn't saying: . . . *if we never make it back from the other world.*

Watching the smile play over Finn's face—leave it to Finn to smile even in his sleep, even the night before heading into danger—Chess understood exactly why Natalie wanted to keep Finn safe. Chess wanted that, too. But as he slid his arms under Finn's neck and knees, Chess made his voice gruff, almost scolding, as he told Natalie, "We promised Finn we'd take him with us. I'm not breaking any promises to Finn."

And then somehow, though Chess could have sworn he got no sleep himself, it was Friday morning, and Emma was cramming their mother's computer with the coded message into her backpack; Chess was helping Finn button his shirt as Finn excitedly chattered, "Mom always said this is her favorite shirt of mine—she'll like that I'm wearing her favorite shirt, won't she?" And then all three Greystones clustered around Natalie at the top of the stairs. Natalie took a deep breath.

"Let me handle Dad when we go down to the kitchen,

okay?" she muttered.

All four kids descended the stairs, maybe for the last time.

Natalie sped into the kitchen, grabbed a box of Pop-Tarts, and made a big show of tossing it to Chess. He added it to his backpack.

"You remember Megan's mom is taking me to school this morning, right?" she asked her dad, who was sitting at the kitchen table, hunched over a cup of coffee. "And then, because she works close by, she'll drop off the Greystone kids at the elementary, too. 'Kay?"

Mr. Mayhew blinked groggily. He wasn't a morning person.

"So . . . you all need a ride to Megan's?" he asked.

"*No*, Dad," Natalie said, with an exasperated eye roll. "Megan's the one who lives in *this* neighborhood. Like, a block away. I don't need a ride."

"Oh," Mr. Mayhew said. "I thought . . . You know I have to work late this afternoon, so . . ."

"Yeah, yeah, we'll be fine. We'll order pizza or Chinese for dinner. See you later!"

Natalie brushed a kiss past the top of her father's head, on the spot where his hair was a little thin.

"Bye, Mr. Mayhew!" Finn chirped. Chess and Emma

waved, but Chess could tell that Mr. Mayhew barely noticed, because he was watching Natalie vanish around the corner.

The kids made it out to the garage, and Natalie sagged against the handles of her bike.

"He'll know I forgave him for last night, right?" she muttered to Chess. "Because I kissed him on his bald spot? He'll remember that if . . . if . . ."

Once again, Chess knew what Natalie wasn't saying.

"Helmets," he reminded Finn and Emma, even though it seemed crazy to worry about bike helmets when they would be riding toward so much danger.

Natalie still stood there frozen. Chess handed her a helmet, too.

"You're not worried about getting your friend Megan or her mom in trouble?" Chess asked. "You know, if we're . . . gone for a while?"

He wasn't going to let his voice just trail off. He wasn't going to acknowledge any danger except delays.

"I tried your mom's trick, and set up automatic texts that will go to my dad over the next week, if we're gone that long," Natalie said. "It's all excuses until the last one. And the last one will . . . explain."

Chess wanted to say, *Do you really think explanations* help*? Did we miss our mother any less, knowing why she left?*

But just then, Natalie gifted him with a dazzling smile.

"And don't worry about me getting anybody else in trouble," she added. "I don't have any friends named Megan."

And then she snapped on her helmet, threw her leg over the bicycle, and pushed off, leading all of them out into the early-morning darkness, toward her mother's house.

THIRTEEN

FINN

Finn had never been allowed to ride his bike in the dark before, and he loved it.

Of course, he had Natalie and Emma ahead of him and Chess behind him, so he felt perfectly safe and in no danger of getting lost. He could just savor the fact that the route from Mr. Mayhew's house to Ms. Morales's neighborhood was downhill. The first mile or so, he barely had to pedal.

Then there was a straightaway for a while, where they all pedaled hard.

We're finally going back to get Mom! Finn wanted to shout at everyone they passed—the joggers and the other cyclists and the cars inching around them, making room. The words sang in his head, working into the rhythm of his pedaling. He hadn't felt this happy in weeks.

They turned into Ms. Morales's neighborhood, which was full of even bigger mansions than Mr. Mayhew's neighborhood, and even bigger yards, too. It took Finn at least five times of saying, *We're finally going back to get Mom!* to get past each house. And then Ms. Morales's house lay right ahead and above them, just as the sun broke over the horizon.

Natalie screeched to a halt.

"What?" she exclaimed. "Is that—?"

Just as abruptly as she'd stopped, she hopped back on her bike and started pedaling furiously toward her mother's house.

Finn pulled up beside Emma, who was still stopped and peering off after Natalie.

"What happened?" Finn asked. "What got into her?"

Emma squinted into the distance. She shaded her eyes with her hand to block the glare of the rising sun.

"I think . . . ," she began. "I think . . . Finn, why would there be a For Sale sign in Ms. Morales's yard?"

FOURTEEN

EMMA

By the time Emma, Finn, and Chess caught up with Natalie, she'd yanked the Realtor's sign out of her mother's yard and stomped it down flat on the grass.

"I hate him!" she shouted. "He didn't even tell me! How could Dad put Mom's house on the market—Mom's and *my* house on the market—and not—not—"

"I was wrong. That sign actually just says 'Coming Soon,' not 'For Sale,'" Emma said, squinting down at the sign. "That's not as bad, is it?"

"And why do you think it was your dad who did this?" Chess asked. "Your parents are divorced. So wouldn't your mom have had arrangements for someone else to—"

"Who cares?" Natalie said, jumping up and down on the sign. "*Somebody* gave up on Mom ever coming back. *Somebody* thinks she's dead, and Dad didn't even have the courage to tell me what . . . what . . ."

Natalie's long, dark hair flew out in all directions as she jumped and screamed. The part of Emma's mind that always analyzed things scientifically thought it was a beautiful demonstration of kinetic energy.

The part of Emma's brain that felt angry all the time wanted to join Natalie in stomping on the sign.

"Natalie," Chess said softly. "We wanted to sneak into your mom's house without anyone seeing or hearing us."

Natalie ignored him.

"Maybe you'd feel better throwing that sign into the trash?" Emma asked.

"Good idea," Natalie said. She lifted the sign from the ground and stomped over to punch in the garage code on the side of the house. Before the garage door was even halfway up, she ducked under it and slammed the sign down into the trash can in the garage. Then she kicked the can.

The three Greystones dashed after her into the garage. Chess hit the control pad to shut the door from the inside, hiding all four of them.

"Natalie, nobody would have changed anything in your

mom's office, right?" Emma asked. "It's still soundproof, isn't it?"

"How would I know?" Natalie growled. "Nobody tells me anything!"

"Let's go check," Emma said.

She and Natalie raced toward Ms. Morales's office. Emma shut the door behind them, pausing only to tell Chess and Finn, "You two stay outside. Knock on the door if you hear anything." Then Emma turned to Natalie and told her, "Scream as loud as you want. Say bad words if you have to."

"AHHHH!" Natalie shrieked.

Emma put her hands over her ears to keep from being deafened. But she could still hear Natalie shouting: "Nobody should give up on my mom! She can take care of herself! She's *fine*! She's still alive! And we're going to rescue her! It's not going to be like Grandma. . . ."

Natalie suddenly went silent.

"Wait, what?" Emma asked, taking the hands off her ears. "'Like Grandma'—what does that mean? You've never told us about any grandma."

Natalie's face quivered.

"She died," Natalie said. "A year ago. She was my favorite person in the whole world, and . . . I don't talk about it. I can't talk about it, not when Mom's missing, and Dad . . .

and Mom . . . I hate how people say, 'I'm sorry,' and it doesn't mean *anything*. . . ."

Emma knew what that was like.

"You can keep screaming if you want," she offered.

Natalie screeched even louder than the first time. Emma joined in, yelling at the top of her lungs, "Natalie's so right! Nobody else is going to die!"

Ms. Morales was a Realtor herself, and she had half a dozen signs with her face on them stacked behind her enormous desk.

"That woman is still alive!" Emma shouted, pointing at the signs. "My mom is still alive, too! They're both fine! So's Joe!"

Natalie and Emma stopped screaming at the exact same time. Natalie blinked in the unexpected quiet.

"Emma . . . that really helped," she said, sounding surprised. "How did you know? Is there some scientific study you read somewhere, about how screaming can make you feel better?"

"Nope," Emma said. "It's just what I would want to do, if I were you. It's . . . what I've wanted to do for the past two weeks."

Natalie had an expression of wonder on her face.

"Emma, I think we're a lot alike," she said. "Who knew?"

Emma gritted her teeth. She liked Natalie a lot more

than she had when she first met her, and she was pretty sure Natalie liked her, too. Emma kind of wanted to say, *I am sorry about your grandma dying, even if it makes you mad to hear that.* She wanted to say, *You can talk to me about her if you want.* Or maybe, *You know you can tell Finn and Chess, too.*

But there were other things Emma needed to talk about right now.

"Natalie," Emma began. "When we go over into the other world, you can't . . . you can't freak out again. No matter how mad you get. We need you. You're the best at lying, and you're the only one who can look like you belong there. So . . . oh, my gosh. I think I've heard too many of your dad's sports shows. I was about to say, 'You've got to keep your head in the game.'"

Natalie let out a sad sound that might have been a laugh.

"I know," Natalie said. "I do need to keep my head in the game."

"Okay," Emma said. She put her hand on the doorknob. "Ready?"

"Yeah," Natalie said. "Let's go save our moms!"

FIFTEEN

CHESS

Chess had no idea what Emma and Natalie talked about in Ms. Morales's office, but when they came out, they were both calm and resolute.

"Basement," Emma said, turning with almost military precision toward the door that led to the basement stairs. "That's where we try this. Because that's where we're least likely to run into anybody on the other side."

"Makes sense," Natalie agreed.

And then Chess *couldn't* say how much he hated basements now, how much they made him feel trapped.

All four kids trooped down the stairs. Ms. Morales's

basement was immense and practically empty, with an expanse of cream-colored carpet that looked like no one ever walked on it.

Natalie gulped.

"This . . . used to be Dad's man cave," she mumbled. "It was, like, sports fan kingdom. When he moved out, he took all the furniture. Mom didn't do anything but replace the carpet and have the walls repainted."

"Okay," Chess said.

"I'm just telling you," Natalie said. "In case what we see on the other side is . . . different."

"Let's just focus on *getting* to the other side for now, all right?" Emma asked.

"Let's go! I'm ready!" Finn jumped up and down, tugging on Chess's arm.

"I've got the lever," Chess said, because he had the biggest backpack, the only one that the lever could fit into. He took the backpack from his shoulders and pulled out the lever, still wrapped in Finn's shirt from the day before.

Were we stupid, that we didn't work harder at checking for fingerprints? Chess wondered. *Or was Emma right, that we really need to solve all of Mom's coded message before we go back?*

Chess was so sick of second-guessing everything. He handed the lever to Emma.

"Lever, wall," Emma said, as if she needed to remind

herself. She took five steps back, moving under the stairs, behind the furnace. "Let's try this back here. So we'll be hidden if, you know, the basement's laid out the same way in the other world."

Chess, Natalie, and Finn clustered around Emma. Emma swung the lever out and then forward, like it was a bat and she was determined to hit a home run.

The lever made a strange thud colliding against the wall. It didn't sound like metal banging against plaster and wood; it sounded more like stone on stone. And then, somehow, the lever seemed to become part of the wall; it looked like it had been built that way.

"That . . . that . . . ," Natalie stammered.

"That isn't how it worked before, back at Mr. Mayhew's house," Finn said. "Emma, you did it!"

"Not until we turn the lever," Emma said.

Chess looked from Finn to Emma to Natalie. If he hadn't known better, he might have thought it was Natalie who was related to the younger kids, instead of him. Not because their features were so similar—though, with all three having dark hair and dark eyes, they were close enough. No, what made Finn, Emma, and Natalie look so much alike was their expressions: They all carried the same mix of awe and hope and excitement in their eyes and written across their faces. Finn and Natalie put their hands on the lever beside

Emma's; all of them wanted to open a tunnel to the other world together.

Chess didn't reach out a hand to join them. The thought repeating in his head was, *And we know how to shut off any tunnel to the other world now, too. If it's too scary, if there's too much danger, I'll have to be the one who yanks the lever straight off from the wall, breaking off the connection. I can do that, if I have to. I can keep everyone safe.*

Finn, Emma, and Natalie shoved the lever forward. Chess felt the room around him begin to spin, and all he could do was shut his eyes.

SIXTEEN

FINN

"It's working!" Finn shrieked. "Emma was right!"

But the words were ripped from his mouth by the crazy spinning. He couldn't even hear himself, let alone anyone answering. Finn's body pitched to the right and then to the left. He tried to picture himself like a surfer riding the waves. But the image that came into his head was of him, Chess, Emma, and Natalie slamming around the enormous basement like dice in a cup.

"We survived . . . the spinning . . . before," he shouted, in case any of the others felt panicky, too.

Maybe his mind blanked out between the words; maybe

whole minutes passed between one word and the next. This, too, was a feeling he remembered from crossing into the other world before, from his own basement. Both times he'd hit a moment when he couldn't think. Or see or hear or feel or . . .

Maybe what actually happened was that he stopped existing for an instant?

Finn's brain must be working again, if he could think that. He kept spinning.

And then, suddenly, everything was still.

Finn blinked, his eyes adjusting to . . . well, not darkness, exactly, but dimness. That was different. Hadn't the lights glowed bright as day in Ms. Morales's basement, even though the sun was barely up outdoors?

Woozily, Finn sat up. Chess, Emma, and Natalie were just shadowy shapes on the floor beside him. He reached over and shook Emma by the shoulders.

"Get up!" he whispered. "We made it! I think we did, anyway!"

Emma groaned. Chess staggered to his feet. Beyond Chess, a tunnel stretched off into the distance from an odd, dark hole in the wall.

"It's like . . . how it worked at your house," Natalie whispered, raising her head, too. "The spinning makes the tunnel, and then the tunnel stays open as long as we're here. So we can go back. Anytime we want."

"But if we leave it open, *anyone* can go through," Chess said. "In either direction. Anytime."

He groped around on the wall. His hand caught on something. He bent his knees and shoved.

There was a lever here, too. And Chess was turning the lever in the opposite direction.

The tunnel vanished.

"Chess!" Finn exclaimed. "How did you know that would work? Was there a second lever at the other end of the tunnel in *our* basement?"

"There must have been, but I didn't know enough to look for it," Chess said grimly.

"Mirror . . . image," Emma croaked, still sprawled flat on the floor. "I guess the . . . lever . . . duplicates itself . . . in each world. . . ."

"Oh, like a door has a doorknob on both sides," Finn said. "That makes sense." It was a rare day when he could explain things faster than Emma.

"Are you *sure* it will open back up now?" Natalie asked.

"I—" Chess began. His face flushed.

Finn rushed over to the wall and pushed the lever to the right. The wall started to melt away, showing just a glimpse of the open tunnel again. Quickly, Finn yanked the lever back to the left, and the wall turned completely solid once more.

"Yes!" Finn practically crowed. He shimmied his shoulders in something like a victory dance. "We've got it all figured out now!" He went back to Emma and tugged on her arm. "Did you see that?"

"Need . . . a minute," Emma muttered. "I think . . . I'm the one who has the most trouble . . . adjusting."

Finn giggled.

"Then maybe I'm best," he bragged. "I sat up first!" He leaned down close to her ear. "But don't worry. You'll always be best at math. And science. And lots of other things. Chess, Natalie, and me, we'll just look around while you recover."

His ears felt normal again—they weren't ringing anymore—and he could feel how deeply silent this basement was. It made him feel safe. Nobody could have seen them arrive.

Finn wanted to congratulate Emma for that, too. But first he wanted to *see* his surroundings, and no matter how much his eyes adjusted, they'd never work well without more light.

"Is the light switch over by the stairs?" Finn asked Natalie.

He didn't wait for an answer. The older kids were all so groggy.

Finn tiptoed out from behind the furnace, heading toward the stairs. The basement had to be empty; nobody would sit in such darkness. Only the slightest glow came through the small windows that ringed the top of the room. Finn hit the light switch.

"Natalie!" he cried as the lights sprang to life in such a sudden glow that for a moment, Finn could only see shapes. "This room is full of furniture now! Full to *bursting* with furniture!"

Then Finn's eyes adjusted. Now he could see colors as well as shapes.

And every object in the room—pillars, curtains, couches, wall hangings, carpet, even a *refrigerator*—were either navy blue or orange. The entire basement was like a tribute to orange and blue, a celebration of those colors, a denial that any other colors had a right to exist.

Finn had only ever been in one place that looked anything like this basement: the Public Hall where his mother had been trapped for her trial.

"Natalie!" he cried. "Is your basement *another* place where they punish innocent people?"

SEVENTEEN

EMMA

Emma heard the terror in her little brother's voice.

She was still blinking back her discomfort with the trip through the tunnel, but every blink made her notice something new around her that was navy blue or orange, or both intertwined: the coasters arrayed across a coffee table, the inlaid stone around a section that seemed to have been turned into a jacuzzi, the flags that hung around every pillar.

"Finn! It's just sports stuff!" Emma hissed. "I guess somehow, in this world, this is still Mr. Mayhew's man cave. Natalie, you tell him. Tell him which team your dad loves, where the colors are orange and blue! Or maybe it's your mom who's the sports fan here?"

"The teams my dad likes—and my mom, too—are the Cavs, the Blue Jackets, the Buckeyes, and the Browns," Natalie said dazedly. "*None* of their colors are orange and blue."

"But maybe their team colors are different here?" Emma heard how she sounded like she was begging Natalie to agree. "Or maybe your mom likes a different team here? Or maybe it's *you* in this world who's the big sports fan?"

"I don't know." Natalie shrugged helplessly.

Finn darted back to huddle beside Emma.

"We never knew what it meant, that almost everyone was wearing orange and blue the last time we were in this world," Chess said, as if he was trying to sound reasonable and unafraid. "It might not have meant anything. It just seemed . . ."

"Bad," Finn muttered, clinging to Emma.

"No, it seemed *evil*," Natalie said. "Like someone having Nazi swastikas everywhere, or seeing KKK members wearing white hoods, or—"

Emma opened her mouth to warn Natalie, *Can't you see you're terrifying Finn even worse?*

But just then Emma heard a door open, followed by a voice coming from the top of the basement stairs: "Natalie, is that you down there? Why aren't you at school?"

It was Ms. Morales.

For an instant, Emma felt her heart jump. Ms. Morales was such a *mom*. Staying with Ms. Morales after their own mom vanished had been nightmarish for the Greystones, but Ms. Morales had always been kind. And Emma knew how Natalie longed to get her mother back; Emma could see joy burst over Natalie's face at the sound of her mother's voice.

And then, just as quickly, the joy on Natalie's face flipped to fear, and Emma felt her own heart crash. Finn burrowed closer against Emma's side, and Chess pulled them both back into the shadows.

It must have hit the others as quickly as it hit Emma: This wasn't the Ms. Morales they knew. This was the Ms. Morales from the other world.

The evil one.

EIGHTEEN

CHESS

Chess heard Ms. Morales's voice. Then he heard footsteps on the stairs.

Ms. Morales—the other world's Ms. Morales—was coming *down* the stairs.

"Hide!" Natalie whispered, shoving the three Greystone children farther back into the shadows behind the furnace.

"You, too!" Chess begged.

"No—she already knows I'm here!" Natalie whispered back. "She'll look for me—it'll just make her find the three of you. . . ."

There was nothing Chess could do to help Natalie.

Natalie—brave, brave Natalie—stepped away from where the Greystones were crouched. She stopped by the bottom of the stairs.

"Natalie, answer me!" Ms. Morales demanded, her heels clicking on the stairs.

Even hiding, Chess was still at the right angle to see the play of emotions on Natalie's face at the sound of her mother's voice.

No, don't think of her as Natalie's mom, Chess thought. *That's too hard, and it's not really her. This woman is the Judge. The Judge who wanted to punish* my *mother.*

And the Judge didn't sound *exactly* like Ms. Morales. Ms. Morales's voice had a lilt to it, a playfulness, even when she was mad at Natalie. Maybe there was just the trace of an accent, too, a hint that she'd be equally comfortable speaking Spanish or English. Chess wasn't sure what made her voice unique, but he liked the way Ms. Morales talked.

The Judge's voice was more boxed-in, tightly controlled. It sounded humorless and angry, with no room for any other emotion.

"M-Mom?" Natalie stammered. "I thought you already left."

"Oh, so you waited until you thought everyone was gone, and *then* you skipped out from school and sneaked back home?" the Judge accused.

"Everyone"? Chess thought. Who else lived here besides Natalie—er, *Other*-Natalie—and her mom?

Natalie seemed to be fighting to control the emotions on her face. She finally settled on a defiant glare toward the Judge, who'd stopped on the bottom step. If he leaned out a little, Chess could see the back of the Judge's head.

"I'm not skipping school!" Natalie protested. "I got sick and they sent me home!"

"Without calling me first?" the Judge mocked. "Come on, Natalie. That's not school policy. How stupid do you think I am, telling such a transparent lie—"

"It's *true*!" Natalie insisted. "They tried to call you and couldn't get through. The school secretary said something about lots of people having cell phone problems today. . . . Anyhow, my friend Megan's mom was there, and she said she'd bring me home, since she was coming this way anyway."

"Lies, lies, lies." The Judge's voice was truly cutting now. "You don't have any friends named Megan."

Well, Chess thought. *Score one for the Judge for knowing that.*

"She's a *new* friend," Natalie said. "You haven't met her yet."

And . . . score one for Natalie for coming up with that so quickly, Chess thought.

Against the odds, he felt hope rising. Natalie sounded

utterly convincing. Maybe she could lie her way out of this.

She had to.

"Natalie . . ." To Chess's surprise, the Judge's voice softened. "We've talked about this. You have to be . . . cautious . . . about people trying to get close to you. You know, because of my position, and your father's, there are people who will try to worm their way into your good graces and *pretend* to like you. When really—"

"Are you saying no one would like me if you and Dad weren't my parents?" Natalie exploded. "Really, Mom? Is that what you want me to think? Are you *trying* to destroy any self-confidence I might have left after . . . after . . . ?"

"Natalie!" The Judge's voice was harsh again. "You know that's not what I'm saying! And regardless, you know this supposed mother of Megan, whoever she is, isn't an approved emergency contact. The school knows there's a very short list of people they should release you to—the school was completely irresponsible, and I fully intend to complain. But your behavior was reprehensible and . . . and reckless. Do you *want* to be kidnapped? Don't you understand how *likely* that could be, given the circumstances? And I *know* you're not sick. Just admit it, and we'll pick up this conversation from there."

The Judge didn't raise her voice, but somehow her biting tone was worse than yelling. Chess was behind the furnace, not in the direct line of the Judge's fury, and he still felt like withering. He still felt like begging for mercy and apologizing, *I'm sorry! I'm sorry Natalie had to lie!*

He almost felt like creeping out from behind the furnace and telling the Judge, *I'm sorry for sneaking into your house from a different dimension! I'm sorry you don't even know Finn and Emma and I are here!*

But that was crazy.

Chess swallowed hard and watched to see what Natalie would do.

Natalie's face convulsed like she was about to cry. Then she ran to the side—Chess had to crane his neck to see where she went—and she grabbed a navy blue-and-orange metal trash can. She held the rim so tightly Chess could see her knuckles turning white.

Then Chess heard the unmistakable sound of retching. And . . . vomiting.

"She can make herself throw up?" Finn whispered beside Chess. "She's that good of an actress?"

Emma slid her hand over Finn's mouth and shook her head warningly. Chess put a finger over his lips.

"Oh, Natalie. Honey." The Judge sighed, and in that moment she didn't sound like the Judge anymore. This time her voice was an exact match for Ms. Morales's. "Come on. Let's take you upstairs and get you cleaned up. And then . . .

let's make sure nobody poisoned you."

Chess huddled even more tightly with Emma and Finn, hoping all three of them fit into the shadows as Ms. Morales took a few steps across the basement's navy blue carpet to reach Natalie and guide her back toward the stairs. He kept his head down, peering at his little brother and sister, because he didn't trust himself to look toward Natalie and the Judge.

If the Judge sees us, I *need to come up with a convincing story,* he told himself. *We can't just count on Natalie to lie for us. And when the Judge turns around, we'll be in her direct line of sight if she glances in this direction. . . .*

But evidently, walking back to the stairs, the Judge looked only at Natalie. Chess didn't hear her gasp in sudden horror or scream, *Who are you? What are you doing here? I'm calling the police!*

Still, Chess stayed tensed and braced to run. Or maybe braced to jump out and cause a distraction and hope the Judge saw only him, not Emma and Finn. Wasn't that a better plan?

He didn't let himself relax until he heard Natalie's and the Judge's footsteps at the top of the stairs, followed by the door shutting behind them.

And then Finn shook off Emma's hand over his mouth and tilted back his head to gaze up at Chess and asked, in his most innocent Finn whisper, "Poison? There's poison here in this world? Like, anyone could be poisoned, out of the blue?"

"I don't know anything about that, Finn," Chess said. "I guess . . . I guess it's a good thing we brought our own food."

"But . . . Mom's here," Finn said. "And Ms. Morales. And Joe. And now Natalie's up there, and she left her backpack down here with us, and we just heard her mother say that she could be kidnapped or poisoned. . . ."

Neither Chess nor Emma reminded Finn that the Judge wasn't Natalie's mother. Not *their* Natalie's mother.

"Finn, we'll make sure Natalie's okay," Emma finally whispered. "We'll get her back, and we'll rescue Mom and Ms. Morales and Joe, and then we'll go home."

But Emma didn't step out of the shadows, any more than Chess did. Chess couldn't even bear to lift his head to look at the glaring orange and blue of the rest of the basement. It had never occurred to him that they wouldn't have Natalie with them the entire time they spent in this world. How much had he come to rely on Natalie?

What would they do if she never came back?

NINETEEN

FINN

What if Natalie dies? Finn wondered.

This was such an unusual thought to find in his brain that he actually tilted his head to the side and smacked the palm of his hand against his temple, the way he would if he had water stuck in his ear.

He reminded himself that he'd been with Natalie until two minutes ago; he'd seen her eat a cinnamon-and-brown-sugar Pop-Tart as she pedaled her bike to her mom's house. It had come out of the same pack as one Finn ate as he waited in Ms. Morales's hallway while the girls were in Ms. Morales's office. And his stomach felt fine. He *knew* Natalie hadn't been poisoned.

But he'd watched Ms. Morales—no, the evil judge lady—as she rushed to Natalie's side, and it was hard to remember what was real and what was fake. It was hard not to believe his own eyes. The Judge really did act like she thought Natalie could have been poisoned; the Judge totally *looked* like she believed her daughter was in danger.

What is wrong with this world? Finn wondered. *Why is it so different from ours?*

He was thinking wrong again. The world he thought of as his, the world where he'd spent almost his entire life, wasn't really where he belonged. This awful world—with its mean people and its ugly orange-and-blue flags and banners and clothes and furniture—was where Finn and his family were supposed to fit.

How could we be from a place that stinks so bad? he wondered, sniffing sadly.

And . . . he didn't smell anything.

He tugged on Chess's arm and poked Emma in the back.

"Hey—did you notice? This house doesn't stink like the other places we went, the last time we came to this world," he told them.

Emma raised both eyebrows and then squinted—this

was her "I'm a scientist, and I'm going to test a hypothesis" look. She inhaled so deeply and for so long that Finn wondered if her lungs were twice as big as his.

Then she let the air out and grinned and patted Finn's shoulder.

"He's right!" she exclaimed. "I don't smell anything. What does that *mean*?"

"Maybe no one's being controlled in this house," Chess said. His words should have been comforting, but he said them with a bitter twist. Finn gazed up at his brother, and Chess's skin seemed stretched too tightly across the bones of his face.

"No odor, no control," Emma murmured. "Sounds like a logical conclusion."

Finn remembered that Emma had come up with a theory the last time they'd been in this world. It was when the kids were at the bizarre, awful trial where their mother was up on the stage—handcuffed to a chair. (Finn couldn't forget that detail, even though he wanted to.) And Mom couldn't even defend herself, because there was fake video making her seem guilty. And, if Emma's theory was right, the people in charge had also released something into the air that made the crowd scared and angry and cruel. It made the kids feel defeated and hopeless, too.

Emma thought whenever the stink got worse, the bad

stuff in the air was worse, too.

"Of course the Judge wouldn't be controlled in her own home," Chess said. "She's the one doing the controlling."

"We don't know that for sure," Emma said.

"She was the one running Mom's trial," Chess said. "She . . ." For a moment Chess's face looked like he was trying, two weeks late, to fit in with all the angry, bitter faces in the crowd at Mom's trial. He didn't look like himself at all. Maybe he smelled the bad odor, even if Finn and Emma couldn't.

Finn sneaked his hand into Chess's, as if he could pull Chess back to being himself. Chess looked down at Finn, and his face softened.

"Never mind," Chess said. "Let's figure out how to find Mom."

Emma pulled a laptop from her backpack. But it wasn't the one with Mom's secret codes—it was one of Natalie's. Evidently Emma had brought two laptops with her.

"We need to find Wi-Fi first," Emma announced. "We do that, and I bet there's a way to . . . to see where Mom was sent to prison."

"Mom's in prison?" Finn said. His voice shook.

The whole time they'd talked about coming back to rescue Mom, somehow he'd imagined her frozen in place, just where they'd left her. Somehow he'd believed the Greystone kids and Natalie could just run back to the huge auditorium where the trial was, and Mom and Joe would still be onstage.

And then, he thought, Mom and Joe could figure out how to rescue Ms. Morales, too.

"Finn, you saw that trial," Emma said. "No way were they going to find her not guilty."

He was glad it was Emma, not Chess, who answered. Emma could make the awful words sound brisk and matter-of-fact.

Chess would have made Finn *feel*.

"But *we* know Mom isn't guilty!" Finn protested anyway. "We know she didn't do anything wrong!"

"Finn," Chess said gently. "Yes, we know she didn't do anything wrong. She *wouldn't*. But we don't know how many things they've made illegal here. Things are backward in this world. Mom said it wasn't even legal to tell the *truth*. Not if it makes the leaders look bad."

"Yeah, but . . ."

Finn didn't know what argument he could use, if truth was illegal.

Emma looked up from the laptop, which she'd turned on while Finn and Chess were talking.

"Okay, I can't log on to anything from here," Emma reported. "We need to sneak out and find a place where I can. Do you think they have public libraries here, like we do? Or

Starbucks or Panera or . . . ?"

"Last time, Natalie couldn't get her phone to work in this world," Chess pointed out. "Maybe computers from the other world won't work here, either."

"I think Natalie's phone problem was because she was out of range," Emma said, shutting the computer and slipping it into her backpack again. "You know, because she was in a different *dimension* from the cell towers she was trying to connect to. With a computer—"

"With a computer, the leaders might be able to see who's trying to log on, and where they are," Chess said. "What if there's something about that computer that lets them see we're from the other world?"

"Chess," Emma said. "We can't just sit in this basement doing nothing."

Finn saw Chess dip his head down, giving a quick glance toward Finn. Chess wasn't just looking at Finn; Chess was trying to get Emma to look, too. It was like Chess and Emma were arguing, and Finn was the argument. He was caught between his brother and sister.

Chess and Emma didn't usually argue. And they *never* made Finn choose sides.

Finn's stomach churned. Maybe his Pop-Tart had been bad after all. Maybe he was getting food poisoning, just like Natalie.

Or maybe it was this world that made people sick, even without the bad smell. Looking out at the blue-and-orange basement made Finn's stomach queasier; remembering all the angry faces at Mom's trial made him want to grab the lever on the wall and open the tunnel again and run back to the other world. The better world.

Except, how could anything be better without Mom?

Just then, Finn heard a door clunk against a wall above him. The basement door was open again, and someone was running down the stairs. Finn could hear every pounding footstep.

"Guys!" It was Natalie. She didn't sound sick now. She sounded ecstatic. "Guys, listen. Mom and Dad are gone now, so you can come out. Did you hear me? I said Mom *and* Dad. I love this place! Mom and Dad are still married here. Isn't that great?"

TWENTY

EMMA

"They aren't *your* mom and dad," Emma said.

Natalie's face hardened.

"I know," she said. "It's just, for so long I . . ." She clutched her head with both hands, her palms pressing in on her cheekbones, her fingers tented over her eyes. Then she shook her head and dropped her hands. She peered back at Emma. "Never mind. Let's . . . get moving."

"First things first," Emma said. "Wi-Fi. So we know where to go. And maybe we should use a computer that's already in this house, so no one detects ours. Do you think this world's Natalie might have a spare laptop in her room?"

Chess patted her shoulder approvingly.

See, Chess? Emma wanted to argue. *We're doing this* safely. *We're going to approach this logically, and that's how we'll succeed.*

"*I* have a new laptop I take to school and an old one I keep as backup, just in case, so maybe the other Natalie does, too," Natalie said. Then she frowned. "Except Dad surprised me with the new computer the day the divorce went through, and I think it was kind of a . . . bribe . . . related to the divorce. So maybe this world's Natalie *doesn't* have a spare."

"How about we just go find out?" Finn asked, smiling so sweetly that there was no way he'd hurt Natalie's feelings.

Emma rushed toward the stairs, her brothers following a few steps behind her. At the top of the stairs, Chess drew Emma and Finn back and told Natalie, "Why don't you go ahead of us and close the curtains and blinds so no one sees us from outside? Just to be careful."

"Don't worry—that won't be a problem," Natalie said. She pressed her lips together, the corners of her mouth tugging in opposite directions. "You'll see."

Emma stepped out into the kitchen of Ms. Morales's house—no, *Judge* Morales's house, which maybe Emma should start thinking of as the Morales-Mayhew house instead. To Emma's relief, the kitchen was not all navy blue and orange like the basement; the granite counters seemed extra shiny, but otherwise everything looked familiar. Finn darted past Emma into the dining room.

"What?" he exclaimed. "Natalie—what happened to all your neighbors?"

Emma joined him at the dining room window.

The version of Ms. Morales's house that Emma knew sat at the top of a hill with a large yard, but it had been surrounded by other equally large mansions. This house stood alone and seemed to have sprawled across the equivalent of several other lots. Maybe it had expanded and gobbled up the other houses. Beyond the last wing of the house, the yard sloped downward into a bunch of trees nestled against something solid and gray—a stone wall?

"Oh, wait, I see *one* other roof," Finn said, standing on tiptoes and craning his neck.

"That's a guard tower," Natalie said grimly behind them. "I think. Mom—I mean, Other-Mom, the Judge—she asked how Megan's mom was allowed past the guards, and I had to pretend I knew what she was talking about."

"Natalie, your house is like a *compound* now," Emma said. "Or like the White House, where it's really, really protected. . . ."

"This world's version of your house had a fence, too," Natalie reminded her.

It wasn't the same. In the Greystones' neighborhood in

this world, all the houses were cut off from one another by tall hedges and ugly, battered wooden fences. Just picturing that in her mind's eye made Emma feel afraid. It made her feel like she was smelling the stink that infested this world's version of her family's neighborhood all over again.

Here, the imposing wall mostly hidden by trees seemed to say, *The people who live in this house matter more than anyone else. That's why they can't have neighbors; that's why they need guards to protect them.*

"How *did* you convince the Judge you knew what you were talking about, Natalie?" Chess asked, coming up behind the others. "And were you just acting when you threw up, or are you really sick?"

Emma caught a look that passed between Chess and Natalie. If Emma had to analyze it, she would have said Natalie liked Chess asking about her. She liked that he was worried about her.

But Natalie also winced and rolled her eyes.

"I think it was just nerves," she admitted. "But then, making myself retch again and again was a good way to avoid answering Mom's questions. Er, the Judge's questions." She twisted her mouth, running her tongue over her teeth, then wrinkling her nose. "Ugh. Do you think it'd be wrong to use Other-Natalie's toothbrush?"

"What if it's poisoned?" Finn asked.

"It won't be poisoned," Natalie said confidently. "That's just Mom being paranoid. I mean, the Judge." But she didn't turn and walk toward the stairs. "You'll . . . you'll all come upstairs with me, right?"

Is Natalie chickening out now, too? Emma wondered. *Is she as frightened as Chess? And . . . me?*

"If there's a chance we'll find a usable laptop, of course we're going upstairs," Emma said.

But all four of them tiptoed rather than running to the next flight of stairs, and then up to the second floor.

Natalie was the first to reach the doorway that corresponded to her room in her own world.

"Oh," she said, sounding surprised.

Emma stepped up behind her.

When the three Greystones had stayed with Natalie and Ms. Morales—Real–Ms. Morales—in the better world, Emma had been so focused on getting her mother back that she'd barely glanced at Natalie's room. But this room looked virtually the same as Emma remembered: clothes strewn across the floor, pictures of Natalie and her friends tacked up on the wall, a puffy white comforter slipping off the unmade bed. The only big difference here was . . .

"That," Chess said, pointing toward a vast poster hanging over the bed. "That's . . ."

"Scary," Finn filled in.

The poster showed a large group of kids in navy blue and orange, holding lit candles and staring grimly out at the camera. Solemn lettering at the top of the poster announced, "When we stand together, no one can oppose us."

In the picture, Natalie stood in the middle of the front row of grim-looking kids. Her expression was the sternest, the most forbidding.

No, it's Other-Natalie, Emma told herself. *She just* looks *like our Natalie.*

"Maybe this is a sports thing," Natalie said weakly. "Like . . . team-building. I want to go out for lacrosse next year. Maybe I—I mean, Other-Natalie—maybe she's already on the team here, and they changed the school colors, and . . ."

Natalie was trying so hard to make it seem like Other-Natalie wasn't involved in the evil of this world.

Emma held back a shiver and tried to stay analytical. Blue and orange were just colors, after all. The kids in the picture were just teenagers. So why was that poster so creepy? Why did it make her, Finn, and Chess huddle together without even thinking? What was the difference between those kids on the poster wanting to stand together, and the Greystones' personal motto (thanks to Mom) of "We'll always have each other"?

It's the word "oppose," Emma decided. *Having us Greystones stick together doesn't mean we won't be nice to other people, too. But that poster, that sentence . . . it's like they're saying anyone who doesn't stand with them is an enemy.*

Emma knew barely anything about this world, but it was clear: Those kids would consider Mom an enemy.

That meant the Greystone kids would be those kids' enemies, too.

And Natalie? Emma wondered. *What about* our *Natalie?*

Natalie took four steps across the bedroom floor, scrambled up to stand on the bed, and yanked on the top two corners of the poster. They sagged. Natalie let go, and the top half of the poster plunged down, hiding the bottom half.

"Natalie," Chess said softly. "This world's Natalie wouldn't—"

"I don't *care*," Natalie said. "If anyone here sees this, let them think the poster just fell on its own. Or—half fell."

"Let's get Mom and Ms. Morales and Joe and get out of here before anyone sees that," Finn said.

"Right," Natalie said.

She jumped down from the bed and went over to open a desk drawer.

"Bingo," Natalie said, pulling out a laptop. "Other-Natalie even keeps it in the same place I do."

Emma's hands tingled with impatience.

"Give that to me, and I can—" she began.

"Emma," Chess said. "Natalie's the fastest at finding stuff online."

Emma held up her hands as if surrendering.

"I know! I know!" she said. "But, Natalie—hurry!"

Natalie nodded, already plopping onto the bed and opening the laptop. Her fingers flew across the keyboard. Chess put his arms around Emma and Finn and drew them close as all three kids hovered by Natalie.

"Okay, it connected to the internet automatically, so I don't have to guess any passwords," Natalie reported.

"Looking up Susanna Morales in this world is just going to lead to the Judge, and we don't know Joe's last name, so you should start your search by looking for our mom," Emma suggested.

Natalie cocked an eyebrow at Emma.

"Emma, I'm on it," she said. "Don't worry. I'm sure it will just take a moment before . . ."

She jerked her head back and scowled at the screen.

"What?" Emma asked. "What just happened?"

Natalie didn't answer. She leaned closer to the laptop and typed faster. Emma stepped to the side and craned her neck, trying to see the screen, but Natalie's long hair slipped forward, blocking Emma's view.

"Natalie?" Finn whispered.

Natalie didn't answer him either. She seemed to be in her

own little world, just her and the computer. Emma felt like she'd zipped back to the first time she'd met Natalie, when Natalie did nothing but hunch over her cell phone and text.

Then suddenly Natalie's head dropped even farther forward, her forehead coming to rest on the rim of the laptop. Now she was neither typing nor looking at the screen.

"Natalie, what's going on?" Chess asked. His grip tightened on Emma's shoulder. "You're scaring us."

Natalie groaned and lifted her head. She spun the laptop around so the Greystones could see four words glowing on an otherwise blank screen: "Search term not found."

"I can't find *anything* about your mom," Natalie wailed. "It's like she doesn't even exist!"

TWENTY-ONE

CHESS

Chess went numb. Distantly, he could hear Emma and Finn suggesting possibilities Natalie might not have thought of: "Did you try . . ." He blanked out on registering their ideas, but he heard Natalie's repeated responses: "Yes, I already tried that. . . ." "Yes, that, too. . . ."

He stumbled away from the other kids, toward the backpack he'd brought from the other world, lugged up from the basement, and then dropped on the floor when they'd first come into Natalie's room. He rifled through it, pulling out a stiff sheet of paper folded into fourths. He carried it over to Natalie without unfolding it. Because that would *hurt*.

Even thinking about this paper was painful.

"Here," he said gruffly, sliding the paper into Natalie's hand. "Do an image search."

Natalie unfolded the paper, and Emma and Finn recoiled along with Chess.

This was the sign Chess had ripped off a pole the last time they'd been in this world. Under the words "CRIMINAL CAUGHT!" it held a scary, odd picture of Mom, and announced that she was an enemy of the people.

The sign also ordered everyone to go to her public trial and sentencing—the horrifying sham trial where the Greystones and Natalie had tried and failed to rescue her.

How could anyone think a trial would be fair if everyone knew from the beginning that it included a sentencing?

But at that trial, their mother had begged them to run away and rescue the three Gustano kids instead of her. So the Greystones never heard the verdict; they never heard her sentence.

Was there any way for Chess *not* to feel guilty looking at this sign or thinking about that trial?

"I—I didn't know you kept that," Emma gasped.

Chess shrugged, because what could he say? He didn't want to admit how many times, in his room back at Mr. Mayhew's house, he'd secretly unfolded this sign and stared at Mom's picture, even though it only made him feel worse.

"What if . . . what if it was dangerous bringing that back here?" Natalie asked.

Chess shrugged again, almost recklessly, which wasn't like him.

"I bet Other–Ms. Morales—the Judge, who's definitely not *your* mom—I bet she has a whole stack of signs like this somewhere in this house," he said, his voice cruel and cutting, which was even less like him.

"I *know* she's not my mom," Natalie said. She pointed at the poster sagging down from the wall. "I don't want to be *that* Natalie. Okay? I just . . . If you had divorced parents, you'd understand."

"Yeah, well, our dad's dead, remember?" Emma asked. "So we do know what it's like to wish things were different. We understand the . . . temptation."

Chess gazed at his sister in surprise. Her voice was gentle, her expression soft. Emma wasn't usually the peacemaker, the compassionate one. That was his role.

Was it possible that Emma missed their dad, too, even though she'd been so young when he died that she didn't actually remember him?

Was there anything today that wouldn't make Chess feel sad?

Yeah—finding Mom, he thought.

"*Can* you do an image search, Natalie?" Finn asked.

"Sure," Natalie said, shaking back her hair as if she could shake off the whole conversation. She reached for the phone in her back pocket. "I just have to take a picture and then . . ." She positioned the phone above the poster, then lowered it. "Oh, right. I keep forgetting. My phone won't automatically connect to the internet here." She bit her lip and squinted off into the distance. Then she tucked both the sign and the laptop under her arm and hopped up from the bed. "Come on. Let's go use the scanner in Mom's office. That'll be fastest."

She was out the door before Chess, Emma, and Finn could remind her that the office in this house didn't belong to *her* mom—and there was no guarantee that it contained a scanner. They just shouldered their backpacks again and trailed along behind her.

Once they were downstairs, they found Natalie standing before an imposing wood door full of ornate carvings—totally different from Real–Ms. Morales's office door. The wooden animals and birds and leaves (and were those faces? *Screaming* faces?) reminded Chess a little too much of the stone carvings at the Public Hall where his mother's trial had been held. So it took Chess a moment to realize that Natalie was twisting her hand uselessly on the doorknob, back and forth.

The door was locked.

"Seriously?" Natalie muttered. "She locks the door when she knows I'm home alone?"

"*And* when the house is surrounded by guard towers?" Finn added.

"Maybe this Ms. Morales would hide a key the same place your mom would," Emma suggested. "Do you know . . ."

Natalie dashed toward the kitchen and came back a moment later with a shiny key in her hand.

"Yep," she said. "Same flour-jar hiding spot, same ribbon on the key, same . . . How can they be so much the same and so different, all at once?"

Natalie seemed to be trying to speak jauntily, but she kept her head down and didn't look directly at anyone.

Natalie won't look at us because . . . she's trying not to cry? Chess thought.

He had seen and heard recordings of Kate Gustano, the alternate version of his own mother, when she was begging for the release of her kidnapped children. That had been horrible enough. Wouldn't it be worse for Natalie, to have *met* the Judge and seen so many similarities to her own mom—and yet know that the Judge was a terrible person?

Natalie unlocked the office door and shoved it open.

Emma's jaw dropped. Finn's eyes grew huge.

"I think this Ms. Morales likes pictures of herself even

more than the real one does!" Finn exclaimed.

Chess switched from watching the other kids to peering into the office.

Natalie's real mom was a Realtor, so her office back in the better world had held several real estate signs with her picture.

But this office held even more signs stacked against the walls—and all of them contained *huge* pictures of the Judge. Chess was tall for a sixth grader, but if he stood by one of these signs, his head wouldn't have even come to the bottom of the Judge's nose. Chess thought Real–Ms. Morales was pretty; he could see where Natalie got her long, curly, dark hair and her sparkling brown eyes and her high cheekbones and . . .

Probably not the best time to start thinking about how pretty Natalie is, Chess told himself.

He forced himself to focus on the Judge signs again. In these pictures, the Judge wasn't just pretty. She looked like a movie star or an actress or a singer—someone who seemed too beautiful to be real.

Natalie made a sound that came out as a strangled snort. "That's how happy Mom always looked before . . . before she and Dad started fighting and . . ." She gulped. "I can't look."

She turned and bent over a printer to lift the lid and slap

the horrible picture of Chess's mom onto the glass of the scanner.

Finn tugged on Chess's arm.

"Why do those signs say VOTE SUSANNA MORALES FOR JUDGE?" he asked. "I thought Other–Ms. Morales already *was* a judge."

"She's running for reelection, I guess," Chess said. "That's how government works. People elect public officials, and then every so often people have the chance to vote again, so they can decide if they like the way the officials are doing their jobs, or if they think someone else would be better. . . ."

"If *I* lived here, I'd vote against her," Finn said. He stuck his tongue out at the giant picture. "Because she was mean to our mom." Then he glanced toward Natalie. "Sorry, Natalie. I'd vote for your *real* mom. She's nice."

Natalie didn't answer. She'd moved from scanning the picture of the Greystones' mom to hunching over the laptop again. Emma was right at her elbow.

"Is anything coming up?" Chess asked, circling the huge desk in the center of the office to peer down at the laptop with the two girls.

"Nothing useful," Natalie said. "Not yet."

Chess saw that the screen was filled with image matches—but every single one showed only a sign on a pole in the background of some other scene.

"Try refreshing it," Finn said, jostling against Chess's elbow. "Maybe it just wasn't thinking hard enough the first time."

"Finn, that's not how the internet works," Emma said, though she ruffled Finn's hair, too, so it wasn't like she was calling him stupid.

Natalie flashed him an indulgent smile and hit Enter again. Then she leaned closer to the screen.

"Wait," she said. "Why did some of the matches disappear?"

Chess saw that now only half the screen was filled with rows of matched images.

Natalie hit Enter a third time.

Now the bottom row of matches disappeared. It had only contained two pictures, but when Natalie hit Enter yet again, half of the second-to-last row vanished as well.

"The images of your mom—they're being erased!" Natalie gasped. "Someone's deleting them *right now*!"

TWENTY-TWO

FINN

"Then save them!" Finn yelped. He yanked on Natalie's arm as hard as he could, so she would listen. "Save the pictures of Mom while you still can!"

Natalie glanced dazedly down at him, then her gaze sharpened.

"He's right," she muttered. "Finn's totally right. We should save copies of those images to check . . ."

She jerked away from him to reach for the computer again. But that threw Finn off balance. He stumbled to the side, waving his arms wildly. His right elbow hit something solid. At least he *thought* it was solid. Then he heard a ripping sound.

Finn looked down to see that he'd put his elbow through one of the VOTE SUSANNA MORALES signs.

"Oops," Finn whispered.

"Don't worry about it, Finn," Natalie said. She grinned a little wickedly. "I've wanted to vandalize those signs ever since we walked in here."

"But you'll get in trouble when the Judge comes back, and—"

"Just hide it behind the others," Emma suggested.

Finn looked back at the punctured sign.

"No, wait, it's like there are two layers," he said, tugging on the torn canvas. "I only broke one layer, so . . ." He made the hole in the sign even bigger. "Yes! It's still the word 'VOTE' right below where I stabbed it, so I can pull away the top layer and . . ."

Recklessly, he yanked harder. The entire top layer of the sign fell away, revealing a second layer that was just as glossy and gleaming as the first. And it held another familiar smiling face.

But this was a giant photo of Natalie's dad, not her mom.

Finn took a step back so he could read all the words under the picture: VOTE FOR ROGER MAYHEW. Confused, he swiveled his head back toward the older kids.

"Natalie, are *both* your parents judges here?" he asked. "In charge of everything?"

"I . . ." She stumbled toward Finn and clutched his shoulder as if she were comforting him. Or trying to hold herself up. "Is it possible? Maybe if my parents hadn't gotten divorced . . . If they'd stayed happy together in *my* world, if they hadn't spent so much time and energy fighting . . ."

Emma had replaced Natalie at the laptop and was typing fast.

"This says Mr. Mayhew is currently mayor of the city," she reported. "And he's running for governor."

"Governor?" Finn said, gazing up at her in awe. "Natalie, your family's, like, really important here!"

"These people aren't her family, remember?" Emma shoved the laptop back a little too roughly.

"Other-Natalie's family, then," Finn said. "But why is Mr. Mayhew's sign hidden under Ms. Morales's?"

"Can we think about that after we save the pictures of Mom?" Chess asked.

"Oh!" Natalie rushed back to the computer.

Finn followed. Emma was already switching away from the information about Mr. Mayhew. Natalie typed in a command. The screen flickered and went blank.

"I thought we were going back to the pictures of Mom," Finn complained.

The other kids huddled close around him. Chess put his arm around Finn's shoulders. Emma patted his arm. And

Natalie dropped her hands from the keyboard.

"I'm sorry, Finn," she said. "All the images are gone. Her name, and now her pictures, too. . . . *Everything* about your mom has vanished from the internet."

TWENTY-THREE

EMMA

“This is my fault,” Emma said. “I shouldn’t have switched over to looking up Mr. Mayhew.”

“I shouldn’t have put my elbow through that sign,” Finn said.

“Stop it!” Natalie told them. “None of you are to blame for the weird stuff in this world. And anyhow, I might be able to see what happened to those images of your mom.”

“You can?” Emma asked.

“Just give me a minute,” Natalie said.

Emma walked over to examine the sign, so she wouldn’t hang over Natalie’s shoulder and distract her.

"What if there's a Mayor Mayhew sign behind every single one of the VOTE SUSANNA MORALES signs?" she asked. She moved the mayor sign to the back of the stack, so she could look at the others.

"Why would there be?" Chess asked, stepping up beside her. "None of this makes sense. I mean, some people might reuse signs to save money or be environmental. But in this house . . ."

He looked up. For the first time, Emma noticed that there were elaborate wood carvings on the ceiling of the office, just like on the door. Real–Ms. Morales's office wasn't like that at all. Emma didn't know what carved ceilings and doors cost—or, oh, look, carved wooden pillars in every corner of the room, too.

Judge Morales and Mayor Mayhew aren't worried about saving money at all, Emma thought.

"Ugh," Natalie sighed behind them. "The wayback function isn't working. But before we lost everything, I did see one web address for your mom's image, and . . . What?"

Emma, Chess, and Finn all rushed to Natalie's side.

"You're just looking at stuff about your dad again?" Finn asked. The image on the screen showed a picture on a signpost—but the photo was indeed Mayor Mayhew's election pose, not anything about the Greystones' mom.

"N-No," Natalie said. "That's from the day of your

mom's trial. It's timestamped and everything. Five minutes ago, this timestamped picture showed a signpost from two weeks ago with your mom's picture on it. We *saw* that signpost in real life! Not just on the internet!"

The picture was grainy and barely in color—it seemed to come from a security camera. But Emma recognized the surroundings. It was a scene right beside the Public Hall where her mother's trial had been held.

Emma gasped.

"Who would make it seem like that was a picture of your dad instead of our mom? And why?" she asked. "Why try to make people think they don't remember things right?"

"I . . . I don't know," Natalie stammered.

Emma's head swam. It was all too strange—Mayor Mayhew's face hidden under Judge Morales's in this office; Mom's image being replaced by Mayor Mayhew's online. It made her think of when she was a little kid learning how to play rock-paper-scissors; she'd asked again and again, "But which one's really the strongest? Which one has the most power?"

Mom doesn't have any power in this horrible world, Emma thought. *She's trapped. But Judge Morales, Mayor Mayhew . . .*

Just then, there was a loud crash outside the office.

"I thought you said everyone else in the house was gone!" Emma hissed at Natalie. "And why isn't this room soundproof, like your mother's office back home?"

Emma whirled toward the door and saw the answer to her own question. They'd left the office door hanging wide open, the key with its green ribbon still jammed into the lock.

"Oh, I'll shut—" she began, taking a step forward. But before she could go any farther, Chess slammed into her.

"Get down!" he whispered, his long arms pulling Finn and Natalie, too. "Everybody has to hide!"

TWENTY-FOUR

CHESS

Protect the others, thrummed in Chess's brain. *Protect the others. Whatever else happens, I have to protect the others. . . .*

He really wasn't sure Emma, Finn, or Natalie had any instincts for self-preservation. Emma had even been ready to walk to the door, where anybody standing outside the office might have seen her.

Am I the only one who remembers how scary this world is? he wondered.

He realized he wasn't just thinking about their last trip to this world, when they'd failed to rescue their mother and ended up barely escaping from the cops. Something about being back here again was jarring loose older memories, older thought patterns.

When I was a little boy and we lived in this world, he thought. *When Daddy was still alive. Back then . . . Mommy and Daddy were scared all the time.*

He saw that now, though he hadn't understood as a three- or four-year-old.

Why was that coming back now, as he crouched behind the desk in the Judge's office with Natalie, Emma, and Finn?

Was there any chance he'd been in this house as a little boy?

He caught only flashes of old memories and old feelings, too brief and mysterious to interpret. They were like insects that landed for only an instant, then flew away. And the more he tried to chase them, the faster they left.

It dawned on him that Emma was squirming away from him.

"Chess, this *isn't* a good place to hide," she whispered. "Not with that door open, not if that sound was Judge Morales coming back . . ."

"I'll shut the door," Natalie whispered. She squared her shoulders, her back pressed hard against the Judge's desk drawers. "It has to be me. I live here."

She flashed the three Greystones a crooked smile, and Chess saw that she was saying that like an actress preparing for a role, psyching herself up.

"What if that sound was Other-*Natalie* coming back?" Finn asked. "What if *she* got sick at school today and had to come home and then she sees you and . . ."

"Well, then, I'll . . . overpower her," Natalie said grimly, her voice filled with even more bravado. Even more falseness. "I'll have the element of surprise on my side. I'll overpower her and lock her in her own closet and . . ."

Chess put his hand on Natalie's arm.

"Just wait," he begged. "Wait and listen, and let's see what you might have to deal with. . . ."

He broke off, because now he could hear voices outside the office, probably coming from the kitchen or dining room. They were indistinct at first, then got closer and louder.

"—I'll start scrubbing the bathrooms, if you do the vacuuming upstairs . . ."

"Cleaners," Natalie said, slumping in a way that let Chess see that she'd been as terrified as him. Maybe even more so. "This is easy, then. I'll send them away. I'll say I'm contagious."

She jutted her chin into the air, shoved her hair back, and shook Chess's hand off her arm. Then she stood up and seemed to change her mind about the hair, running her hand through it backward to mess it up. She pinched her cheeks until they turned red.

"Have to look sick," she muttered.

"Be careful," Chess whispered, though he was pretty sure Natalie didn't hear him.

She'd barely stepped away from the desk when Chess heard a woman's voice exclaim from the doorway, "Oh! Miss Natalie!"

Chess clutched Finn and Emma and pulled them closer, drawing them into the recessed portion under the desk. Now all he could see of Natalie were her sneakers and her jeans from the knees down.

"Yeah . . . hi." Natalie's voice was barely a croak. "I'm *really* sick." She swayed convincingly. "That's why I'm home from school. Believe me, you don't want to catch what I've got. So you should go. Mom will reschedule after I'm better—who knows how long it'll take?"

"Oh, yes, Miss Natalie, your mother already called and told us you would be here." The cleaner somehow managed to sound both subservient and scolding, all at once. "She said you would stay in your room, away from us. And she said very definitely that we should still clean the rest of the house, because your parents are having five hundred people at their fund-raiser here tonight. Are you so sick that you forgot?"

Emma turned an anguished face toward Chess; Finn waggled his eyebrows and mouthed the words "Five hundred people?" in disbelief.

Chess's heart sank.

"Oh . . . yeah," Natalie said weakly. "You know my parents have fund-raisers all the time. I can't keep them straight." Chess saw Natalie shuffle her feet. Then she planted them more firmly, and Chess could tell she'd probably straightened her spine and done her chin-jutting move again, too, because she sounded more imposing when she spoke again. "Well, I'll hide out in here, not my room, because it makes me feel better to sleep on my mom's office couch when I'm sick. So don't clean this room or mine, okay? Thanks."

"You know we never step foot in your mother's office, Miss Natalie," the cleaner said. "It's forbidden. I've never even seen this door open before."

There was curiosity in the woman's voice, as if she wanted to come in and look around.

"Oh, right," Natalie said. "Sometime when I haven't filled the place with germs, you should ask Mom for a tour."

"You know that wouldn't be allowed," the cleaner said stiffly. "I hope you feel better soon, Miss Natalie."

The way she spoke those words, Chess thought she might have even bowed in reverence to Natalie and her family. Chess heard footsteps receding. Natalie dashed out of sight, and a moment later he heard the office door slam. Then Natalie was back, crouching by the desk to peer at the three Greystones hiding under it.

"There's, like, an *army* of cleaners here," Natalie reported. "But I locked the door and remembered to take the key out this time, so we're safe here until they're gone. We should probably be quiet in case there's *not* soundproofing . . . or, no, I could always say I'm watching something online. . . ."

"What if those cleaners are here for hours?" Emma wailed. "We should climb out the window."

"And go where?" Chess asked quietly.

"To—to—" Emma began.

Chess glanced reflexively toward the window. Strangely, even though the sun should be fully up by now, the light outside was still dim and hazy. So it took him a minute to make sense of the huddled shapes along the long rows of hedges and flowers on the other side of the window. By then, Natalie was already running toward the window. She grabbed the blind and yanked it down, shutting off any view the kids could have of the outdoors.

Or any view anyone outdoors could have of the kids.

"Wh-Why'd you do that?" Finn stammered, his faced twisted in puzzlement.

"There's like, an army of workers outside, too," Natalie hissed.

"Landscapers, gardeners . . . ," Emma added, as if it might

help somehow to categorize everyone.

"But . . . ," Finn began.

"Finn, don't you see?" Chess asked, his voice ragged and frantic. "We can't let any workers know we're here—indoors or out. We're trapped!"

TWENTY-FIVE

FINN

"I still don't understand," Finn persisted. "Natalie can pretend to be Other-Natalie. We can pretend to be, I don't know, friends who brought her homework when we heard she was sick? I mean, we really are friends, so that doesn't take much pretending. Or, hey, Natalie can say she got better, like, really fast, so she invited us over to play, and . . ."

None of the others jumped up and said, *Oh, you're right, Finn—those are great ideas!*

"Finn," Chess said gently. "There's too much we don't understand. We can't start telling lies like that until we know what will and won't sound true. It's more dangerous for us

Greystones than it is for Natalie. We can't risk being seen until we have to. Until we know where to find Mom and Ms. Morales and Joe."

"But Mom and the real Ms. Morales and Joe aren't *here*," Finn protested. "So we know we'll have to go *somewhere* else. . . ."

Finn saw Chess bite his lip. And his voice had come out really, really shaky. Natalie twisted a strand of hair around her finger again and again. Even Emma—Emma who was always so brave—did nothing but hug her laptop. She stayed huddled under the desk.

"Oh," Finn said. "Are you guys all scared again? A lot more scared than me?"

There'd been a time or two on their last trip to this world when the big kids had been afraid and frozen and Finn had been fearless. The first time, Finn had forced everyone else to be brave, too. But the second . . .

"It's not like we just want to hide here doing nothing," Emma said softly. "Natalie can do more computer research. So can Chess. And I can take another crack at Mom's code."

"What am I supposed to do?" Finn asked. No matter how much he tried to hold on to the idea *I'm fearless! I can help the others!* his voice came out sounding like he was just a whiny little kid.

"Maybe you look around the Judge's office for clues?"

Chess suggested. "After all, she was in charge of Mom's, uh, trial, and maybe she has papers somewhere about the . . . sentencing and where Mom is now."

"Wouldn't she just have all that on her computer?" Finn asked grumpily.

"We don't know how things are done in this world," Natalie said. "Why don't I try to get past the security passwords on that laptop"—she pointed to the one on the otherwise empty desk—"and you look for paper files."

"And, Finn, we're not staying here forever," Emma assured him. "I bet the workers will take a lunch break, and we can sneak out then. If we do enough research first, we'll know where to go. And how to get Mom back. And Ms. Morales and Joe, too."

Finn saw Natalie glance toward a fancy clock on the wall. Finn wasn't as good at reading clocks with hands as ones with glowing numbers, but he was pretty sure it was barely nine o'clock.

"Guys, I'm not sure we have until lunchtime," Natalie said nervously. "Remember, the Judge was going to call the school and complain about them supposedly letting me leave with another kid's mom, and the school's going to say, 'What are you talking about? Your daughter's right here in history class.' . . ."

From the stricken looks on Chess's and Emma's faces,

Finn could tell they hadn't thought of that problem.

"We'll do research *fast*," Emma said, scooting up to the couch and dipping her head down over the computer with Mom's secret code.

It could have been funny, how Chess plopped down on the other end of the couch and Natalie dropped into the desk chair and both of them hunched over the two laptops nearest them at the exact same time as Emma. In another mood, Finn would have laughed and shouted, *The three of you look like robots! Or synchronized swimmers! Only—not swimming! Is synchronized computer-hacking a thing?*

Instead, Finn slumped his shoulders and shuffled toward the closet on the other side of the room. It, too, had a fancy carved door. Maybe the Judge had filing cabinets in that closet. Maybe Finn would open a drawer and see his mother's name right away and . . .

And then I'd hand off everything to the big kids, he thought. Because that way, he'd get to help rescue Mom without having to look at anything else describing her as a criminal.

It was kind of like how, back in the better world, he'd helped the other kids by playing pitch-and-catch with Mr. Mayhew while they did all the work.

But Finn had had fun with Mr. Mayhew. There was nothing scary about pitch-and-catch.

What was Mr. Mayhew doing now? Could the Greystones and Natalie—and Mom and Ms. Morales and Joe—make it back before he even knew they were gone?

Thinking about Mr. Mayhew carried Finn all the way over to the closet. He took a deep breath, pulled open the door, and . . .

The closet held nothing but shelves of office supplies: boxes of pens, unopened packs of paper. . . . Or, no—there were also stacks of flyers that were smaller versions of the signs that said ELECT SUSANNA MORALES JUDGE.

Finn really did not want to keep looking at Ms. Morales's face when it wasn't the *real* Ms. Morales.

Halfheartedly, he ran his thumb along the edge of the papers, just to make sure that something more interesting wasn't hidden beneath them. But all the flyers seemed the same. There weren't even any ELECT ROGER MAYHEW flyers mixed in.

He turned around. As fancy as it was, the Judge's office was still *boring*. The laptop was the only thing on the desk; the end table beside the office couch contained nothing but a lamp. Finn bet that when the Judge was a little girl, she kept her bedroom neat and tidy and boring, too.

Finn remembered that sometimes when Mom made him clean his room, he shoved everything under the bed and pulled the comforter down to hide the fun stuff, and then his room looked neat and tidy and boring, too.

Where does the Judge hide things she *doesn't want anyone to see?* Finn wondered. What if there were all sorts of things like the ELECT ROGER MAYHEW sign, hidden beneath something else?

Finn walked back to the Judge's desk. He opened all the drawers but only saw more boring stuff like staplers and computer adapters and cords.

"Natalie, can you move over, so I can get under the desk again?" Finn asked.

"Oh, um, sure . . . ," Natalie murmured, as if she'd barely heard him. She coiled up her legs in the office chair and slid the computer from the desk into her lap without even glancing up. Then she shoved the chair away from the desk.

Finn crawled back into the cubbyhole beneath the desk, where all three Greystones had hidden just a few minutes ago. Finn wasn't trying to hide now but to, well, seek. He'd had the idea that maybe there was some secret door concealed behind the drawers, or an extra drawer tucked away behind a secret panel.

Maybe the Judge has something like the Bat Cave hidden under her office, and I just have to find the latch to open it. . . .

The last night Finn had spent with Mom at home, before she vanished into the alternate world, she'd watched *The*

Lego Batman Movie with Finn and the others.

It really wasn't good for Finn to think about that right now.

He tilted his head back, because he'd learned that was a good way to keep himself from crying. Even if he failed, at least the tears wouldn't run down his cheeks, but sideways, into his hair, mostly out of sight.

Then he forgot about crying and tilted his head even farther back, so he was looking straight up, toward the bottom of the top part of the desk. The Judge had the same kind of ornate carving on the underside of her desk as she had on her doors.

Why would anyone put such a fancy carving *under* a desk, where nobody would see it?

"Natalie?" Finn said, because he wanted to ask if the real Ms. Morales had anything like that in her house back in the better world.

"Mmm?" Natalie said without looking up.

Finn could tell: Now she wasn't paying any attention to him at all.

He ran his hand over the wood carving. Maybe he was wrong—maybe this carving wasn't like the one on the door. It was a little hard to see in the shadows under the desk, but the carvings here seemed to be of angels and lambs and flowers instead of demons and wolves and thorns.

Finn's finger caught on a bump on one of the angels' wings. No, it wasn't a bump—it was a button.

Finn pushed the button.

And then a man's voice came out of nowhere, as if a speaker had crackled to life right over his head, giving Finn the power to eavesdrop on a conversation somewhere else in the house. Maybe even somewhere else in the *world*.

And what the voice said was: "What's this lever doing here?"

TWENTY-SIX

EMMA

“What? Who’s there?” Emma jolted to alertness, yanked away from the jumble of letters and numbers in Mom’s coded message. The laptop braced against her knees slid to the side as she peered around for a place to hide. Or run. She scooped the laptop into her arms and scrambled to her feet, hoping Chess, Finn, and Natalie were ready to run, too.

Or maybe she hoped they’d already found safety, away from that deep male voice whose source she still couldn’t locate, even though she glanced all around. Natalie was still in a chair by the desk, and Chess was at the other end of the couch from Emma. But Finn . . .

Oh, Finn, Emma thought, her heart pounding.

Finn poked his head out from beneath the desk.

"Shh, Emma," he hissed. "I think I found an intercom! Be quiet!"

If it was an intercom, whoever was on the other end would have heard Finn say her name.

Natalie slid down to the floor beside Finn. She reached under the desk—maybe she was searching for an off switch. Emma jumped up and rushed toward Finn and Natalie. She realized Chess had scrambled up right beside her.

And then, before Emma and Chess even reached the desk, an image appeared on the blank wall across from them. It was a scene in a location Emma recognized: a man and a woman standing in front of the lever the kids had left behind in the Morales-Mayhew basement.

Only then did the words Emma had heard fully register: *What's this lever doing here?*

"Don't touch it!" Emma pleaded. She instantly felt foolish, because hadn't she just wanted *Finn* to be quiet?

The man and the woman in the scene projected onto the wall didn't seem to hear Emma. They didn't seem to have heard Finn either. They just stared at the lever, their backs turned to whatever camera was recording them.

Then the woman chuckled deep in her throat, almost like a growl.

"What do you bet Mayor Mayhew heard that all the other mayors in the country have fake levers in *their* houses, and so he had to have one, too?" she asked.

"As long as it doesn't interfere with our goals, Mayhew could put a lever on his head, and I wouldn't care," the man said bitterly.

"Yeah, a lever on his head would flip open the top of his skull and reveal that he doesn't have a brain," the woman said.

"A lever on his chest would open his rib cage and reveal that he doesn't have a heart," the man countered.

The woman started to laugh, then pursed her lips.

"Enough," she said. "We can't be heard speaking like this. We can't endanger our mission."

She glanced around as if it had just occurred to her that someone else might be listening. Then she picked up an industrial-looking vacuum cleaner from the floor behind her. Emma hadn't noticed it before.

"They're more cleaners," Natalie burst out. "They're wearing the same uniforms as the woman I talked to."

Emma had been so focused on the conversation, she hadn't paid attention to the fact that both the man and the woman were wearing baggy brown uniforms that covered their whole bodies except for their hands and feet and heads. Apart from the uniforms, the only distinguishing features

Emma could see were that the woman's hair was red and straggly, barely skimming her shoulders, and the man's was black and clipped short. And the man was much taller than the woman.

"So why are they talking about a mission?" Chess asked quietly. "And their mission being *endangered*?"

"Why does the Judge have some crazy system set up to *spy* on people in her own basement?" Finn asked. "Does she know people go around saying mean things about Fake–Mr. Mayhew? Does she want to be able to *fire* people who say mean things?"

"Finn, remember, Mr. Mayhew—*our* Mr. Mayhew—he had a video security system at his house, where we could see who was at the front door through our computers," Emma said. "Maybe it's just one of those things that, um, rich people have, that we never did."

If Natalie hadn't been standing right there, Emma would have gone on: *You know, because rich people have* things *they worry about thieves stealing. Us Greystones, we never had anything anyone would want to steal, so we didn't have to worry about it.*

But she didn't want Natalie to think Emma was insulting *her.*

"Emma, my dad didn't get that security system until Mom disappeared," Natalie said. "Because . . . I don't know. I guess not knowing what happened to Mom made him worry that something could happen to . . . me."

Natalie's face quivered. Just as Emma could watch the sky and understand what it meant when dark storm clouds rolled in, she could watch Natalie now and see the stew of the older girl's emotions: *She's still mad at her dad, but she misses him, too, and she feels guilty for not telling him the truth, but she wants to protect him, and . . .*

Analyzing every cheek twitch and jaw clench of Natalie's expressions was so much easier than figuring out what "mission" the cleaners meant or why the Judge spied on her workers.

"They can't see or hear us, right?" Finn asked, scrambling out from behind the desk and going over to touch the image on the wall.

The cleaners in the basement seemed entirely focused on dusting and vacuuming now. Emma noticed, though, that the camera angle followed them from behind, rather than staying in one place.

So it's a portable camera unit, maybe motion-activated like the lights in the school bathroom. . . . Something struck her that stopped her dispassionate analysis.

Wait—if there's security footage of what's happening in the basement now, then . . . is there security footage from half an hour ago?

Emma wondered. *From when Chess, Finn, Natalie, and I arrived from the better world? How long do we have before the Judge or someone else sees it? Is this room the only place the security footage can be accessed? Or . . .*

"The Judge wouldn't have things set up so *she* could be spied on," Natalie sniffed, answering Finn. "So I think we're safe in here. But why would she watch the basement? Are there security cameras in other places in the house, too?"

Natalie dived down under the desk where Finn had been. A second later, the scene on the wall changed. Now Emma could see Mr. Mayhew in a vast office with lots of leather chairs and floor-to-ceiling windows that showed skyscrapers behind him.

"She spies on your *dad* when he's at work?" Finn gasped. "Er . . . Other–Mr. Mayhew . . ."

Natalie had just poked her head out from under the desk. She grimaced and reached her hand toward the bottom of the desk once more.

The scene on the wall changed again, and now it looked completely familiar: It was Other-Natalie's bedroom, with the poster sagging from the wall, the clothing scattered across the floor, and the desk drawer hanging open where Natalie had pulled out the laptop.

"The Judge spies on her daughter, too?" Natalie gasped.

"In her *bedroom*? Even *my* mom wouldn't do that!"

"We already knew Judge Morales was a horrible person," Chess said quietly.

"But what's she spying on people *for*?" Emma asked.

In the scene on the wall, the bedroom door opened. A woman in the same kind of brown uniform as the cleaners in the basement entered the room and bent down to dust the woodwork.

"That's the cleaner I talked to!" Natalie said. "I told her not to go in there!" She started to bolt away from the desk, toward the door. "I'm going to order her to leave!"

"And how would you tell her that you knew she was there?" Chess asked.

"I—I—" Natalie gasped. Still, she stopped moving toward the door.

In the scene on the wall, the cleaner threw a quick glance over her shoulder.

She's being . . . furtive, Emma thought, remembering a word from the vocabulary list her teacher had handed out just the week before at school.

It made sense that this cleaner didn't want to get caught, if she was going into Other-Natalie's room when she wasn't supposed to. But hadn't the cleaners in the basement moved and talked in the same way, just as furtively?

Why?

And why did Emma feel there was something almost familiar about the man and the woman in the basement?

"You don't really care what the cleaner does to the other Natalie's room, do you?" Emma asked Natalie. "Could you show us the basement again, please? I want to check something."

Natalie pursed her lips, but she reached under the desk once more, and the scene on the wall changed back to the cleaners vacuuming and dusting in the sea of navy blue and orange in the basement. The man had advanced to a coffee table stacked with blue-and-orange coasters. He polished the top of each stack, looked around, and then went on, clearly only pretending to clean the rest of the table.

"Hey—he's cheating! Cutting corners—that's what Mom calls it when I clean my room like that," Finn said. "Maybe that's why the Judge watches. To make sure her employees do a good job."

Emma didn't care about the man's cleaning skills.

"Can't we see their faces directly, not just from the side or the back?" Emma groaned.

"I don't think— Oh!" Natalie sounded surprised. "I *can* direct the camera. The top of this button is like a trackpad. . . ."

The view shifted. Now Emma could see the two cleaners

head-on: The man had a chiseled face and a thick, muscular neck above his baggy uniform. Beside him, the woman's limp red hair slid back to reveal a wrinkled face.

Emma gasped.

"I know who that man is!" she exclaimed. "No, wait—we know them both!"

CHESS

"That man . . . he's the man who tackled us . . . the, the security guard." Chess could barely get his words out.

"Emma, Chess, you're *right*!" Natalie exclaimed. "That cleaner does look like the security guard my dad hired to watch your house!"

Just seeing the man made Chess feel like he'd been tackled again. Or, like he was about to be tackled.

"But it's not him, right?" Finn piped up. "He's just this world's version of that guard. Not 'Ace Private Security' guy, but . . . Ace Two."

Finn sounded proud to figure that out on his own. And he'd even given the cleaner a name.

"Uh, right, Finn," Chess said, trying to hide a gulp. "Ace Two. But, Emma, what do you mean, saying we know *both* those cleaners? Even the woman? I don't recognize her. Who is she?"

Natalie's eyes grew wide, but she didn't say anything. Before Chess could figure out what that meant, he heard Finn say hesitantly, "Maybe I know?"

Emma locked eyes with Finn, and Chess felt oddly left out.

"At Mom's trial, right?" Emma asked Finn. "The old lady who helped you and then disappeared into the crowd? It *is* the same woman, isn't it?"

Could this get any worse? Chess didn't want to think about the trial any more than he had to.

"You said you barely saw that woman." Chess knew he sounded like he was accusing Finn and Emma of lying. But he couldn't help it. "She stayed in the shadows, and Natalie and I were so far away then, we're no help. But, Emma, you told us you and Finn really only saw that she was wearing a navy blue cap. So were a lot of people at the trial. This woman has such odd red hair—wouldn't you have noticed that?"

"Don't you think that's a wig?" Emma asked. "Or dyed? The woman who helped us—she might wear all kinds of disguises. Maybe she even makes her face look more or less wrinkled. But Finn, just watch how the woman *moves*."

Chess watched too, as the elderly cleaner hoisted the vacuum with ease, moving across the carpet with brisk energy. Finn whistled.

"Disguise Lady is *fast*," he said. "It *is* the same woman!"

Maybe it was just the power of suggestion—or the younger kids' certainty persuading him—but Chess could imagine this being the same woman who'd hidden Finn at Mom's trial.

"This *isn't* just a coincidence," Emma said. Her dark eyes glowed; her cheeks had turned an excited pink. She was practically beaming. "That woman being in Judge Morales's basement after she rescued Finn at Mom's trial—a trial Judge Morales was *running*—that means something. We just have to figure out *what*."

Yeah, because we were doing so well figuring out the mysteries we already have, Chess thought.

Why did the same details that thrilled Emma make him feel even more discouraged?

In the scene on the wall, the woman—Disguise Lady—suddenly dropped the vacuum. But she left it on, its roar continuing. Meanwhile, the woman glanced around, then tiptoed back to the muscular man, Ace Two. She must have said something, because the man raised his head, gazing her way.

"Natalie!" Emma exclaimed. "Angle the camera to see both of their faces! We may have to read lips."

Natalie whipped the viewpoint around so quickly that Chess felt dizzy.

Maybe Natalie found some way to control the volume, too, because now Chess could just barely hear the woman in the basement over the roar of the vacuum.

"—maybe we should disobey," Disguise Lady was saying, pursing her lips. Maybe Chess actually was half lip-reading, half hearing.

"What?" Ace Two said. "But the boss said—"

"I know, I know, she's protecting the girl," Disguise Lady said. "Just because the girl came home sick, that changed the timing. But who do *we* need to protect the most? The boss? Some bratty, spoiled girl who can't be trusted? Who no one will *ever* be able to trust, because she's never known anything but lies?"

"You're saying we should go ahead and do the transfer now," the man whispered. "Because waiting until tonight puts *us* more at risk."

"No—it puts the people we care about in greater danger," the woman countered. "The people we're rescuing. If I cared about my own safety, would I be doing this in the first place?"

Somehow Natalie had angled the camera to zoom in, so Chess could see the agony and indecision play over Ace Two's face. The man no longer looked like someone capable of pulverizing Chess. Instead, he looked as helpless and lost as Chess himself felt.

Then Ace Two clenched his jaw.

"We don't know enough," he said. "We don't understand enough of the rest of the plan to be able to carry off switching the timing of the transfer. We don't know who's an ally, and who's an enemy. I don't know if I can even trust *you*!"

Chess expected Disguise Lady to start protesting, "Of course you can trust me!" But for a moment her eyes just swam with sadness.

"Are you old enough to remember before?" she whispered. "When you could assume most people were good, and the world was mostly a safe place? When doing the right thing didn't mean hiding in the shadows and wearing disguises and lying to everyone you met—even people on the same side as you? Or *supposedly* on the same side as you? Because you never actually know for sure? Do you remember when we could believe the news we saw, and if some government official lied, there'd be a free press to show what the truth actually was, and then—"

"She sounds like Mom!" Finn said, jumping up and down. "She helped us before—she's someone we can trust! What she's saying—it means she would be on our side!"

"Shh!" Chess, Emma, and Natalie all whirled on Finn at once.

Finn clapped his hands over his mouth. Chess bent down to put his arm around his brother's shoulder, so he wouldn't feel too bad about being silenced.

When Chess looked back at the scene on the wall, Ace Two's eyes seemed as sad as the woman's.

"You could just be saying that," he murmured. "You could be trying to entrap me, to get me to say something that would be evidence if you're ever caught, and you need to betray others to save yourself. . . ."

The woman shook her head mournfully.

"Doesn't that just prove what I'm saying?" she asked. "How can civilization survive when nobody trusts anyone? When no one dares to tell the truth? Or believe it?"

"We trust each other enough to work together," the man said firmly, turning back to his fake-dusting. "Tonight. Like we told the boss."

"We don't even trust each other enough to tell our real names," the woman said, still shaking her head.

Just then the vacuum noise cut out abruptly, as if someone had yanked the plug. The old woman dipped down to the ground.

"What is the meaning of this?" a surly voice called from above, as if someone had just opened the door to the basement and was standing at the top of the stairs. "Why is the vacuum running, but you're five steps away?"

The woman sprang back up.

"I thought I saw something caught in the carpeting," she said. "My apologies."

"Don't let me catch you shirking again!"

The vacuum started up again, and the woman scurried over to pick it up once more. But she stayed close to Ace Two, and Chess saw her turn her back to the door—making it seem like a natural part of the vacuuming—and mouth one more word to the man.

"Did she just say 'tonight'?" Chess asked. "So they're doing *something* tonight? Some sort of 'transfer'?"

"Something that would have happened today, if Natalie weren't here," Emma agreed.

"But we don't know what," Finn said softly, like he wasn't sure he was allowed to speak again. "Unless—does everybody else understand? Am I the only one who doesn't?"

"Sorry," Chess said, ruffling his brother's hair. "We're just as clueless as you are."

Natalie shoved herself away from the desk.

"That's why I have to go down there and find out what's going on," she announced.

"Natalie—" Chess began.

She looked him straight in the eye. Chess had wanted Natalie to look at him that way for as long as he'd known her—as if she really saw him and what he was thinking. As if she really cared. But then her expression hardened. It felt to Chess as though she was shoving him away—*rejecting* him.

"I have to," she repeated.

And then she walked to the door.

PART TWO

TWENTY-EIGHT

NATALIE

You should have told them, Natalie thought as she stepped unsteadily into the hallway outside her mother's office. Er, the Judge's office. Whatever.

For just an instant, while she still held on to the doorknob, Natalie imagined telling the three Greystone kids—the three sweet, innocent, unsuspecting Greystone kids—what was running through her brain: *She's alive! I just saw a dead person alive again! And that's all I can think about right now!*

But how could they understand? How could they be happy for her when this world was nothing but terrible for them and their family? When they had no family left except the mother they were searching for?

Natalie pulled the office door firmly shut behind her, locking the Greystones in. Keeping them safe.

Me, on the other hand . . .

It was impossible to train her gaze anywhere in this house without seeing something that brought forth a tidal wave of memory and pain. She tried to make herself look instead for ways this house was different from her own: Had the foyer doubled in size? Was there some sort of greenhouse or giant sunporch jutting out at the side, which showed itself in the glint of light off dozens of windows that shouldn't be there? But Natalie kept getting distracted by details that made her feel like she'd gone back in time, not to a different world. There was Dad's showcase of golf trophies back in the corner of the dining room, right where they belonged. There was Mom and Dad's wedding picture back on the wall in the living room: Mom in white lace, Dad in a tux, both of them looking so young and ecstatic and deeply, endlessly in love. There was . . .

Stop it! Natalie told herself. *Just look down at your feet. Make sure you're walking straight.*

There was the Persian-style rug that used to run down this hallway, before.

Before everything fell apart.

Before anyone died.

"Miss?"

It was another cleaner, one she hadn't seen before. Natalie knew she should raise her head and look closely—if nothing else, to make sure this wasn't someone else familiar, masquerading in a brown uniform.

But Natalie was having enough problems just staying upright.

"I'm getting a drink of water," she mumbled. "Stay away from me. I'm sick. Probably contagious."

It took no acting skill whatsoever for Natalie to sway dizzily. She could feel the prickles of sweat along her hairline, the light-headedness that probably also meant the color had drained from her face.

She saw a pair of brown work boots take a respectful step back. The cleaner must have smashed himself against the wall, giving her space to pass.

Natalie wobbled forward.

She knew how to tell convincing lies, how to back them up. She knew that now she really did need to stop in the kitchen and turn on the faucet for a few minutes, or grab a glass and press it against the water dispenser. It would help to be heard gulping down water.

But Natalie didn't have the patience for that right now. She went straight to the basement door. She flung it open and raced down the stairs, then flew across the carpet.

The closer she got to the woman with the vacuum cleaner, the more certain Natalie was of the woman's identity. In her mind's eye, she could picture throwing herself at the woman, wrapping her arms around her just as Natalie had always done when she was little.

But Natalie wasn't three or six or nine anymore. Or eleven.

Natalie had grown a lot in the past two years, and this woman . . . hadn't.

Natalie was taller than this woman now.

Over the roar of the vacuum, the woman didn't even hear Natalie approach. Natalie stood behind her for an instant, towering over her. Then Natalie reached out one shaking hand and tapped the woman on the shoulder.

"Abuela?" Natalie called, her voice shaking. "Grandma? Why are you pretending to be a house cleaner?"

TWENTY-NINE

NATALIE

In the instant before the woman turned, Natalie saw everything she'd done wrong. She should have made sure the other cleaner was too far away to hear them. She should have let the woman see her first, and take cues from her about whether this world's Natalie would or wouldn't be surprised to see her grandmother in a cleaner's uniform; whether this world's Natalie would or wouldn't alternate between calling her grandmother "Abuela" and "Grandma," as Natalie always had.

She should have made absolutely certain that her eyes weren't tricking her, just because she wanted so badly to see her grandmother again, alive and well.

Grandma shouldn't have died, Natalie thought—the same thought she'd had a million times in the past year. But the doctors said it, too. They blamed Grandma for ignoring the symptoms of her rare cancer until it was too late. Only, Natalie knew why Grandma hadn't gotten help sooner: Grandma had been too busy taking care of Natalie when Natalie's parents were fighting and separating and getting divorced.

But then Natalie forgot all that, because Grandma was facing her directly. Grandma!

"Oh, my baby girl," she sighed, and it was exactly right and exactly wrong, all at once.

This *was* Grandma. But her voice was too husky and deep—suspicious-sounding. And though Grandma had been known to wear silly costumes to entertain Natalie when she was little, she never would have chosen the ugly, wispy red wig she had on now. Even if she had, she never would have looked this beaten-down and meek—she never would have looked so much like she belonged in a brown uniform, cowering behind a battered vacuum.

Natalie didn't care about the wig or the uniform. The worst detail was Grandma's eyes: They didn't soften the way they always had, gazing at Natalie. Instead, Grandma barely glanced at Natalie before turning to peer at the other cleaner.

He was crouched over the back of the couch as if it mattered to wipe away dirt that was already hidden.

He wasn't looking at Natalie or Grandma.

Still, Grandma frowned.

"Shh," she said, even though the vacuum was still on, and its noise filled the basement. "Don't ruin my cover. Don't call me 'Grandma.'"

"But—" Natalie began. Of course she couldn't add, *But I haven't seen you in more than a year! The last time I saw you, it was at your funeral!* Because this wasn't truly her grandmother, her abuela. It was Other-Natalie's.

It wasn't as if she could say, *How are you still alive, when my real grandma isn't?*

Because Other-Natalie's mom and dad didn't fight and separate and get divorced here, and this Grandma must have gotten treatment in time. . . . She never collapsed on our hallway rug and . . . and . . .

"Look," Grandma said, her voice harsh. "Do you think your mother would trust cleaners to just do their jobs right? Without someone watching them?"

"Mom makes you disguise yourself to *spy* on her cleaners?" Natalie asked.

"Shh," Grandma said again.

She switched off the vacuum, and now the silence around them felt too loud.

"Listen," she called to the male cleaner. "The young lady

of the household just came downstairs and now she's feeling ill, and so I'm going to walk her back up to her room."

The other cleaner nodded without turning around, as if he preferred not to look at Natalie. Or maybe he didn't want her to see *his* face.

Are Chess, Emma, and Finn watching this? Natalie wondered. *Do they understand?*

Before she'd met the Greystones, Natalie couldn't have imagined being anything but an only child—and not just an only child, but an only grandchild, too. She'd never been one of those kids who begged their parents for a younger brother or sister. But in the past few weeks, she'd gotten used to having Finn drape himself over her shoulder while they were watching TV, or to hearing Emma bubble over with ideas when she thought she might have a new solution to her mother's coded message. (And, Natalie had to admit, she'd also gotten used to having Chess gaze adoringly at her when he thought she wasn't looking.) So now it made Natalie feel almost lonely to be away from them. It felt like she was missing an arm or a leg. Or maybe three pairs of arms and legs.

But I'm with Grandma now! GRANDMA!

Grandma put her hand on Natalie's arm and tugged her toward the stairs.

"Play along," Grandma muttered under her breath. "A

cleaner can't be seen . . . manhandling the young lady of the house."

Natalie almost giggled. "Manhandle" was such a Grandma word.

Grandma glared at her, and Natalie turned the near-giggle into a cough.

Natalie wanted to nestle her head against Grandma's shoulder. She wanted to spill everything: *Oh, Grandma. In my world, Mom and Dad got divorced and they hate each other. And then Mom got trapped in this world, and I didn't know to pull her to safety; I didn't know the tunnel was going to collapse. . . . And now my friends and I came back to rescue both our moms, and it's so dangerous for Chess and Emma and Finn. But for me, for me . . . Oh, Grandma. You're still alive here, and my parents are still married here, and . . .*

Grandma kept shooting stern looks at Natalie, and that kept Natalie from cuddling against her or saying anything.

But when we get to my room and no one else can hear us . . .

It would be Other-Natalie's room, not hers. And this was Other-Natalie's grandmother, not hers.

Natalie had to remember that.

Natalie kept tripping as she followed Grandma across the expanse of the basement carpet, up the basement stairs, down the hallway again, then up the stairs to the second floor. Anyone who saw her and Grandma together would have every reason to believe that Natalie was sick and weak and in need of someone half carrying, half dragging her to her room. Natalie kept her head down, not even paying attention to whether the other cleaners stepped aside for them or just made themselves scarce.

But finally Natalie and Grandma reached Natalie's room—*no, Other-Natalie's room.*

"Here. I'll tuck you into bed and you can sleep," Grandma said too loudly, as though the words were meant for someone else's ears. "The other cleaners and I, we'll leave you alone."

She pulled Natalie toward the bed. Natalie could imagine Grandma tucking her into bed and smoothing her hair down, just as she'd done many, many times when Natalie was little.

Then Natalie saw the poster half ripped from the wall.

Other-Natalie's poster, Other-Natalie's wall. Other-Natalie's grandma.

Natalie dug her heels into the carpet.

"No, Grandma, you have to explain—"

Grandma leaned close enough to whisper in Natalie's ear: "The less you know, the safer you are. Don't tell anyone you saw me. Not even your mom and dad."

"But—"

Grandma was already turning her back on Natalie, turning to go. Natalie grabbed Grandma's arm.

"I know this isn't just about cleaners!" Natalie said, her voice going shrill with desperation. "I know you disguised yourself at least one other time. To . . . to . . ."

In one smooth motion, Grandma kicked the door shut and then yanked Natalie deeper into the bedroom. Distantly, Natalie realized that Grandma was pulling her toward one corner of the room that was out of sight of both windows.

"You don't know anything," Grandma said.

"You helped . . . other kids," Natalie said, barely stopping herself from saying Finn and Emma's names. "At the trial for . . . for Kate Greystone. You were there in disguise. Pretending to be just part of the crowd. Why? What are you . . ."

Natalie saw surprise flicker across Grandma's face. Then Grandma went back to looking crafty and began, "I wasn't—"

"Don't lie to me!" Natalie protested. "I know what I know!"

"Fine." Grandma practically spat the word. She leaned in close again, but this didn't feel friendly or cozy. "You keep all that knowledge to yourself. Because you don't know who you can trust and who you can't. *I'm* not even sure anymore who's trustworthy. Natalie, cielo, we have enemies. Enemies who are deceivers pretending to be friends . . ."

Was Grandma *begging*?

The doorknob rattled. Then it clicked.

Natalie heard a voice.

"—so if there was some mix-up and Mom thinks I'm home sick from school anyway, then of course I decided to skip the rest of the day! I have an excused absence! Bonus!"

Natalie sprang away from Grandma—Fake-Grandma—and sprinted for the door. She was too late. The door opened, and Natalie came face-to-face with another girl. Or not another girl—just a mirror image of herself, wearing the same jeans and T-shirt, but in a way that made her look less sweaty, less bedraggled, and less scared than Natalie felt. Oh, and somehow the mirror image also made it look like Natalie was talking on a phone.

But mirrors didn't work that way. The world seemed to tilt, and Natalie understood what had happened.

Natalie wasn't facing another girl. She wasn't facing a mirror.

She was facing Other-Natalie.

THIRTY

NATALIE

"No!" Other-Natalie exploded, stepping into the room and shoving Natalie aside. "This isn't happening! I won't put up with it! How could Mom and Dad have gotten me a body double, like they've been threatening to? An impersonator? And they didn't warn me, they just . . . sprang it on me by having you show up in my room? No way!" She stalked over and slammed her phone down on her desk, then seemed to change her mind and pulled it back up again. "I'm calling Dad!"

"Child," Grandma said softly from behind Natalie. "My sweet baby girl. Calm down. Let's talk about this quietly.

There *are* others in the house right now."

Natalie turned. Somehow in the instant while it was just Natalie facing Other-Natalie, Grandma had shucked off the red wig and the brown uniform, dropped them to the floor, and kicked them under the bed. Grandma's stylish short gray hair was a little mashed, and her mauve sweater was a little crumpled, but otherwise she looked perfectly normal.

Perfectly like Natalie's own grandmother if she'd been miraculously brought back to life.

"I am not going to calm down!" Other-Natalie wailed. "Are you kidding? Mom and Dad were too cowardly to break this news themselves? They're making you do it, Grandma? This isn't even a good imitation of me! I bet you can still see plastic surgery scars on her face!"

Carelessly, as if Natalie were just some unwanted doll or stuffed animal someone had dropped off in Other-Natalie's room, Other-Natalie pushed back the hair by Natalie's face. She was clearly looking for proof that Natalie was in disguise.

Natalie shoved Other-Natalie's hand away.

"Who is this, this *fake*?" Natalie countered, too late and too feebly. "*I'm* Natalie Mayhew. This is *my* room and *my* house, and *she's* the impostor! The deceiver!" Maybe Natalie wasn't as good a liar as she thought. Her voice wobbled. Then she added, "And you're *my* grandma!" and that came out right.

Grandma—Almost-Grandma—looked back and forth between the two girls.

"And I thought King Solomon had it rough," she muttered.

"That was someone offering to cut a baby in half because two woman both claimed it," Other-Natalie began. "And this is—"

"—you being asked to tell the difference between your own granddaughter and some *fake*!" Natalie finished for her.

Other-Natalie shot her a startled look. Maybe Natalie had chosen the exact words the other girl had planned to say.

"Stop that!" Other-Natalie scolded. "Stop imitating me! This is freaking me out. I guess Dad—or Mom; it was probably Mom who actually made the arrangements—I guess they must have told you to stay completely in character. But this isn't funny. This is going to ruin my life." She turned to appeal to her grandmother again. "Grandma, you have to talk to Mom and Dad. They're just being paranoid. I *know* the world's a dangerous place, and we're living in dangerous times. But I can take care of myself—I took that self-defense class, remember? You can't let them just lock me in my room all the time while this girl is out going places, living *my* life. She'll ruin my reputation. I mean, just look at her! I don't think she even combs her hair!"

Self-consciously, Natalie smoothed back a strand of hair

that had been hanging down into her eyes. It was true that she'd mashed her hair under her bike helmet that morning and then ignored it ever since. No—then she'd mussed it on purpose, trying to look sick.

"Who cares about hair?" Natalie asked, and both Almost-Grandma and Other-Natalie squinted doubtfully at her.

Oh, right, because that's probably not something Other-Natalie would say, Natalie thought. *It's not even something* I *would have said before a few weeks ago. Other-Natalie is like me before my parents got divorced, before I lost Grandma, before Mom disappeared. . . .*

Natalie had to squeeze her eyes shut for a moment to pull herself back together. This was not going well. She was probably only seconds away from both Other-Natalie and Almost-Grandma screaming for security guards to come and take her away.

She opened her eyes wide and directed her gaze at Grandma.

"Please," she said. "Please help me."

Natalie had thought Almost-Grandma's eyes were wrong before, when she first stood before her in the basement, and her face didn't go all soft and mushy and loving. The old woman's gaze now was so hard and heartless that Natalie wondered how Other-Natalie could stand it. Did this version of Grandma love her granddaughter at all?

Was she capable of loving anyone?

"You know what, girls?" Almost-Grandma said. "I don't have time for this. You work things out on your own. You'll be safe here, doing that."

And then, before Natalie had a chance to react, Almost-Grandma scooped up her clothes and wig from the floor, stalked out the door, and shut it behind her.

Belatedly, Natalie dashed to the door and tried to spin the knob.

It was locked.

Natalie whirled back toward Other-Natalie.

"You let people lock you in your own room?" she asked. With Almost-Grandma gone, there was no reason to keep trying to pretend she was Other-Natalie, and Other-Natalie was the fake.

Other-Natalie gave a combination shrug, eye roll, and head tilt. Natalie recognized the gesture as her own go-to reaction when she was pretending that something didn't bother her—when really she wanted to cry and scream and stomp her feet.

"Welcome to being Natalie Mayhew," Other-Natalie said, her voice flattened so completely that Natalie had to wonder, *Is that how I sound when* I'm *pretending I don't care? Or is she even better at hiding her feelings than I am?*

Natalie half expected the other girl to go back to screaming at her. Or to scream for her grandmother or someone else to come and release her from her room. Instead, Other-Natalie slipped into her desk chair and spun it to the side, studying Natalie closely.

"You haven't had plastic surgery," Other-Natalie said. "You don't have scars. I would have seen them, and they would have been fresh. But . . . you do look like me."

"No," Natalie admitted cautiously. "And yes."

The real Other-Natalie twisted in her chair, turning it side to side.

"Of course Mom and Dad would have paid for the most expensive option," she mused. "The highest quality. The most foolproof. But this . . . I'm guessing all you really need to look exactly like me is better hair-care products. When was the last time you used conditioner? Or—wherever you came from, did they only let you use the cheap stuff?"

In spite of herself, Natalie almost giggled. Or maybe it was a cry she held back. Before the divorce, before Grandma's death, before Mom vanished, Natalie had also been a true believer in the amazing power of the right hair conditioner.

Now—well, honestly, half the time when she'd taken a shower lately, she couldn't remember if she'd bothered using soap and shampoo, let alone conditioner. Most of the time, she'd just stood under the water plotting how to get Mom back, trying to figure out what solution she and the

Greystones had missed.

"Did Mom and Dad have me *cloned*?" Other-Natalie continued. "I mean, it sounds crazy, but . . . let's think about this. If they made a clone of me now—or nine months ago, whatever—you'd just be a baby. But you're the exact same height as me, you look like you're the exact same age, so . . . did they have me cloned when I was *born*? Is that even possible?" Other-Natalie stood up and walked all the way around Natalie, studying her. "I don't understand."

Natalie remembered the Greystone kids telling her about the wild theories they'd come up with when they first heard about the Gustano kids having the same names and birthdates as them. "Cloning" had been on their list of possibilities, too, even though it made no sense. Natalie wished the Greystones were here now—Finn could distract Other-Natalie with his charm, Emma could come up with strange scientific theories to lead her astray, and Chess . . . well, it would help just to have Chess there gazing sympathetically at Natalie.

But the Greystones weren't there. Natalie had to take control of this situation on her own.

"You want to know what's going on?" Natalie asked. "How it's possible for you and me to look identical when we've never seen each other before in our lives?"

"Yes," Other-Natalie said.

Oops. Now Natalie really did have to come up with

an explanation. Some convincing lie, something that made Other-Natalie want to help her.

She opened her mouth and gazed pointedly into Other-Natalie's eyes. Often the key to a good lie was just looking someone directly in the eye.

But looking into Other-Natalie's eyes was too much like gazing into a mirror. She saw the hurt and confusion the other girl was trying to hide. She saw how much Other-Natalie was trying to be her own person, and how sometimes it felt like the whole world was trying to stop her. She saw how many millions of ways she and Other-Natalie were alike.

It wasn't just skin-deep.

Natalie was taken off guard, and the words that slipped out of her mouth were, "I'll tell you the truth. I promise."

THIRTY-ONE

FINN, RIGHT AFTER NATALIE LEFT THE OFFICE

"I'll keep watching," Finn told Chess and Emma. "To see where Natalie goes and what happens."

Chess pressed up alongside Finn and clutched the Judge's desk so tightly that his knuckles turned white.

"I'm watching, too," he said. "And if anything goes wrong . . ." Chess gulped. "I mean, nothing'll go wrong. I just want to watch. Just in case. But Emma, you should keep working on the computer, and see what you find."

"You think I can concentrate at a time like this?" Emma squeaked out.

She joined Chess and Finn, all three of them huddled together by the Judge's desk, all three of them staring at the image on the wall of the cleaners in the Morales-Mayhew basement with its twisted pillars and blue-and-orange banners.

Even Finn knew this was crazy. There was so much they didn't know about this world; they had a million things to look up. Two of them really should be scanning the internet while the third person watched Natalie—that would be the smartest plan.

But Finn didn't say that aloud. It felt too good to have Chess and Natalie pressed in close beside him, bookending his shoulders.

It almost made him feel safe.

And . . . it made him feel like Natalie would be safe, too.

On the wall, Disguise Lady and Ace Two kept working away, vacuuming and scrubbing. And then Natalie appeared in the scene, rushing toward Disguise Lady.

"Can we turn the camera to see Natalie and Disguise Lady from the front, not just the backs of their heads?" Emma asked.

"Natalie did it before, but I saw what she was doing," Finn said. Without taking his eyes off Natalie, he reached under the desk for the button hidden in the carved wooden angel's wing. But maybe he should have looked at what he was doing, because his finger bumped a different part of the wing. The scene on the wall didn't rotate—it changed completely. Now, rather than spying on Natalie and the woman in the basement, the Greystones had a clear view of Other-Natalie's bedroom.

"Go back!" Chess exclaimed.

"Sorry," Finn said. "I'll fix it."

"No—wait! I want to see this!" Emma reached under the desk and grabbed Finn's hand.

"What are you talking about?" Chess asked. "That's just an empty room, and Natalie—"

"It's not empty!" Emma said. "Can't you see the cleaner hiding in the closet? The cleaner Natalie told *not* to go into that room?"

It took Finn a moment to see what Emma meant. At first all he noticed was the closet door sliding to the side, a smidge at a time. Then he saw a woman's face in the crack between the door and the doorframe.

"Are the cleaners playing hide-and-seek?" Finn asked.

The woman squeezed out of the closet, then stepped back in, pulling the door all the way shut this time. Maybe she wasn't actually playing hide-and-seek, but just practicing, the way Finn did when he was looking for new hiding spots and deciding which ones he could get into and out of without making any noise.

Closets were usually too obvious, but Finn did like how Other-Natalie's closet door slid open and shut so silently.

"Okay, the cleaners are doing lots of weird stuff," Chess said. "I don't understand that either. But get back to Natalie! If the cleaners are sneaking around and hiding and, and who knows what else—that means she's in even more danger out there!"

Finn reached under the desk again, more carefully this time. The basement scene reappeared on the wall. But Natalie and Disguise Lady were nowhere in sight. The camera view showed only Ace Two leaning over the couch.

"Maybe they just . . . walked to the back of the basement, to talk privately?" Emma suggested. "Can we see . . ."

Finn ran his finger over the button, and it felt like he was sliding the camera on some sort of railing along the basement ceiling.

"I'm getting the hang of this now!" he exclaimed.

At the back of the basement, there were more shadowy couches, all of them oddly stiff and formal, as well as a dark blue velvet curtain that hung from the ceiling to the floor, right where the basement ended back in Ms. Morales's house in the better world. Why put in such a gigantic curtain just to hide a wall?

Natalie and the old woman were still nowhere in sight.

"Keep going—we've got to find Natalie . . . ," Chess muttered. "Would they have gone toward the stairs?"

Finn made the camera reverse, back toward Ace Two. He was walking away from the couch now, toward the stairs and the wall where the kids had left the lever.

"If Natalie thinks she and that woman can talk privately over by the lever, and then that guy walks over beside them, well . . . I wish we could warn Natalie!" Emma agonized, twisting her hands together.

Finn zoomed the camera ahead of Ace Two. He got the first glimpse of the lever they'd left behind, tucked behind the furnace. No one was standing in this area of the basement, either.

"Maybe Natalie found out Disguise Lady wants to help us again, and so she's bringing that woman up to this office right now," Finn suggested. "Maybe we don't even need to keep watching the basement."

He started to spin the camera view up toward the stairs. But Emma's hand shot out and she grabbed him by the wrist.

"Stop!" she cried.

Finn saw what she was screaming about: Ace Two was beside the lever again. He glanced over his shoulder—once to the left, once to the right, and then once again in both directions, as if he *really* wanted to make sure no one saw him.

And then he put his hands on the lever and yanked it straight off the wall.

THIRTY-TWO

EMMA

"He just, he just—" Emma sputtered.

"Shut off our way back to the other world," Chess finished for her. "He stopped that tunnel from ever working again."

In the scene on the wall, the cleaner gave one more furtive glance over his shoulder, then slid the lever into his uniform, hiding it.

"No, no, no!" Emma cried, circling the desk and aiming for the door.

Chess grabbed her by the shoulder, holding her back.

"Wait—we've got to think this through!" he said.

"I already have," Emma retorted. "If he takes that lever away, we're stuck in this world forever! It won't even matter if we find Mom, because we'll have no way to take her to safety! We've got to get that back!"

"She's right, isn't she?" Finn asked, gazing back and forth between Emma and Chess. "And she's got a plan?"

Emma didn't have a plan. But she couldn't wait. She scrambled for the door.

"You can't go out there by yourself," Chess protested.

Emma saw him peer back at Finn as if he couldn't decide which of them to protect.

"You stay with Finn," Emma said. "I'll be right back."

Chess grabbed Finn's arm, pulling him away from the desk.

"We stick together," Chess said. "All three of us are going to get that lever back."

Maybe Emma was feeling a little torn herself. She wanted Finn—and Chess—to stay safe, but it would also be really nice to have them with her.

"Hurry," Emma said. "Before that man gets away."

Maybe she was also a little afraid that if she waited a second longer, she'd think of all the reasons why going after the lever wasn't logical.

Or she'd just chicken out.

Both Chess and Finn were by her side instantly: Chess

looking white-faced and tense, Finn trying a wobbly smile that was probably supposed to look brave, but mostly just revealed his clenched teeth.

"Should we prop the door open?" Chess asked. "Natalie has the key, but if we want to come back before her, then—"

"Can we make it look like it's locked, but it really isn't?" Finn asked.

"Let's try," Emma said. "Was there a sheet of paper anywhere?"

"Here!" Finn rushed to a closet Emma hadn't noticed, and pulled out a flyer with Judge Morales's face on it.

Emma took the paper and folded it in half and then half again. She turned the doorknob to open the door, and slid the paper into the crack between the door and the doorframe. There was no sound of the lock clicking back into place.

"Okay, that will work," Emma whispered.

Beside her, Chess drew in a deep breath.

"Let's just peek out before we go anywhere," he muttered.

Emma nodded. With Chess and Finn pressed close behind her, she pulled the paper out, turned the doorknob again, and inched the door backward, just enough to see out.

"Nobody's there," she reported.

Chess grimaced and nodded. Emma opened the door the rest of the way and stepped out. The two boys followed her. Quickly, before she lost her nerve, she turned and pulled the door shut behind them, with the folded paper tucked in beside the lock. But maybe the paper was too mashed together this time; maybe the wooden doorframe was imperceptibly angled.

This time the paper slipped as soon as Emma let go, sliding down at least three or four inches.

“Oh no!” Emma exclaimed, grabbing for the doorknob again and twisting it as fast as she could.

But she was too late. The lock clicked, and her hand slid uselessly off the knob.

They’d just locked themselves out of Judge Morales’s office.

THIRTY-THREE

CHESS

Chess felt like he was in a nightmare. He blinked, because maybe his eyes weren't working right; maybe it was just fear making him think they'd just lost any way to get back into the Judge's office on their own.

But it wasn't only his eyes showing him the locked door; he also heard Emma's anguished whisper: "I'm sorry! I'm so sorry! I thought that would work!"

Finn was already patting Emma's back and comforting her: "It's okay! We'll just find Natalie, and she'll unlock the door for us. . . ."

Natalie's vanished! Chess wanted to shout at his siblings.

We don't know where she is! Maybe she's just as lost as Mom and Ms. Morales and Joe. Maybe we'll never find her. And we just left behind our backpacks and computers, which were our only hope of solving Mom's code. And when Judge Morales finds our stuff, she'll see the computers as incriminating evidence. We might have gotten Mom into worse trouble. We definitely just got ourselves *into worse trouble! What if . . .*

Chess couldn't say any of that to Emma and Finn. Not when Emma's eyes were already swimming with unshed tears. Not when Finn was already biting his lip so hard it was surprising he hadn't drawn blood.

They know, he thought.

"Let's go get the lever back," Emma said in a wavery voice. "Then . . ."

"Then we'll worry about what comes next," Chess said, even though he was worried enough about the lever. He hunched his shoulders, a motion that reminded him that they still hurt from being tackled by the guard Mr. Mayhew had hired to watch over the Greystones' house.

What if this world's version of that guy has just as many muscles? Chess wondered. *How do we have any hope of getting the lever back?*

But Emma and Finn were already turning toward the basement door, and Chess scrambled to catch up. They tiptoed and shuffled and darted from doorway to doorway. And maybe their luck was changing, because the only cleaners they saw were facing the other way, intent on shaking out enormous tablecloths or polishing thick, distorting windows or dusting heavy, carved wooden chairs.

The three kids reached the door down to the basement and slipped through it, and Chess let out a deep sigh. He shut the door behind him and sagged against it.

"What's the plan now?" Finn whispered.

Emma threw back her shoulders and held her head high in a way that seemed oddly familiar.

"We're going to act as confident as Natalie," Emma said.

And for a moment, Chess could see it: Emma was impersonating Natalie right down to the way she flipped her thick, dark hair over her shoulder.

Mostly this made Chess miss Natalie more. And worry about her.

He wished he dared to race down the basement stairs and yell, "Natalie! Natalie! Where are you?"

Maybe she and Disguise Lady are still down in this basement, and they were just out of range of the security cameras. Maybe she's already told Ace Two to give the lever back. . . .

But as Chess crept down the stairs behind Emma and Finn, he could tell: Unless the woman and Natalie were crouched down and hiding, they weren't anywhere in the basement.

At the bottom of the stairs, Chess squared his shoulders.

Emma's right, he thought. *We have to act as confident as Natalie. We'll tell that cleaner that's* our *lever, and he had no business taking it off the wall . . . or, no, we tell him it belongs to* Natalie, *and Natalie's parents, and he has to give it back or we'll report him for theft. . . .*

Chess forced his chin up. He tried to clear his brain of everything he was afraid of. He was concentrating so hard on making himself look confident that he walked right into Emma and Finn when they stopped in front of him.

"What's wrong?" he started to ask. But it was apparent as Emma poked her head behind the furnace and as Finn gazed back toward the stairs.

The cleaner who'd taken their lever from the wall had completely disappeared.

THIRTY-FOUR

FINN

"Did he *use* the lever and go back to the other world?" Finn asked.

"Not after yanking it off the wall," Emma said dazedly. "Remember? That keeps it from working again. At least it keeps it from working again in this room. Or this house. Or, well, we really don't know how far out the damage spreads. . . ."

Emma's gaze went vague and unseeing. Finn loved watching Emma's face at times like this. Her eyes narrowed and then grew wide; her lips bunched up and then spread out in a grin. Her eyebrows darted up and down, like gears that drove her brain to work faster and faster.

"The cleaner's still in this basement somewhere," Emma announced, peering all around the vast orange-and-blue room.

"What?" Chess said. "How do you figure that?"

"There wasn't time for him to run up the stairs and leave through that door without us seeing him," Emma said, pointing behind her.

"But there's that sliding door over there—" Chess pointed to the side.

"If he'd run over there and rushed out that door, he would have had to brush past those sheer drapes, and they would still be swaying back and forth," Emma said. "The same goes for that weird velvet curtain at the back of the room."

Finn had no doubt that Emma was right. He wouldn't have been surprised if she'd done some complicated math calculation in her head and figured out exactly how many seconds would have had to pass before the drapes would stop swaying, if the cleaner had used that door.

"So is the cleaner scared of *us*, that he hid when we came downstairs?" Finn asked. He turned toward the vast, open section of the room and called in his sternest voice, "We're not playing hide-and-seek! This isn't the time for that! Come out, come out, wherever you are!"

"Shh," Chess said. "What if the cleaners upstairs hear you?"

"Well, some of them were playing hide-and-seek, too," Finn said, "and it looked like they didn't even know that closets aren't good places to hide. . . ."

Finn glanced around. Back by the furnace, there was a door under the stairs that could easily have been a closet. Was it just Finn's imagination, or had the wooden door vibrated ever so slightly when Finn first glimpsed it? Was that like how Emma said the drapes by the sliding door would have swayed if the cleaner had run that way?

Finn took two steps and whipped open the door.

"Found—" he began.

But he'd found nothing but a nearly empty space with a bucket, a mop, and ugly wood paneling.

Maybe the whole closet was just flimsy—the wood paneling inside the closet seemed to sway slightly, too, as if it had just been moved. Was it still vibrating from the way Chess, Emma, and Finn had come thundering down the stairs overhead just a moment ago? Or just from Finn whipping open the closet door?

Finn had never before wondered about why a wall

would shake, or how long that shaking could last. That kind of thinking fit in Emma's brain, not his.

But the wood paneling made Finn think of an animal breathing in and out; he even felt a little puff of air against his cheek.

There shouldn't be air coming out of a closet. It was a closed space. Wasn't it?

Finn reached for the wood paneling. He felt around the edges.

"Finn, what are you doing?" Chess asked behind him.

"I just thought . . . ," Finn began.

And then his finger hit something in the corner of the closet. Maybe it was just a rough place in the wood, but it made Finn think of the button hidden in the carved angel's wing under Judge Morales's desk. Or, no, maybe it was more like the button hidden between the bookcase and the wall back in the basement of Finn, Emma, and Chess's house.

Something clicked, and Finn tried to shove in on the paneling. Nothing happened, so he tried to pull it out.

"Does it *slide*?" Emma said practically in his ear, and that was the first moment that Finn realized she was right behind him, too, watching intently.

Emma reached out and tugged on the paneling, even digging her fingernails into the narrow wood seam.

The wood paneling separated at the corner of the wall and slid a foot and a half to the right.

"Finn!" Emma exclaimed. "You found another hidden room! And . . . this one is *enormous*!"

THIRTY-FIVE

EMMA

Emma couldn't see all the way into the space behind the closet—that's how big it was. She thought maybe she saw a bobbing light in the darkness—far, far off in the distance. Could it possibly have been a mile away? *Two* miles away?

This isn't just a room, she thought. *It's a tunnel. Like the one we had under our house, when the lever made it possible to go between the worlds there . . .*

The light winked out.

"What? No!" Emma moaned. "I want to see!"

Chess pressed something into her hand. A flashlight.

"There's a whole shelf of them up there," he whispered, pointing over Emma's head.

Emma switched her flashlight on. Chess must have grabbed lights for himself and Finn as well, because soon there were three beams crisscrossing before her. All three kids shone their lights toward the endless space behind the paneling. But in just that instant, everything about the space changed. Now it was small and confined; Emma could see another wall only a few feet behind the paneling.

She waved her flashlight around, and so did Chess and Finn. The three beams of light danced across a solid wall.

And then all three beams came to rest on a lever on the wall, off to the side—a lever seeming to move by itself.

"Are there . . . ghosts?" Finn asked.

For just an instant, Emma was ready to accept that explanation. Then her brain came up with a more logical idea.

"No, this must be what it looks like from the other side when someone closes the tunnel between one world and the other," she breathed, in awe. "Remember how Chess turned the lever right after we came to this world, so we weren't just leaving a tunnel open? That cleaner, Ace Two—he just moved the lever from where we left it, in plain sight, to this hiding spot where the wrong people won't see it. So it's like he helped us! And he proved that once you yank a lever off a wall, it still can work in the same house, just not in the exact same spot. How close can you get, I wonder? Should we—"

"What if Ace Two *keeps* moving it? To someplace we can't find it?" Chess asked, reaching for the lever. He tucked his flashlight under his chin and wrapped both hands firmly around the metal lever. "This is our lever, and when we get Mom and Ms. Morales and Joe back, we need to know where it is!"

"You're right," Emma said. "But can we—"

She wanted to keep figuring out how the lever and the tunnel worked; she wanted to test ideas on Chess and Finn about tracking down Ace Two and getting him to explain everything. But before she could speak another word, she saw Chess's arms slide down.

Oh, he just pulled the whole lever off the wall, she thought. *That was probably smart, though what's the cleaner going to think when he's stuck on the other side, and the lever just disappears?*

Then Emma realized: Chess's hands were empty. His arms hadn't jerked down because he'd pulled the lever off the wall. They'd fallen because the lever in his hands had suddenly vanished.

"W-What? Where . . . ?" Chess stammered. "Where'd it go?"

Emma had everything figured out. But she kept hoping she was wrong.

What if . . . no. But maybe if . . . no, not that either . . .

"I don't understand!" Finn wailed. "What happened to the lever?"

"Oh, Finn," Emma moaned. "Oh, Chess. I think . . . I think the cleaner just pulled the lever off the wall at the other end of the tunnel. In the other world. And that's what made the lever disappear here. He took it to the one place we can't follow him!"

THIRTY-SIX

CHESS

We're trapped, Chess thought. *Stuck in this horrible world forever.*

This was so much worse than being locked out of Judge Morales's office. Chess realized that ever since they'd stepped through the tunnel in the first place, he'd kept an image of the lever in the back of his mind like a safeguard, a protection. A talisman. He'd thought that no matter what else happened, as long as they stayed near the lever, they could always go back to the other world.

"We should have ripped it off the wall ourselves," Chess muttered. "We should have kept it with us so no one else could steal it. . . ."

"But we thought it might not work in this house again, if we did that," Emma said, almost like she was apologizing. "We didn't figure out the rules before we started using it. . . ."

"We just wanted to get Mom and go home!" Finn moaned. "That's all I want *now*!"

Chess clenched and unclenched his fingers, still feeling the ridge where he'd clutched the lever only a moment before. He'd been holding on so tightly it didn't seem fair that the lever could have just vanished. It seemed more likely that he would have cut his hands on the sharp edges, or that he would have imprinted the letters from the message "USE IN A SPOT THAT EXISTS IN BOTH (WORLDS)" onto his fingers.

Wait a minute—sharp edges? he thought. *Were the edges sharp before?*

He took the flashlight in his right hand and shined it onto the palm of his left hand. He had two angry red lines across his hand—one down by the thumb, and the other between the joints of his fingers. The lever hadn't left marks like that before, even when he'd held it just as tightly. How could it have left such marks now? Hadn't the edges always been smooth and rounded?

"What if . . . ," Chess began. He swallowed hard and tried again. "What if that wasn't our lever?"

Emma and Finn stared up at him, matching puzzlement in their eyes. Then Emma's eyes grew wide, and she let out a gasp.

"You think there's more than one lever?" she asked. "Well, of course there's more than one lever, because we know the bad guys didn't come through the tunnel at our house when they kidnapped the Gustano kids. . . . Do you think this lever was in this hiding space in this closet all along? Do you think it was the bad guys' lever? How many levers do you think there are? And—"

Chess held up his hands defensively, because once she got going, Emma could ask *lots* of questions. And he didn't have any answers. But she suddenly stopped mid-sentence and slumped over.

"What's wrong?" Finn asked.

Emma frowned and shook her head.

"Even if that wasn't our lever on this wall, that cleaner guy just escaped to the other world and made it so we can't follow him," she said. "And he must have taken our lever with him—either way, we can't get our lever back."

Don't go on, Chess thought, putting his arms protectively around his little brother. *Don't tell Finn how bad things are.*

He opened his mouth and tried to think of something hopeful to say. For Finn.

But just then, he heard footsteps on the stairs above them.

He reached back and yanked the closet door shut behind them.

"Where are they?" The voice came from overhead. "You say they were last reported down there?"

Finn gave a little jump.

"Mr. Mayhew!" he whispered, as if that was good news.

"*Other*–Mr. Mayhew," Emma corrected. "The Mayor."

Chess shoved both Emma and Finn forward, toward the space behind the wood paneling. Then he reached back and pulled the paneling closed behind them, so it would look like nothing but a solid wall again if anyone opened the closet door.

"Flashlights off!" he hissed, switching off his own.

Emma was almost as quick, and Finn was only a split second behind her.

The darkness that engulfed them was unbearable. Wouldn't the Mayor know about this secret hiding place in his own house, anyhow?

Chess pressed his ear against the back of the paneling, listening intently.

"My wife and I have always screened every single one of our employees thoroughly," the Mayor was saying. "We hire the best security forces in the country. How is it possible that anyone slipped through our defenses? How could there be spies among our cleaners?"

Finn tugged on Chess's arm.

"They're not looking for us!" he rejoiced in a whisper. "They don't know we're here! They're just worried about the cleaners!"

"Shh," Chess warned him. "Don't let them hear. . . ."

"Sir, your enemies are crafty." This was another man's voice, one Chess didn't recognize. "But I assure you, it's because of your superior security force that we were able to discover the infiltration. They've only been setting up their network—we detected their presence before they had a chance to carry out any other plans. This is effective security in action."

"Then why don't I see you carrying out an arrest this very minute?" Mayor Mayhew sounded peevish. "This room's empty! There's nobody here!"

"We'll find them," the other man replied. "No matter where they're hiding."

Chess heard more footsteps pounding down the stairs above him.

Then he heard the closet door open.

THIRTY-SEVEN

NATALIE, A FEW MINUTES EARLIER

"We can trade off," Natalie said, settling down onto Other-Natalie's bed, while Other-Natalie watched her curiously from the desk chair. "We'll take turns asking questions. I'll go first."

"Why don't I get to go first?" Other-Natalie asked. "I'm the real Natalie Mayhew! While you're just . . . what *is* your name?"

"Natalie Mayhew," Natalie responded automatically. "And there. You did get the first question. I even answered it."

Other-Natalie's face flushed, and Natalie knew exactly how she felt, being tricked.

Careful, Natalie told herself. *Don't make her mad.*

"Fine." The other girl all but snarled the word. "Your turn."

See, she's going to play fair, Natalie thought. *Because* I *would play fair, if I were her.*

It was dizzying to peer back at Other-Natalie and try to figure out how to see her. Were Other-Natalie and Natalie exactly alike, pretty much the same person except for living in separate worlds? How different could someone be when she had your same face, your same hair, your same brain, your same parents?

She doesn't have the same parents, Natalie reminded herself. *She has the Judge, not Mom. And her dad's running for governor, not selling sports cars. And she lives in the bad world, so that's got to affect her, too. . . .*

And Other-Natalie's parents were still married. And her grandma was still alive. And *her* mother wasn't missing.

Natalie glanced up at the poster sagging down from the wall, to remind herself of *that* difference with Other-Natalie, too. With the top part of the poster bent over the bottom, Natalie could see only the poster's white backing. But she could remember the menacing look on all the kids' faces in that poster—even Other-Natalie's.

"What are you looking at?" Other-Natalie asked, turning

to follow Natalie's gaze. She let out a loud gasp. "Did you do that? Did you start tearing that down, and Grandma caught you, and, and . . ."

Natalie caught herself flinching guiltily. And Other-Natalie saw. What could Natalie say now? If she lied, Other-Natalie would see straight through her. And if she told the truth . . .

Well, how would I react if some stranger came into my room and started trashing it?

"Hey—it's my turn for questions, remember?" Natalie went for the snarly, defensive mode. But Other-Natalie's eyes were so wide and awestruck, her expression almost hopeful, that Natalie softened her voice. "Let's talk about other stuff first."

Natalie wouldn't have relented if she'd been in Other-Natalie's place. But maybe they weren't completely alike. Other-Natalie only glanced back at the poster once more, tilted her head to the side, and muttered, "So, ask."

It surprised Natalie into blurting, "Are you and your grandma close?"

This wasn't the right question for getting Other-Natalie on her side, for getting her help rescuing Mom, Mrs. Greystone, and Joe. And it was only the beginning of what Natalie wanted to know about Other-Natalie and Almost-Grandma.

She could have gone on, *Are you and your grandma best buddies? Is she the person who cares about you most in all the world? Does she hold you together when everything else goes wrong? Could you ever recover if she died?*

But Other-Natalie recoiled, disbelief spreading over her face.

"Me and *Grandma*?" she asked incredulously. "Are you kidding? Grandma doesn't have time for me. She thinks I'm a spoiled brat. She tells Mom and Dad that every chance she gets. She says I've grown up too sheltered."

Other-Natalie put air quotes around "sheltered," as if she were quoting her grandma exactly.

"But that's . . ." Natalie stopped herself before she could finish her protest: *That's not what Grandma's like.* She switched to "How could she not have time for you?"

Other-Natalie snorted.

"Did you take this job thinking you'd have fun hanging out with a seventy-six-year-old woman?" she asked. "Grandma's busy managing Mom's political career. Don't you watch any news?" Then, to Natalie's surprise, Other-Natalie winced. "I mean, I'm sorry. I guess no one would take this job for *fun*. And maybe you don't have access to any news, or knowing anything. I guess you'd have to be pretty desperate, to be willing to maybe die so that I don't have to be in danger."

That's what Other-Natalie meant, thinking her parents hired me as her body double? Natalie marveled. *People really do that in this world?*

Other-Natalie stared down at her lap for a moment, then peered back at Natalie with a hard-to-read expression.

"Grandma probably is right, that I've been sheltered," Other-Natalie said. "It's like Mom and Dad—especially Dad—they've tried to keep me like some princess in a tower, always protected. Always *ignorant*. They don't tell me anything, and school . . ." She rolled her eyes. "School's *worthless*. But I read things nobody knows I read. I've figured out how to work around most controls on my computer. And I've heard, for people who aren't politicians or business leaders—or their kids—for people who aren't rich . . . I've heard that those people lead horrible lives. People like you. Is that true?"

"Is that your next question?" Natalie asked weakly. She was stalling. As much as she missed Real-Grandma, she longed for someone else now: Mom. Real-Mom. Mom was really, really good at her job as a Realtor, and she'd made a lot of money, but she'd told Natalie a million times that no one should measure their value in money, no one should think a poor person was any less of a human being than a rich person. Other-Natalie sounded like she needed that lecture.

Or does she?

Natalie remembered the desperate people crowded into

the Public Hall two weeks ago for Mrs. Greystone's trial, and the way they'd been lied to and manipulated. She remembered Emma's theory about how there was some chemical released into the air that controlled people's emotions—that made them angry and afraid. And obedient.

That *had* been horrible. Before Emma had figured out what was happening and told Chess, Finn, and Natalie to hold their breath, Natalie had felt all that despair herself. She'd almost gagged over the constant odor and the constant fear and hopelessness.

And . . . there was no hint of that odor here at Other-Natalie's house.

"You've got to tell me," Other-Natalie said, almost begging. She leaned forward, waving her hands emphatically. "I want to know *everything*, and nobody will tell me *anything*!"

Was she acting? Lying? Only pretending to care?

She's genuine, Natalie told herself, because Natalie would have said the same thing the same way, if she'd been in Other-Natalie's shoes.

"I'm not actually from here," Natalie began cautiously. "But I've seen a little of how ordinary people live in your city. It *is* bad. And . . . I think some of it is your mother's fault."

"Of course it is," Other-Natalie replied. "She runs this city. Maybe the whole state. My dad's just a figurehead.

He's worthless. Believe me, I *hate* my parents. They're awful people."

This plunged Natalie into a different memory. The first day she'd met the Greystone kids after their mother went away, Finn, Emma, and Chess had been distraught and confused. Natalie had tried to comfort them by telling them how awful her own parents were; she'd told them that that's just how parents were.

She'd used the word "hate," too.

But her own parents weren't *actually* hateful. They were annoying and difficult, and sometimes they made Natalie's life miserable. Especially during the divorce. But Dad had been a good sport about taking the Greystones in when they had nowhere else to go, and Natalie didn't know anyone else's mom or dad who would do that. And Mom . . . Mom was all about helping other people. That was how she'd ended up trapped and missing. She put herself in danger only because she'd been trying to help the Greystones.

And because she'd been trying to help Natalie.

"Why do you want to know stuff?" Natalie asked Other-Natalie. "Just for the sake of knowing it? Wouldn't you want to change things, if you could? Don't you want to do something to really make a difference?"

Other-Natalie stared into Natalie's face, her intense brown eyes locked onto Natalie's matching pair.

"Yes," Other-Natalie whispered. "I do want to change things."

For a moment, both of them sat frozen in place. Then Other-Natalie whipped her head around, looking back toward the sagging poster. She scrambled to her feet, took a giant step onto the bed, and yanked the poster completely from the wall. She ripped it in half. She kept tearing until the poster was only a pile of scraps on the bed and pillows.

"There," Other-Natalie said, breathing hard and shoving the scraps to the floor. "I finished what you began. Those are the people who don't want change. They want to keep their power and leave everyone else in pain. And I am done pretending I'm one of them! I don't care what Mom or Dad or Grandma think!"

She's braver than me, Natalie thought. *She will help.*

She took a deep breath of her own.

"Okay, then," Natalie began. "Have you ever heard of alternate worlds?"

THIRTY-EIGHT

NATALIE

The minute Natalie finished talking, spilling everything, Other-Natalie spoke just two words: "Prove it."

"How?" Natalie asked. "What would convince you—"

Other-Natalie tilted back in her chair.

"Show me the lever in the basement," she said. "Take me to the other world. *Your* world."

Natalie wasn't sure that was a good idea, but she had more immediate problems.

"Have you forgotten we're locked in this room?" Natalie asked. "*And* that your house is full of cleaners who would freak out seeing you and me together? Even if we screamed for help and one of us hid until we got out . . . we can't risk anyone seeing what they'd think was the same girl coming down the stairs twice."

Other-Natalie tapped a finger against her chin.

"How much do I trust you?" she muttered. "You already saw me tear up the poster, but I could always deny that. . . ."

Other-Natalie bit her lip, then seemed to make a decision. She stood up and went over to her dresser, pulling out a red wool scarf that could have been the twin of one Natalie had worn all last winter.

Why should that surprise Natalie, when she and Other-Natalie appeared to be wearing the exact same dark jeans, the exact same cream-colored T-shirt?

"Blindfold," Other-Natalie said, holding the scarf out to Natalie.

"You think that will keep the cleaners from figuring out I look like you?" Natalie asked. "Wouldn't—"

"No," Other-Natalie said impatiently. "That will keep you from seeing how I get us out of here."

Natalie frowned but put the blindfold on. Other-Natalie spun her around, then guided her forward. The scarf was hot on her face but didn't entirely block her vision.

Didn't Other-Natalie ever play blindfold games when she was little? Doesn't she know you can almost always see out the bottom? Natalie wondered.

Natalie could tell they were walking toward the closet. She heard the closet door sliding open, and hangers being shoved to the side. Possibly shoes being shoved to the side as well.

Doesn't she know my hearing works fine? Natalie wondered.

Then she heard a click.

"What was that?" Natalie asked.

"*That* would be what I didn't want you to see," Other-Natalie said.

There was the sound of something else sliding away, and Other-Natalie pushed Natalie forward again. Natalie forgot herself and cried out, "Are you trying to slam me into the wall?"

But the wall inside the closet had vanished. Natalie could peek out of the bottom of the blindfold, and see her spare pair of Nikes—*oops, no, Other-Natalie's*—pushed messily off to the side, soles up. The toes of the shoes should have been nestled against the closet wall, but instead they pointed into a dark space.

Natalie gasped.

"Your house has secret passageways?" she asked. "Like, like . . ."

"Well, not like the house *you* were telling me about," Other-Natalie said, leading Natalie forward. "This passageway doesn't lead to other worlds. There's nothing like that in my house. I mean, there wasn't until you got here. As far as I know."

They'd only taken about a dozen steps before Other-Natalie warned in a whisper, "Stairs. And be quiet from now on, because someone might be able to hear us through the walls. And we can hear them."

Natalie had a million questions racing through her head, but she stifled them and concentrated on stepping down and down and down, one step at a time. The stairway wrapped around a single pole, like a spiral staircase, and Natalie was on the narrow side of every step. With her eyes still covered, it would have been so easy to fall.

Maybe that's what Other-Natalie wants. Maybe she's trying to get rid of me. . . .

But that was crazy. Other-Natalie could have screamed for a guard when they were back in her room and demanded that Natalie be taken away. She didn't have to go to all this effort, unless she really did believe Natalie.

And trust her.

She does trust me, right? She must look at me and feel like she understands me the same way I feel like I understand her. Doesn't she?

They reached the bottom of the first circular flight of stairs. Somehow all that turning around and around had disoriented Natalie—she couldn't picture where on the first floor they would be now, or which wall they were hidden behind. Somewhere off in the distance she could hear the hum of a vacuum cleaner, but that could have been anywhere in the house.

And then suddenly a door slammed, and Natalie heard a voice over a walkie-talkie somewhere on the other side of the wall from her: "All call for guards! This is not a drill! All guards must report downstairs immediately to deal with intruders!"

Then she heard the sound of running feet.

Natalie felt Other-Natalie's hand freeze on Natalie's arm.

"Maybe we . . . ," Natalie began cautiously, in a whisper.

"I know, I know," Other-Natalie muttered. "Change of plans. We stop in Mom's office and you introduce me to those other kids. No matter how many guards swarm the house, none of them would be allowed in Mom's office. So we'd be safe there."

Would it be dangerous for Other-Natalie to meet the Greystones? Should Natalie suggest just going back up to Other-Natalie's room until the guards were gone?

That would sound suspicious, Natalie decided. *And . . . I want to make sure the Greystones are safe.*

She let Other-Natalie pull her in another direction. Five steps, ten . . . Natalie felt even more disoriented when Other-Natalie stopped her and pressed a hand over Natalie's blindfold, as if to make absolutely certain that Natalie didn't see. This time there were beeps, as if Other-Natalie were entering a code into some sort of electronic lock. Natalie felt a whoosh of air on her face, and then she could see a burst of light even through the wool blindfold.

"I thought you said those other kids were waiting in Mom's office," Other-Natalie muttered, pulling Natalie forward.

Natalie ripped the blindfold from her face. She whirled around, looking everywhere. She and Other-Natalie were indeed back in Judge Morales's office, but Chess, Emma, and Finn were nowhere to be seen. Behind her, Other-Natalie was easing the closet door shut.

"Were you lying?" Other-Natalie asked.

Natalie stumbled forward. Now she could see the backpacks she and the Greystones had dropped on the floor.

"Oh, they'd be smart enough to hide, hearing someone enter the room," Natalie said. "Chess? Emma? Finn?"

No answer. She turned and saw two laptops angled carelessly on the couch—the two laptops Chess and Emma had been using. She walked over and brushed her hands over them. They were still warm; they'd just gone into sleep mode. Natalie's touch brought them back to life. One screen showed Mrs. Greystone's mysterious code; the other showed images of campaign posters.

Chess and Emma would have been smart enough to hide their laptops, too, if they'd heard someone entering the room. For that matter, wouldn't they have hidden the backpacks?

Maybe they just didn't have time. . . .

Natalie glanced under the desk, the best hiding place in the room. No one was there. Fighting panic, Natalie clutched the edge of the desk. Her finger hit the same button Finn had discovered, bringing the projection back to the wall. It showed a view of the basement Natalie had seen before.

It also brought the sound of her father's voice—no, Other-Dad's voice—saying, "Where are they? You say they were last reported down here?"

"Oh no. Oh no," Natalie moaned.

"What?" Other-Natalie asked, craning her neck so she could see the projection on the wall, too. "What's happening?"

"They must have left . . . They must have seen something down there that made them . . ." Natalie could barely get words out. She sprinted for the door. "I've got to find them before he does!"

"Wait! What are you doing?" Other-Natalie reached out to grab Natalie as she ran past.

But here was a difference between the two girls: Right now, Natalie was much more determined. She shoved

Other-Natalie away, practically knocking the girl over. Natalie let out a gasping, "Sorry . . . I can't . . ." before giving up words completely and concentrating only on running. She tore open the office door and slammed it shut behind her.

And then she took off, dashing for the stairs.

THIRTY-NINE

NATALIE

Natalie reached Other-Dad just as he was opening a door under the stairs in the basement. She saw his bald spot first, and that made her heart pound. *Just like Real-Dad, how he tries to comb his hair to hide that. . . .* But the way this man stood was so wrong—too puffed up, somehow, with too much bulk in his chest. This *wasn't* Dad. It was the Mayor.

Natalie slammed into him, knocking the door shut again. She tried to make it look like she was only hugging him.

"Dad, what's going on?" she asked. "I thought you were at work! Why are all these guards here?"

She tilted her head back to gaze worshipfully up at him,

batting her eyes for good measure. She tried to make the expression on her face say, *You're my daddy and I love you and I know you love me and would do anything for me. . . .* To achieve that look, she had to clear her brain of thinking, *You're not actually my father and you're married to a horrible person, so you might be horrible, too. But right now I just care about protecting Chess, Emma, and Finn. And finding Mom. And you—you're just an obstacle to all that. . . .*

This version of her father was just as deeply tan as her real father, and his teeth were just as perfectly white. But his blue eyes held a hardness that Natalie hadn't expected. And the way he looked down at her, it was like he didn't quite see her—or didn't *want* to see her.

Well, fine. That way he won't see that I'm not actually his daughter, Natalie told herself. But it hurt to have someone who looked so much like Dad gaze at her as if he'd rather see past her.

As if he, like Almost-Grandma, didn't have time for her.

She went back to telling herself how much she loved him.

"Natalie!" the Mayor scolded. "Go back to your room! This is just a . . . minor security issue. The guards are here as a precaution. Nothing to worry about! It's all being taken care of!"

That's what I'm afraid of. . . .

"But if it's only a precaution . . . I'm feeling better now, and it's so boring staying in my room by myself. Can't I hang out with you? Please?" Natalie smiled as sweetly as she could. "Why don't you send the guards away, and we can have some daddy-daughter time?"

Natalie saw a flicker of emotion on the Mayor's face. It was almost like a look her own father got sometimes, a combination of pride (*Look what a great dad I am, that my daughter loves me so much!*) and something more like insecurity (*I am a great dad, aren't I? Natalie's a great kid—doesn't that prove I'm great, too?*). But there was something deeper on the Mayor's face, something Natalie couldn't decipher. It was too disorienting, because this wasn't her father, wasn't anyone she knew at all.

"Oh, honey," the Mayor said, flashing a smile that was fake, fake, fake. He glanced around, as if he wanted the nearest guards to hear every word. "That's so sweet, you wanting bonding time. But Daddy's a little busy right now. Keeping *you* safe."

"Daddy"? Natalie thought, barely managing to keep the disgust off her face. *Is that what Other-Natalie calls him?*

It threw her off so much, she didn't know what to say next. The horde of guards in their dark uniforms flowed across the basement like so many ants. The ones in the front reached the back wall and whipped aside an odd velvet curtain that seemed so out of place—Natalie's own basement back in the real world held nothing like it. Then Natalie gaped—there wasn't a wall on the other side of the curtain. Instead, the basement went on and on, as broad and vast as a football field. One of the guards pressed a button on the wall, and both the floor and the ceiling of that extra space began to pull away, revealing a soaring glass roof overhead and levels of terracing below. The floor at the far end of the regular basement began to slide away, too; cabinets opened in the wall to swallow up some of the furniture.

Natalie blinked. This wasn't a basement anymore. It was more like a party hall. Or perhaps a cathedral—one designed to make everyone who walked into it feel small and powerless.

Just like the Public Hall where Mrs. Greystone's trial had been held.

"Roger? What's wrong?" It was Almost-Grandma. She spoke from the top of the stairs, and Natalie heard a smacking sound, as if Almost-Grandma had hit some control button up above. The moving floor at the other end of the room froze in place, and the guards seemed to freeze, too, as if waiting for their next command.

Natalie heard a *click-click* of heels; Almost-Grandma was descending the steps. As soon as she came into view, Natalie had to correct herself—this was Wowza-Grandma. *Boss*-Grandma.

Grandma had always been someone who took care with her appearance—she'd once made Natalie promise that if Grandma ever got so infirm that she couldn't put on her own lipstick, Natalie would do it for her. Every day. But Grandma's style had always been understated and classy. *Not* about showing off.

This version of Grandma was extra-everything. She wore a regal bright orange silk dress that seemed to say, *I have money, and I'm not afraid to use it*. And Natalie was pretty sure that the huge diamonds of her tiered necklace were real.

Her outfit seemed overpowering even in this newly huge space.

"You're dressed for the fund-raiser already?" the Mayor asked, barely concealed contempt in his voice. "It's not until tonight!"

"I was trying on my clothes to see if they needed further alterations, when I heard the all-call for guards. I came right away." Almost-Grandma punctuated her last word with a stiletto heel stabbed into the carpet at the bottom of the stairs. She turned to face the Mayor head-on. Too late, Natalie realized she should have scurried out of sight rather than gaping. From behind the Mayor's back, Natalie tried to signal Almost-Grandma with one raised eyebrow and a finger on her lips. She also tried telepathy: *Please, Grandma, don't ask how I got out of the locked bedroom, or whether I'm real or fake Natalie or . . .* But Almost-Grandma's gaze just skated coldly across Natalie's face before she went back to glaring at the Mayor. It was like Natalie was completely beneath Almost-Grandma's notice.

Fine. That's what I want right now. Isn't it?

But when the Mayor turned to the side, Almost-Grandma gave an almost-imperceptible shake of her head to Natalie. Was she telling *Natalie* to stay quiet? Why would she do that?

"These guards are too loud, and they don't seem to be trained very well," Almost-Grandma said dismissively. "Are you certain they've all been screened for duty in the house, with full access to your family? And your *daughter*?" Almost-Grandma darted another glance at Natalie, but this one was even more painful. It was like Natalie wasn't a person, just a thing. An object that needed to be kept behind glass. Almost-Grandma sniffed and waved her hand imperiously. "Send these guards away immediately."

Oh, yes, please send them away, Natalie thought. *Now, before they find Chess, Emma, and Finn . . . wherever they are. And then you go away, too, so* I *can find the Greystones. . . .*

"But—" The Mayor seemed baffled about what to do next.

Almost-Grandma sighed and stepped close enough to whisper in the Mayor's ear, "If you're afraid of losing face, pretend you've just heard that the intruders have been caught, and no one is in any danger any longer. Pretend you've *solved* the problem."

"But if there really is a threat, if any of the cleaners are traitors, then—"

Wait a minute—they're looking for cleaners who are traitors? Natalie thought. *Not the Greystone kids?* Relief flowed through her. She could fix this.

"Dad, don't you know Grandma was—" she began, ready to spill everything about how Almost-Grandma had disguised herself to spy on the cleaners.

Subtly, without even seeming to move, Almost-Grandma stepped on Natalie's foot. It felt like a warning—but why? At the same time, Almost-Grandma took the Mayor's arm and turned him to the side, away from Natalie.

"Trust me, you and your family are in no danger from any *cleaner*," Almost-Grandma said, rolling her eyes, as if suspecting a cleaner was the most ludicrous thing ever. "I was right there when my daughter hired this crew. Are you doubting Susanna's judgment now?"

"N-No, no, of course not," the Mayor stammered. He cleared his throat, then shouted, "Men! False alarm. Thank you for your assistance. Now—back to your assigned stations!"

"Yes, sir."

"As you say, sir."

"So noted . . ."

The guards turned and began streaming out the sliding glass door at the far side of the room, their movements almost robotically obedient. Natalie tried to make sense of what she'd just witnessed.

Even if the guards weren't looking for the Greystones, they would have found them if they'd kept searching, she thought. *So Almost-Grandma just helped me, even though she didn't want me to talk. . . .*

Why hadn't Almost-Grandma wanted Natalie to talk?

That didn't matter as much as figuring out what to do next.

Get rid of Almost-Grandma and the Mayor, find the Greystones, make sure Other-Natalie hasn't come out of the office yet and doesn't reveal me as a fake. . . .

How could Natalie do all that at once?

Then Natalie heard a voice from the top of the stairs.

"Roger? Mother? *Natalie?* I was informed I needed to come home immediately. . . . What are the three of you doing down there?"

It was so wrong, how Natalie's heart could jump at the sound of her mother's voice—even as her brain cautioned, *No, that's* not *Mom. Not, not, not. It's the Judge. Be careful.*

"Resolving a security issue, dear," the Mayor called, taking a few steps back to peer toward the top of the stairs.

Don't listen to how he *still calls the Judge "dear"; don't think about how they're still married and still happy together. . . .*

But did he actually sound happy? The Mayor's voice had an edge to it. Even before Natalie had learned that her parents were getting divorced, she'd started listening closely to how they talked to each other, how they talked *about* each other. Mom saying, "Dad has to work late, so it's just you and me for dinner," sometimes meant that Mom and Dad had had a terrible fight and couldn't stand being in the same room together. Other times, it really was about Dad's job. Natalie had once prided herself on instantly being able to tell the difference. Sometimes, during the worst of her parents' fighting, that had felt like the only power she possessed. Now she was out of practice—ever since Mom had vanished, Dad actually did sound like he missed her and worried about her constantly. But Natalie still knew her own parents so well she rarely needed more than one syllable of any word to figure them out.

Everything was different with the Mayor and the Judge. It felt like more than just Natalie not knowing them as well. The Mayor and the Judge seemed to be talking from behind guard towers, or through locked doors—even their simplest statements seemed to hide undercurrents that Natalie needed to decode.

Either that, or Natalie just couldn't think straight because she was too panicked about being in this dangerous world and too worried about everyone she loved who had vanished here.

"You shouldn't speak of security issues in such a public area," the Judge said icily.

Public? Natalie thought. *The Mayor's standing in his own basement. Or, well, his party hall. But there's no one nearby but family. How is that public?*

She remembered the way she and the Greystones had watched the basement from the Judge's office; she remembered the guard towers visible from the first-floor windows. What if guards there were watching security footage from inside the house? Natalie moved closer to the Mayor so she could peer up at the Judge as well. The Judge's face looked so much like Mom's and so wrong all at once—her expression was hard as rock.

Mom isn't even capable of looking that heartless, Natalie thought. And then she had to stop herself from thinking about Mom, before it made her cry.

"I just—" the Mayor began. He sounded as helpless as Natalie felt.

"We should discuss this someplace else. Privately," Almost-Grandma said quietly, stepping up behind the Mayor and Natalie, and herding them toward the stairs. "Perhaps in your office, Susanna?"

"Excellent idea," the Judge said.

Her voice was once again so chilling that Natalie's brain went numb. Or maybe Natalie just didn't want to put together all the possibilities:

Other-Natalie was undoubtedly either still standing in the Judge's office where Natalie had left her, or on her way to find out what Natalie and the Mayor were up to in the basement.

The Judge was already turning back toward her office; Almost-Grandma was already nudging Natalie and the Mayor toward the stairs.

No matter what Natalie did, there seemed to be no way she could stop the Judge, the Mayor, and Almost-Grandma from running into Other-Natalie.

In a matter of minutes, *everyone* was going to find out that Natalie was a fake.

FORTY

FINN

Finn snuggled close to Chess and Emma in the darkness of the secret compartment behind the closet. He could hear footsteps overhead—two pairs of high heels, perhaps, clicking against the tile; one set of footfalls that sounded like a kid in sneakers; and one that sounded heavier, as if they belonged to a tall man. Finn tugged on Chess and Emma's arms wrapped around him.

"I think they're gone now," Finn announced. "Shouldn't we . . . uh, what should we do?"

He didn't have a clue, but that was the great thing about

being the youngest: He didn't have to. He could let Chess and Emma figure everything out.

Neither Chess nor Emma answered.

"Hello?" Finn said, daring to switch his flashlight back on.

Maybe that wasn't such a great idea. Finn could remember playing around with flashlights back home with his best friend, Tyrell. They always laughed at how the dim light and shadows made their faces look spooky and ghoulish.

Now that there was actual danger and Mom was missing, it wasn't the least bit funny to see how the flashlight glow made Emma's and Chess's faces look too pale, and as though they had no eyes, just dark, empty eye sockets.

"I . . . I don't know what to do," Chess said, and this was worse than no answer at all.

"Emma?" Finn said, because surely she would be brimming with ideas. She'd been quiet for whole *minutes*; she'd had loads of time to figure out all sorts of plans.

But Emma *still* didn't answer. Finn shone the flashlight directly on her face, straight into her eyes. Emma put her hands up, blocking the light.

"Oh no," she moaned. "Noooo . . ."

"Okay, I won't shine it right in your face," Finn said, lowering the flashlight even though this made Emma look eyeless and ghostly again.

"No—it wasn't the light," Emma muttered. "It was . . . oh, this is so great, this is so terrible . . . why didn't I see this last night?"

She really wasn't making sense.

"Emma, what are you talking about?" Chess asked. "How is *anything* great right now?"

Emma reached for the sliding panel that sectioned them off from the front of the closet.

"We've got to go back to the Judge's office!" Emma cried. "I've got to get my computer!"

Chess pulled Emma away from the panel.

"Are you nuts?" he asked. "Weren't you listening? That's where the Judge and the Mayor are headed. Along with Natalie and someone I couldn't hear very well . . ."

"Shouldn't we go rescue Natalie?" Finn asked.

Chess was already frowning and shaking his head.

"Believe me, I'd like to, but . . . we'd just blow her cover," Chess muttered. He clutched his head as if the light hurt his eyes.

"If I'd just figured this out sooner, we'd have all the answers now!" Emma moaned.

"If you figured out anything, doesn't that mean you have *some* answers now?" Finn asked hopefully.

"I would if I had my computer!" Emma practically shouted.

She brushed past Chess, as if she was going to try again to open the sliding panel. Chess responded by grabbing her hands and clutching them tightly in his.

"Emma, shh!" he begged. "Are you *trying* to make the guards find us?"

"No, Chess, but . . ." Maybe it was just the eerie effect of the flashlight beam across her face, but Emma seemed dazed. "I finally figured out how to decode the rest of Mom's letter! *That's* why we have to go back for the computer. It'll tell us everything!"

"You did?" Even Chess forgot to whisper for a moment. He clutched Emma's hands even tighter. Then he sagged, his back hitting the wall behind him. "Are you sure? You've thought you'd figured out the key a couple hundred times before and . . ."

"I'm sure! I translated the first line in my head—I had it memorized. It says, 'If you got this far . . . ,' And that's all I know right now, but—"

Chess let go of Emma's hands and went back to clutching his head. In the dim glow of the flashlight, it almost looked like he was holding his hands over his ears, trying not to hear. Or just trying to hold his head together.

"It's not safe to go back to the Judge's office," Chess said. "And we were locked out, remember? We can't do anything without Natalie. And Natalie's with the Judge and the Mayor on the way to the Judge's office, so . . ."

Chess—big, strong Chess—sounded like he was about to cry.

"But I have to solve Mom's code!" Emma insisted. "Now that I know how!"

Finn loved how Emma could still sound so determined, so single-minded. So stubborn. He actually touched his hand to his heart. Something crinkled in his shirt pocket, and he almost gasped with laughter.

"Emma!" he cried. "You don't actually need the *computer* to solve the code, right? Don't you just need to see the code Mom left behind?"

"Right, but—" Emma began.

Finn drew a folded-over paper out of his shirt pocket and handed it to his sister.

"Mom's letter she sent through the mail," he said. "The *paper* copy of her code."

For a second, Finn wondered if he should have admitted that he'd tucked Mom's letter into his pocket last night when everyone else was packing up computers and food. At the time, it had seemed silly to bring the letter—maybe even dangerous—so he hadn't said anything about it. But it was a piece of Mom, a connection. He couldn't leave it behind.

And now, even in the flashlight's dim glow, he could see

Emma's eyes light up. She threw her arms around Finn, hugging him and the letter as tight as possible.

"Finn, you're the best!" she cried. "I bet you just saved us—and Mom and Joe and Ms. Morales, too!"

FORTY-ONE

EMMA

Emma unfolded the letter, flattening it against the concrete floor of the small hidden room behind the closet. It felt almost sacred to touch the same paper Mom had touched, on the last day she'd spent in the safer world.

Focus, Emma told herself. *Just solve this as fast as you can.*

She was only dimly aware of Finn and Chess crouching beside her, helpfully directing flashlight beams at the garbled mix of letters and numbers on the paper. Emma put her finger on the exact spot in the letter where she'd stopped deciphering Mom's code before.

"Okay, it's 'If you got this far . . . ,' then . . ." She glanced up. "This would be a lot easier if we had a pencil or a pen, and I wouldn't have to keep everything in my head. Finn, you don't have one of those tucked away, too, do you? Or Chess—?"

Finn turned his empty jeans pockets inside out, as if to prove he didn't have some pencil even he had forgotten. Chess settled for patting his pockets, then turned toward the sliding panel.

"There's got to be one somewhere in the basement," he whispered. "I'll go get it."

"No, Chess, that's not—" Emma began. But she couldn't decide if it was too much of a risk or not.

"I've been worthless all along—let me be brave just this once," Chess muttered.

Chess, worthless? How could he think that? Somebody should tell him that wasn't true.

But Emma couldn't even watch as he squeezed out through the sliding panel. She peered back down at Mom's code, letting it distract her.

Only a moment passed before Chess was back and shoving a fat, fancy pen into Emma's hand. It had lettering on the side that said *We stand together against our enemies*—almost the same motto as on the poster in Other-Natalie's room.

Emma wished she hadn't seen that.

"I wanted to find pencils or pens for all of us, and extra

paper, too, but I thought it was more important to get back fast," Chess muttered.

Emma decided to pretend not to notice that he was sweating, and huffing and puffing as though he'd run a mile, not just taken a few steps.

Or, as if he'd been really, really scared.

"Okay, here's the key I figured out," Emma said, writing twenty-six letters across the top of Mom's letter: USE IN A SPOT THAT EXISTS IN BOTH.

"What?" Finn said. "The words from the lever? *That's* the key? But you forgot the word 'worlds' at the end. . . ."

"Yeah," Emma said. "And that's what tipped me off. Why was 'worlds' in parentheses? I thought it was weird last night, but I was too distracted then. Parentheses means something is optional, and why would 'worlds' be optional in that sentence? Only if that sentence has another purpose."

Did she need to confess how scared she'd been? Did she need to confess that she'd started counting the letters in the phrase "use in a spot that exists in both" only to keep herself her from freaking out?

She glanced at Chess, still red-faced and sweaty. She should let him know she'd been frightened, too.

"I needed *something* to think about to keep from being scared," she said. "So I was lucky. It was the right theory to test. *Finally*."

"But that *isn't* a good key, is it?" Chess asked. He pointed at all the duplicated letters. "There are, what, five *T*s? Four *S*s, three *I*s . . ."

"Yeah, you told us the perfect key for a code would have twenty-six *different* letters!" Finn added, sounding indignant. "So you don't get confused about which letter to use where!"

"Right, but that's where the numbers come in," Emma said. "I thought they were separate, but look . . ."

Quickly, she added the alphabet under the key. Then she added numbers, so the full key was:

U	S	E	I	N	A	S2	P	O	T
A	B	C	D	E	F	G	H	I	J

T2	H	A2	T3	E2	X	I2	S3	T4	S4
K	L	M	N	O	P	Q	R	S	T

I3	N2	B	O2	T5	H2
U	V	W	X	Y	Z

"Oh," Chess said.

Maybe Finn asked more questions, but Emma let Chess answer after that. Having the key written out meant that she could work so much faster, since she didn't have to count letters in her head. In no time at all, she'd translated the first two and a half sentences: "If you got this far, you know about the lever. And if you know about the lever, you are bound to face the temptation to use it. But you shouldn't do that until . . ."

Oh, Mom, Emma thought, her heart throbbing. *Don't you know we used the lever the instant we found it, before we understood anything?*

But of course Mom couldn't have known that, writing this letter. When she'd written this, Chess, Emma, and Finn had been safely asleep in their beds back home, totally ignorant of levers, secret rooms, secret codes, or alternate worlds. Back then, they hadn't even known Natalie.

"I wish I could skip ahead," Emma muttered. "I think the next few sentences are just going to be stuff we already know, from being in this world. But I don't want to go too far ahead and miss something important."

"You skip ahead," Chess said. "Finn and I'll work on the sentences in order, and we'll borrow the pen and write it down every time we have a long phrase."

"But I can't—" Finn started to complain.

"You can if we work together," Chess said, patting Finn's shoulder.

Oh, Chess, you are so not worthless, Emma thought.

But she was already back in the code. She lost track of time, attacking a sentence here and there, and passing the pen back and forth with Chess. She barely listened as her brothers worked out parts of the code she'd skipped: "*A* here, *N* there, then *D*, okay, that's 'and' . . ."

She tried a sentence in the next paragraph down, but it seemed to be about politicians and lies.

We know about those already, Emma thought, remembering how much of her mother's trial had been fake.

Another paragraph talked about the network of journalists Mom had worked with who were trying to preserve and reveal the truth. They believed people had to know the truth to make good decisions about their leaders. But the letter didn't reveal any names of the people in the network because, Mom wrote, "There is still too much of a chance that this letter will fall into the wrong hands, and I can't risk destroying an ally. There are too few of us even now."

Instead, Mom told how the allies might identify themselves to the kids: "I left something behind that you kids will recognize, and you will know that it's out of place. You will know where it comes from, too, and who first created it. *That* is the symbol an ally would show you to prove they can be trusted."

Oh, Mom, Emma thought sadly. *Why didn't you put that in the* first *part of your letter, that we decoded before we went to your trial? That would have saved us so much trouble and worry!*

She knew Mom was talking about the crooked heart Finn had once drawn on Mom's phone case. Emma had found a copy of that heart image in Mom's desk drawer, even though Mom normally kept nothing personal in her desk. And then, at Mom's trial, the mysterious man they knew only as Joe had shown them a smaller copy of the same image.

That heart image was the only way they'd known to trust Joe.

If we'd known about the heart signal from the start, we would have trusted Joe sooner. Then we might have gotten to Mom sooner; we might have managed to rescue her at her trial and not have had to come back. . . . We would have been so fast, we wouldn't have lost Ms. Morales, either. . . .

Emma needed to stop thinking about their last trip and focus on *now*. And this paragraph was just more information that she, Chess, Finn, and Natalie already knew. She skipped down another paragraph.

B *is* W, N *is* E. . . .

This time, Emma was only partway into translating the sentence before she gasped. And then she threw her arms around her brothers and called out, "This is it! This is exactly what we need!"

"You know where to find Mom, and how to rescue her?" Finn asked breathlessly.

"Well, no, but—it's a first step, anyway! Our first helpful clue since we got here!" Emma hugged her brothers even tighter.

"What'd you figure out?" Chess asked, and for once he sounded as hopeful and excited as Finn.

Emma pointed to the line of crooked printing she'd added above her mother's coded words. Then, realizing Chess and Finn probably couldn't read her hasty scrawl, she read it to them: "'We have an ally inside the Morales-Mayhew household who can help you.' Chess, Finn, that's *here*. Someone in this house is on our side!"

FORTY-TWO

CHESS

"But who is it?" Chess asked. "Doesn't Mom say? What good is it to know that if we don't know a name?"

It felt cruel to say this when Emma was practically jumping up and down beside him, and Finn was grinning ear-to-ear. It felt as mean as kicking a kitten or pulling a puppy dog's tail.

"Well, no, I don't . . ." Emma paused to decode another line. "Yeah, that's what I thought. Mom's all about protecting 'allies,' because she's afraid this letter could fall into the wrong hands. But she also talks about the heart symbol Joe showed us. What if we showed that symbol to people we think we might be able to trust? We don't have one with us, but if Finn drew one, then—"

"I just need a red marker," Finn said. "And paper. Once we have that, I can draw as many hearts as we need!"

Sometimes Finn and Emma broke Chess's heart. Didn't they see how the fear had practically killed him, when he'd just tiptoed out to grab a pen? Weren't they thinking about guards and danger and spy cameras, like he was? Even if they could find a red marker and paper, they couldn't risk roaming around the Morales-Mayhew house showing anyone crookedly drawn hearts.

Now, if we still had Natalie with us, there might be some hope. . . .

Natalie.

Chess was pretty sure that the panic coursing through his body was mostly because he was so worried about Natalie. Where was she? What was happening to her? Was she in danger? Was there anything Chess could do for her?

He hoped she understood that if he could think of any way to help, he'd be doing it.

Chess felt like he might explode with all the worry and questions. He didn't think he could stand sitting in this closet a second longer.

"I'll go look for a marker and paper," he muttered to Finn and Emma, even though he thought that was a pointless plan, and he was terrified of stepping outside the closet again. He had to do something, and decoding information they already knew just made him feel worse.

"Chess, be careful," Emma whispered. She pressed her hands against her cheeks, and even in the dim, eerie glow from the flashlights, he could see that she was scared, too.

Maybe she did know how dangerous their hope was. Maybe only Finn was still too innocent to see that.

Chess eased the wooden panel open, stepped through, and then slid it back into place, protecting Emma and Finn. Cautiously, he opened the closet door a crack.

The vast room before him was still silent and empty and dim. Rather than just darting for the nearest coffee table, as he had before, this time he forced himself to stare all the way to the end of the room. And—were his eyes tricking him? It seemed to go on endlessly now, dissolving into a lit-up maze of orange-and-blue banners in a glass-ceilinged space far beyond.

What? This isn't a basement anymore! It's a . . .

"Shrine" was the word that came to mind. It was a shrine to whatever those orange-and-blue banners stood for—the same orange-and-blue banners that had been everywhere leading to his mother's trial.

Banners can't hurt you, Chess told himself. He inched out of the closet and, again, shut the door behind him. Now he was almost mad at himself—mad that he felt so hopeless, mad that he was such a coward, mad that he hadn't managed to protect everyone from the very beginning, mad that he'd let Natalie rush away on her own when there was so much danger. . . .

He went back to the nearest coffee table and yanked out the drawer where he'd found the pen before. No markers, no paper. He already knew that. Angrily, he shoved the drawer back and stood up again.

And then there was a sound at the other side of the room: someone trying to stifle a gasp, maybe.

Chess dived back down, hiding behind the coffee table. No—that wasn't enough. He scrambled backward so he was better hidden, crouched beside a navy blue couch. His heart pounded so loudly he could barely hear the whisper from across the room: "Chess?"

It was Natalie's voice.

Chess sprang back up, peeking over the edge of the couch, and there was Natalie, peeking out from behind a desk at the other side of the room.

She didn't see where he'd gone. She was gazing around, probably looking for Emma and Finn, too. For a moment, Chess could only watch her. She shook her hair back from her face, and it rippled and glistened like it had the first time Chess had ever talked to her, when he'd sounded like a fool.

Even that memory didn't seem so horrifying now, because Natalie was back, and that was like the sun being back, like hope returning, like everything that had seemed impossible a moment ago seeming possible once again.

Because Natalie was alone, not with anyone from this horrible world. She'd escaped, and somehow she'd known to come down to the basement to look for Chess, Emma, and Finn. And now they would be able to find the ally in this house and rescue their mothers and Joe.

"Natalie," Chess said, and her name felt like the most beautiful word in the world on his tongue. He began rushing toward her. He kind of wished he was Finn's age, because if he were, he could just run over and hug her.

Finn could do that; Chess couldn't. But he still kept dashing toward her, calling her name. She flinched slightly at the sound of his voice, and that made him worry.

"Natalie?" he said. "Are you all right? Is everything okay? Did—"

Her eyes met his, and Chess stumbled. Because in that moment, Chess saw: Natalie *wasn't* all right. Everything *wasn't* okay.

Chess, Emma, Finn, and Natalie were in even more danger than he'd thought.

Because this wasn't Natalie.

FORTY-THREE

NATALIE, A FEW MINUTES EARLIER

When they figure out I'm not Other-Natalie, I'll have to . . . I'll . . .

All the way up the stairs, Natalie's brain kept sputtering out the same useless thought, breaking off, and starting over. There didn't seem to be any way to fix this. She felt like a prisoner being escorted to her jail cell as the Judge walked ahead of her, leading the way toward her office, and Almost-Grandma in her regal orange gown brought up the rear, as if making sure that Natalie wouldn't escape.

At least the Mayor's not walking beside me like a third jailer, Natalie thought.

Instead, he kept moving out in front of her, as if he were

trying to catch up with the Judge. But she kept walking faster and faster.

The Judge reached the door of her office and a key glinted in her hand, as if she'd had it out and ready all along.

Just like Mom, Natalie thought sadly. *Always prepared . . .*

The Judge turned the key in the lock, but she didn't instantly shove the door all the way open the way Natalie expected.

"What's this?" the Judge asked, bending down and picking up a folded-up paper that fell out of the door. Had it been there before, and Natalie just hadn't noticed?

The Judge unfolded the paper. It was a flyer announcing the Judge's reelection campaign, surely something the Judge had seen many times. But the Judge kept her head bent over the paper for a long time, as if she needed to study it carefully.

Or . . . as if she's looking for a secret message or a secret code, Natalie thought. *Is she looking for traces of invisible ink or patterns of letters almost inconspicuously blacked out or . . . ?*

Natalie decided she'd spent too much time with Emma, and too much time listening to Emma's descriptions of hidden messages left in innocuous places.

But the Judge seemed to shoot a significant glance at Almost-Grandma before refolding the paper and tucking it into her pants pocket.

Then she pushed the door of her office open all the way.

"I can explain," Natalie burst out, deciding to go on the offensive and start talking before the adults saw Other-Natalie, who would undoubtedly be right there in the office, in plain sight.

"Explain what?" the Judge asked, stepping into the office.

Natalie brushed past the Judge, barely believing her eyes. But it was true: Except for the Judge and Natalie, the office was empty. Natalie tiptoed past the desk and got a second surprise: All the backpacks and extra computers were gone, too.

"Explain . . . why I went downstairs, even though I was sick and . . . and could have exposed other people to my germs." Natalie tried to cover her blunder. "I didn't want to make anyone else sick, but I felt better, and—"

"Oh, who cares about guards or cleaners?" The Mayor waved his hand impatiently.

He and Almost-Grandma had stepped into the office now too, and Almost-Grandma closed the door behind them. The Mayor peered back at the door as if he were the one longing for escape now.

"Why did you summon me here?" he asked.

"Oh, have a seat, *dear*," the Judge said, gesturing toward the couch.

There was that pet name again—"dear"—but it sounded as wrong coming from the Judge as it had coming from the Mayor. Natalie had a sudden memory of the last time she'd heard her own mother tell her father "I love you." She'd been in the car with Mom and Dad and Grandma on the way home from her fifth-grade school play—Mom and Dad in the front, Grandma and Natalie in the back. She'd heard Mom say, "Of course I love you, Roger," but her tone was more like *I can barely stand to be in the same car as you.* Then Grandma had said, "Could you turn the radio up? Natalie, isn't this your favorite song?" And even though it wasn't Natalie's favorite song, she nodded anyway. More than anything else, she hadn't wanted to hear Mom and Dad fighting.

That might have been the very first time Natalie lied to her grandmother.

That might have been the very last time she, Mom, Dad, and Grandma were all together.

But now here the four of them were again—or at least *versions* of the four of them.

Natalie felt her throat tighten. She was glad nobody was asking her anything right now. She couldn't have answered.

The Mayor sat down on the couch, but the Judge and Almost-Grandma kept standing, towering over him. Natalie hung back by the desk. Maybe the adults would forget she was there. Also, she thought she might have to lean on the desk to stay upright, if things got worse.

After a moment, the Mayor stood up again, drawing himself to his full height.

"I have every right to address security concerns in my own house," he said. "It's not fair for you to make it seem like it's all *your* decision, like you're the ultimate control."

"You're going to be governor," the Judge said. "With my help."

That sounded like a threat—not like she was promising help, but as if she was warning him she'd withdraw it unless the Mayor did what she wanted.

But what did the Judge want?

"You . . . you . . ." The Mayor swung his hands out wide, almost helplessly. "You make me look like a fool."

"*Look*?" the Judge said acidly. "You know what they say: If the shoe fits . . ."

The Mayor balled up his hands into fists. He took a step toward the Judge. She kept staring him down.

"You—you're up to something," the Mayor accused. He turned his head frantically side to side, his gaze taking in Almost-Grandma, too. "Both of you—there's something you're hiding from me, something you're lying about. . . ."

"*You're* going to accuse *us* of lying?" Almost-Grandma asked, stepping up beside the Judge, her orange dress rustling. "You?"

"When has anything in our marriage been based on truth?" the Judge asked. "When has the actual truth ever meant anything to either one of us? Or—to anyone in our country?"

"This is different," the Mayor insisted.

Natalie's head spun. The Mayor's words did something strange to her eyes, to her ears, to her brain. It no longer felt like she was watching three strangers who only resembled her parents and grandmother. It no longer felt like she could hold on to the idea of alternate worlds and alternate versions of her own family. The Mayor's words zoomed her back to a specific moment with her own parents more than a year earlier.

A moment that she would never in a million years have wanted to relive.

Natalie couldn't help herself. She gasped.

"You're getting a divorce," she cried, the words coming out ragged and fearful. "That's what this is about. The two of you don't trust each other anymore and you, you've lied to each other, and you don't love each other anymore and . . ."

If this were a strict reenactment, one of the worst moments of Natalie's life replayed in this alternate universe—as if the worlds really did mirror each other, just on a strange time delay—Almost-Grandma would be at her side in an instant, holding her up, murmuring, "But *you're* okay. You've got me. I promise. Always."

So Natalie wasn't surprised to find strong arms engulfing her instantly, wasn't surprised to hear a soothing, "Shh, shh," whispered in her ear.

But it was the Judge, not Almost-Grandma, holding her. And the Judge's shushing blended into a murmured, "Thank you. You gave us a way out of this . . ." before the Judge whipped her head back to accuse the Mayor, "See what you've done? You've convinced our daughter we're getting *divorced*! You've traumatized her!"

Almost-Grandma had her hands on her hips as she glared at the Mayor.

"You know your political campaign can't afford even *rumors* of discord between you and Susanna," she told him. "Whatever problems you have in private, you can't let anything show in public."

"I know, I know," the Mayor said, wiping a hand across his sweaty forehead. "I just don't—I can't—"

"You can't afford to mess up anything else," the Judge said. "Mother will handle the security for tonight's fundraiser, and you'll do nothing but shake hands and smile. And you and I will gaze adoringly at one another anytime there's a camera around."

"There's always a camera around," the Mayor murmured.

"Exactly," the Judge said, gifting the Mayor with the full wattage of her most dazzling smile. Anyone who didn't know the Judge—or Ms. Morales—probably would have believed it was real. But Natalie could see through that smile.

She despises him, Natalie thought. *More than Mom ever hated Dad.*

This was so much worse than her own parents. The way the Judge was smiling at the Mayor now made Natalie think of knives encrusted in jewels; murder weapons masquerading as art.

"Of course I'll do what you want, dear," the Mayor said, smiling back. "Anything for you."

Those words, dripping with falseness, felt like a sword plunged into Natalie's heart. This was unbearable. She'd lived through her parents' squabbling and splitting up; she could see through trembling smiles and transparent lies.

And . . . Natalie wasn't a fifth grader anymore. She wasn't the innocent, unsuspecting kid who'd had no idea her parents were so miserable together. She'd gone through watching her parents get divorced and her grandmother die—and her mother go missing—and she'd survived all that. She wasn't going to suffer through this a second time in silence.

"You two are both horrible people," she said aloud. She didn't quite turn to face Almost-Grandma as well; she couldn't decide if she wanted to include her in her sweeping statement or not. She settled for narrowing her eyes at the Mayor, whose familiar tanned face looked particularly repulsive now. He was so pathetic: pathetic and weak and sniveling and . . . fake. All his teeth were capped. He'd had plastic surgery to erase his frown and smile lines.

"Are you spying on Mom, too?" she asked cuttingly. "The same way she's—"

Before Natalie could get to the rest of her accusation, the Mayor jerked his head toward Natalie and asked in a suspicious voice, "*Who's* your mother spying on, Natalie? What do *you* know about all of this?"

"She means Susanna's spying on the cleaners, of course." Almost-Grandma stepped between the Mayor and Natalie. "Susanna's monitoring *all* your family's employees, just as you would want her to, Roger. She's protecting you *and* Natalie. Everything you and Susanna have built together, all the power you've consolidated—Susanna's making sure you keep it."

Natalie hadn't meant that. She'd meant that the Judge was spying on the Mayor. But before she could protest, she felt the Judge's hand encircling her arm.

"Get Natalie out of here, Mother," the Judge demanded, practically shoving Natalie toward Almost-Grandma. "She doesn't need to witness this. *She* needs to be able to act for all the world as though she knows her parents are deeply in love, a unified team. As we are."

Now Natalie was the target of the Judge's dazzling smile. Up close, the smile was blinding—so alike and so different from Mom's, all at once. The mouth was the same shape; the smile lines were just as deep; the eyes gleamed just as brightly. The *surface* details were the same. But Mom's smile would have felt like the warmth of the sun just then; the Judge's smile was like a lightbulb in a freezer.

Mom's smiles were real; the Judge's was just another lie.

This woman doesn't even remember how to tell the truth, Natalie thought.

Natalie was so disoriented by the Judge's smile and her own thoughts—and the near-reenactment of one of the top three worst moments of her life—that she barely noticed Almost-Grandma tugging her toward the door.

Should I resist? Natalie wondered. *Or is it* better *for me to go? Should I be trying to find out as much as I can from the adults, or trying to get away so I can find the Greystones?*

It would probably be a good idea to track down Other-Natalie, too.

And we're no closer to finding Mom, Mrs. Greystone, and Joe than we were an hour ago. . . .

Almost-Grandma had the door open and was shoving Natalie through before Natalie gathered her wits enough to ask, "Where are you taking me?"

"We need to have a talk," Almost-Grandma said. "Downstairs."

Downstairs—where the Greystones might be out in plain sight now. Where Almost-Grandma might easily see them.

Almost-Grandma's fingers dug into Natalie's arm, making dents in Natalie's skin.

And if this is how she treats someone who could be her own granddaughter, Natalie wondered, *what will she do to the Greystones?*

FORTY-FOUR

FINN

"Emma!" Finn cried, tugging on his sister's arm. "Did you hear that? Chess is out there talking to Natalie! Natalie's back!"

Emma raised her head from staring at Mom's code, but her eyes remained unfocused, as if her brain was still deciphering. Finn didn't wait for her answer. He slid aside the wood panel of the closet's false back and darted out the door after Chess. Emma could catch up if she wanted.

Finn dropped the flashlight because there was enough light coming from the other end of the basement. The clatter of the flashlight hitting the floor made Chess and Natalie turn their heads toward Finn; Chess began shaking his head warningly.

It's just Natalie, not bad guys, Finn wanted to holler at Chess, because sometimes Chess really did worry too much. But Finn poured all his energy into running toward Natalie, far across the basement. Finn couldn't understand why Chess wasn't running alongside him, dashing over to welcome her back. Finn darted right past Chess, who seemed frozen in place.

And then a second later, Finn was sprawled out on the floor. He glanced back, and Chess was drawing his foot back. Finn put it all together: Chess's green running shoe, still touching Finn's ankle; Finn's unexpected tumble . . .

Chess tripped me, Finn thought. And then, because it was so startling, *Chess tripped me?*

Chess wouldn't do that. Finn's friends might, as a joke; Emma might—but not *Chess.*

Chess bent over Finn, reaching down to help Finn up.

"Are you all right?" Chess asked, loudly, as if he wanted Natalie to hear. Then, as he tugged Finn upright again, Chess added in a whisper, "That's not her. Maybe we'll have to pretend that we think it is. But don't tell her any—"

Chess broke off, probably because Natalie—or Not-Natalie?—rushed toward them, calling, "Finn? Are you hurt?"

"He's fine," Chess said, brushing off Finn's backside, as

though Finn had fallen onto a pile of dirt instead of a stretch of navy blue carpet that had just been vacuumed. Oh—Chess was stalling, his eyes begging Finn to understand.

Then Natalie/Not-Natalie was right beside them, reaching awkwardly to join Chess in helping Finn up.

But Finn didn't feel like hugging her anymore. Because one glance, close up, made him totally understand.

This girl had Natalie's pretty hair, her heart-shaped face, her friendly smile. Her *clothes*. But her eyes were all wrong. They were too cautious, too guarded, too much like Natalie's had been the day Finn first met her.

This wasn't Natalie. It was *Other*-Natalie.

"Tell me everything I missed," Other-Natalie said, still smiling. "Why'd you leave Mom's—I mean, the Judge's—office? What happened?"

"You go first," Chess said. "Tell us everything you saw."

Oh, Finn thought. *Oh oh oh.*

He crossed his arms over his chest and turned to stand shoulder to shoulder with Chess. (Though, with the height difference, it was more like shoulder to elbow.) He tried so hard to look strong. But his arms trembled, and then his bottom lip started trembling, too. This wasn't right. The Greystones and Natalie were friends. And even though this *wasn't* Natalie, she looked so much like her that it felt wrong to glare at her, to keep secrets from her.

Then Finn heard the basement door opening at the top of the stairs.

"Quick! Hide!" Chess whispered, shoving Finn down again, as he crouched low himself.

Other-Natalie froze in place.

Finn reached up for her hand.

"You, too!" he insisted. "Be safe!"

And Finn couldn't have said if he was doing that because she looked so much like Natalie, or because he knew he needed to pretend she was Natalie—or just because she was a person, and he didn't want to see anyone in danger.

But he noticed that Chess tugged on her other arm, trying just as hard as Finn to save her.

Other-Natalie barely hesitated before she dropped to the floor alongside the two boys.

"If it's someone I can send away, I'll do that," she whispered. "If I can, I'll keep *you* safe."

How was Finn supposed to know if she was still pretending, or if that was for real?

FORTY-FIVE

EMMA

When Finn started shouting about Natalie, Emma had just translated a phrase that began, "But don't go to the Morales-Mayhew house unless . . ."

"Just let me finish this sentence," Emma muttered. But Finn had already bolted from the closet before she got the words out.

Chess and Natalie are out there, she told herself. *He'll be fine. And I can go see Natalie, too, in just a minute. . . .*

She went back to substituting letters and scrawling them above her mother's writing.

The one sentence turned into a full paragraph that Emma *had* to figure out. When she finally dropped her pen, she'd written: "But don't go to the Morales-Mayhew house unless you absolutely have to. It is a place of subterfuge, intrigue, and constantly shifting alliances, and there is only one person there I trust completely. But again, I can't tell you a name because it's too much of a risk if this letter falls into the wrong hands."

So frustrating. And Mom must have thought the kids would be a lot older before they figured out this code. Emma had only the vaguest idea what "subterfuge" and "intrigue" meant.

They're bad things, right, Mom? Emma thought, as if her mother were right there, available for questions.

The secret hiding space behind the closet felt particularly silent after that. Emma listened hard, hoping to hear happy chatter—maybe even laughter—from outside, where Finn and Chess had just reunited with Natalie.

Nothing.

Oh, well, Emma thought. *I'll just go out* with *the others. Maybe Chess and Natalie will know what "subterfuge" and "intrigue" mean.*

She stood and tucked her mother's letter and the pen into her blue jeans pocket. She'd just put her hand on the paneling to slide it aside when she heard footsteps overhead. And then . . . voices.

"What do you need to tell me?"

It was Natalie. What was she doing at the top of the stairs? And why did it sound like the footsteps overhead were going down instead of up? Hadn't Natalie already been in the basement? Wasn't she with Finn and Chess?

Emma heard a long, drawn-out "Shhh . . ." and then a whispered "Wait."

The footsteps reached the bottom of the stairs and turned the corner toward the closet where Emma was hiding. Then they stopped. Someone cleared a throat.

"You have to go home. It isn't safe for you here. You don't know anything, and that puts you in constant danger."

Now Emma recognized the voice. It was the same one that had said, "Shh," and "Wait." And it belonged to the female cleaner, the same woman who'd kept Finn safe during a dangerous moment at Mom's trial. Emma's heart jumped. So Natalie had found Disguise Lady, and it sounded like she wanted to help.

But . . . by sending Natalie home?

"Then tell me what I need to know to be safe," Natalie said. Emma wanted to cheer her on—that was the perfect answer.

"No," Disguise Lady said. "There isn't enough time to tell you everything. And . . . I don't want your blood on my hands."

Blood? Emma thought.

Surely the woman was exaggerating. Surely she was only trying to scare Natalie into leaving.

Emma listened even more intently. It sounded like the closet door was opening. Instinctively, Emma backed away from the wood panel separating her hiding space from the main part of the closet. She shut off her flashlight.

A split second later, the panel slid back, and light flowed in. Emma tried to squeeze herself back, out of sight, but it was too late—the woman was already peering at Emma in surprise. Emma was glad she'd already recognized Disguise Lady's voice, because this woman looked different once again: Now she wore a dramatic orange dress, heavy makeup, and tiers of diamond necklaces. The weird red wig was gone, too; now her hair was sleek and gray, elegantly arranged.

And . . . the woman looked as surprised to see Emma as Emma was to see her.

Does she recognize me from Mom's trial? Emma wondered. *Does she know who* I *am?*

Without knowing the answer to that question, Emma

was paralyzed, unable to speak.

"Friend of yours?" Disguise Lady asked, glancing back over her shoulder at Natalie.

"What will you do if I say yes? Or no?" Natalie asked.

Would it help for Emma to reply instead? But what could Emma say?

Disguise Lady snorted.

"There's my answer," she muttered. "And here's yours—I'm sending *both* of you back where you belong."

She grabbed Natalie by the arm.

"But—" Natalie protested.

Emma saw the struggle Natalie was having.

Don't blurt out that we're here looking for our moms, Emma wanted to tell Natalie. *Not yet. Not until we know for sure that we can trust this woman . . .*

Emma glanced at Disguise Lady's hands. Was she about to show them a heart symbol, to prove she was trustworthy? Or . . . what if the woman was on their side, but just didn't have a heart symbol with her? Would Emma need to make the first move? Not that Emma had a heart symbol with her either, because Chess hadn't come back yet with a red marker and more paper.

Disguise Lady only tugged on Natalie's arm, pulling her toward the closet. Emma took a step forward, as if to help

Natalie fend off the woman. Something in her jeans pocket stabbed her leg. Emma couldn't be sure if it was the pen or her mother's folded-up, half-transcribed letter.

At least I've got paper and something to write with, Emma thought. *Could I maybe draw the heart and just say it's supposed to be red?*

"Really, I've got to go," Disguise Lady said, still pulling on Natalie. "I promise you, this is for the best. For everyone."

She stepped into the closet. Then she froze, staring over Emma's head. Her jaw dropped.

Emma turned to see where the woman was looking. It was just a blank section of wall. Emma decided she could take one risk.

"You expected to see a lever there, didn't you?" Emma asked the woman.

"I—" Disguise Lady began. "I can't . . ." She shoved Natalie forward, and the older girl crashed into Emma. "Just stay hidden," Disguise Lady said, and now it almost sounded like she was begging. "That's the only way to stay safe for now. I'll find . . . I'll find out what to do next. . . ."

Disguise Lady had her hand on the wooden panel like she was about to close it on Emma and Natalie.

"Wait!" Emma said, wedging her knee into the opening.

The panel slammed into Emma's leg, but Emma ignored the pain. With a shaking hand, she reached back into her jeans pocket and pulled out the pen and the folded-over letter. Was this the right choice?

We have to know if Disguise Lady is on our side or not, Emma thought.

"Look at this first," Emma said. "This should be red, but I don't have a marker right now, and . . ." Her hands shook, but she managed a passable imitation of Finn's crooked heart on the back of the letter, in a section without words. She held the folded-up letter out past the paneling, where there was enough light for the faint drawing to show up. "Do you understand?"

For an instant, Disguise Lady seemed to freeze again.

"I don't have my reading glasses with me," she muttered.

Then she did something terrifying: She took the letter from Emma's hand.

"I wasn't giving that to you," Emma said, reaching out to grab Mom's letter back. "I just wanted to show you—"

"What is this?" Disguise Lady said, unfolding the letter and holding it up high. Emma couldn't tell if she was trying to look at it more closely or if she was just keeping it out of Emma's reach.

"Give it back!" Emma insisted, leaping past the panel and lunging for the letter.

"What are you doing?" Natalie said, in a whisper that would have been easy for Disguise Lady to hear, too.

Natalie doesn't even know, Emma thought, in a panic. *She doesn't know that's Mom's letter; she doesn't know we can't let Disguise Lady keep it. . . .*

"I've got to get that back!" Emma shrieked, jumping toward Disguise Lady once again.

But this time the woman swung to the side. Emma's shoulders jammed between the doorway and the door. Natalie shoved the wood panel completely open and joined Emma in scrambling for the letter. Emma half expected Disguise Lady to run for the stairs, but she darted back toward the furnace instead. This meant that Emma and Natalie dodged the wrong way, giving Disguise Lady even more time to peer at the letter.

"You can't show this to people," Disguise Lady said. "Not in this house. It's too dangerous. I've got to keep you safe. . . ."

She bent down.

We've got her cornered, Emma thought. *There's nowhere for her to go. She's got to give that back. And maybe answer some questions, too.*

Emma took a step back, waiting. The woman had helped them before—surely she could be reasonable now.

But the woman touched something at the bottom of the furnace. No—she touched the *letter* to something at the bottom of the furnace, inside a little door.

When she stood up and turned around, the letter was on fire.

FORTY-SIX

CHESS

Chess sprang to his feet and started running as soon as he heard Emma shriek, “Give it back!” But a second later, he stumbled.

Finn! Is it safer to grab him, or to leave him here with Other-Natalie?

“Chess! What’s happening?” Finn moaned, blinking up at him.

That helped Chess make up his mind—he scooped up Finn and went back to running, even as he muttered in Finn’s ear, “I don’t know, but let’s go find out. Shh. We have to be sneaky. . . .”

Chess switched to darting from one hiding place to another. He crouched behind a couch, then behind a coffee table, then behind a row of chairs. . . . He reached a counter—the hiding spot closest to Emma, Natalie, and Disguise Lady—in time to see Emma swat at the woman's arm as she held a flaming torch high above Emma's head. No, it wasn't a torch. It was flaming . . . paper?

"Finn, stay here out of sight while I—" Chess began, easing Finn down to the floor.

But Other-Natalie grabbed his forearm, holding him back.

"No! It's not safe for you to be seen, either," she hissed. "Grandma can act kind of crazy when—"

"Grandma?" Chess whispered. "That's your grandma?"

Other-Natalie winced. "Never mind," she said.

Finn tugged on Chess's arm as he tried to peer around the side of the counter.

"Is that woman hurting Emma?" he asked.

Emma did sound like she was in pain.

"Stop! Don't! I mean—blow it out!" Emma screamed, leaping helplessly for the flaming paper. The woman kept it too high overhead for Emma to even come near the flames.

"What *is* that?" Other-Natalie whispered.

Only one set of papers could send Emma into such a panic, the only one set of papers they'd seen in this basement:

Mom's letter. But why hadn't Emma kept it hidden?

Why would this woman burn it?

The tips of Other-Natalie's hair tickled Chess's arm, and it was so wrong to have her, not Natalie, beside him.

"Never mind," he muttered to Other-Natalie.

Would she realize he was just quoting her?

Across the room, Emma had stopped shrieking and was now huddled over something on the floor and moaning, "No, no, no . . ."

It was the ashes of the paper that Disguise Lady—Other-Natalie's grandmother—had burned only a moment earlier.

"Is your grandmother always so cruel?" he asked Other-Natalie.

Other-Natalie didn't answer, but it almost seemed as if the woman did. Standing over Emma's wailing, the woman hissed, "I'm sure this is hard to understand, but that was the kindest thing I could have done for you right now. Now, hide before somebody else comes—someone who won't be so kind. And don't worry. I'll be back for you later. I'll do everything I can to get you out of here. I would suggest cleaning up this mess, so it doesn't alert anyone's suspicions."

She pointed back toward the closet the Greystones had hidden in before. And then, with the long skirt of her orange dress rustling around her legs, she strode back to the stairs.

Emma stayed crumpled on the floor, grabbing ashes that disintegrated at her touch. Natalie stood helplessly off to the side. As the grandmother swished past, Natalie reached out an arm, then let the arm fall uselessly to her side. She didn't do anything else as the grandmother mounted the stairs, stepped out into the hallway beyond, and shut the door behind her.

Both girls seemed to be in shock.

Chess thought maybe he was, too.

"Emma!" Finn cried, racing toward his sister's side as soon as the grandmother was out of sight. "Are you okay?"

Chess took off after him, even though he couldn't think of a thing to do for Emma. Maybe he just didn't want to be left behind with Other-Natalie.

Emma raised her head to peer up at both brothers. Tears trembled in her eyelashes.

"I messed up so bad," she said. "That woman saw Mom's letter, and what we'd translated so far. She saw the code key! And then she destroyed it. . . ."

"Did she have matches with her, because she was *planning* to burn things?" Finn asked. "Did she have a lighter?"

Trust Finn to ask a question like that. Chess turned his head and caught a glimpse of Finn's face and understood: It was almost like Finn was afraid the woman had superpowers somehow, and could set things on fire just by touching them.

She did seem about that fierce. And scary.

Emma sniffed.

"She used . . . she used the pilot light on the furnace," she muttered. Finn and Chess and Natalie all stared at her blankly, and she went on. "I guess it's a gas furnace, so there's a little flame at the bottom that's on all the time. . . ."

Emma would know something like that.

"Guys, I hate to say this, but maybe Almo . . . I mean, that woman . . . maybe she was right," Natalie said. "Maybe it is too dangerous for us here, and we should go home, while we still can. I don't know why she'd think our lever was in the closet, but . . . Maybe we can go back and figure out more from the other world, where we're safe, and then—"

Chess saw her glance toward the wall by the furnace where their lever had been before the cleaner guy had torn it off the wall, carried it into the closet hiding space, and then cut off that route back to the other world, too. Chess knew the exact moment when Natalie saw the lever was missing. Her eyes widened with panic.

"Our lever's gone," Finn said. "The—"

Chess bent down and clapped his hand over Finn's mouth because he saw Other-Natalie sidle up behind them just then.

Emma stared back and forth between Natalie and Other-Natalie.

"You're . . . you're . . . ," she stammered.

"The *real* Natalie Mayhew," Other-Natalie said scornfully. "The real one here, anyway. Oh, yes, I know about your alternate world. And I know there was supposed to be a lever for getting back and forth down here. Why's it gone? What happened to it?"

None of the Greystones answered her. Natalie looked too stunned to say anything.

"Oh, so you're *all* going to be like that," Other-Natalie muttered sarcastically. "Great."

If it had been Natalie speaking, Chess would have recognized the tone as a cover for pain—that was how she often sounded, talking to her dad. And that was how she'd sounded sometimes talking to her mom, before her mom vanished.

But this isn't *Natalie, and I can't think I understand Other-Natalie just because I understand Natalie,* Chess told himself.

"How do you know about our lever?" Finn asked.

Other-Natalie lifted a mocking eyebrow.

"If you don't tell me things, I don't tell you things," she said.

Chess could still hear the pain in her voice.

Is she . . . lonely? he wondered. *Doesn't she have lots of friends, like our Natalie does?*

But he caught the way Other-Natalie darted a glance at

Natalie, and Natalie flushed.

Did Natalie tell Other-Natalie about the lever? Does Natalie trust Other-Natalie?

Emma sniffed again, a sad punctuation to this weird conversation where more was being left unsaid than said.

"Anyway," she said. "Even if we had access to, um, any lever right now, we couldn't go back yet. Not without, you know. Getting the backpacks and, um, other things we left in the Judge's office . . ."

She means our computers, Chess thought, his heart sinking. *The only place we have Mom's letter anymore.*

"All that's gone," Natalie muttered. "When I went back with, well, *this* Natalie's parents and her horrible grandmother, everything was missing."

"Nooo," Emma gasped.

Finn patted her shoulder comfortingly. Chess reached out as if he planned to do the same, but he let his hand fall into dead air. He couldn't provide any comfort. Not now.

We all messed up, he wanted to tell Emma. *We all messed up so bad. . . .*

But Other-Natalie smiled. It was so strange how the same arrangement of features that could look so beautiful on Natalie just looked smug and annoying—frightening, even—on Other-Natalie.

"*I* know where your things are," Other-Natalie said. Was there a hint of triumph in her voice? "I moved them, because they weren't safe in Mom's office. Come on. I'll show you."

"Why should we trust you?" Emma asked, and in spite of everything, Chess felt a little surge of pride that she was brave enough to ask that question.

Other-Natalie's smile only broadened.

"Do you have any other choice?" she asked.

FORTY-SEVEN

NATALIE

"Other-Natalie's on our side," Natalie whispered to Chess as the four kids threaded their way across the basement. Or, Natalie couldn't really think of it as a basement anymore, now that it opened out into both a glass-ceilinged addition and a dark, open pit. Right now, the space seemed caught in transition, with the floor at the other end of the room partially retracted, and some of the blue-and-orange furniture partially rolled back into the walls. Natalie couldn't quite make herself see either what the room had been or what it was becoming, but she was pretty sure someone was bound to come down here soon to finish the changes.

She kept her gaze on Chess and tried harder to explain about Other-Natalie.

"Remember that scary poster in her room? The one I wanted to tear down? She ripped it to bits," Natalie said. "She—"

"If you trust her, I trust her," Chess said, with such loyalty that Natalie almost gasped.

I am right about Other-Natalie—aren't I?

Or was Chess just pretending to be so trusting, because Other-Natalie could hear him, too?

Natalie couldn't quite figure out how to see Chess right now, either.

Emma bobbed up between them.

"What *was* that poster in your room about?" she called ahead to Other-Natalie. Her voice rang out too loudly in the odd room. "Who were those other kids?"

"The children of our country's leaders," Other-Natalie said, without looking back. "The ones who will be leaders themselves. Their pictures will be on these walls in thirty years." She pointed toward elaborately framed portraits Natalie hadn't noticed before. All of them showed cold-eyed adults in stiff, regal poses. Natalie recognized no one but the Judge and the Mayor.

"What if someone like me wanted to be a leader?" Finn piped up. "Someone whose parents *haven't* been in charge?"

"That's not how it works here," Other-Natalie said, biting off the words. She reached an open, blank section of the wall. "Now, turn around. I don't want you to see how I open this door."

"What door?" Finn asked. "Please let us see! We won't tell anyone! Who would we tell?"

Natalie held her breath. How could anyone resist Finn?

Other-Natalie sagged against the wall.

"I'm . . . not used to trusting anyone," she muttered. "It's always been . . . too dangerous. . . ."

But she didn't repeat her command for them not to watch. She touched some sort of release on the nearest picture frame, and a small panel on the wall slid away, revealing a numbered keypad. Other-Natalie quickly hit a series of numbers Natalie couldn't follow, and then a door-sized opening appeared.

"Oh, *cool*," Finn raved as the wall rolled away. "It's another secret room!"

"Mostly just secret stairs, here," Other-Natalie corrected, pointing into the dim space that had opened up behind the moving wall. Only the bottom steps of yet another spiral staircase showed in the distance.

Finn rushed into the darkness and then, more hesitantly, Chess, Emma, and Natalie followed. Natalie's eyes adjusted even as Other-Natalie shut the door behind them. After the grandness of the transformed basement, everything in this space seemed bland and forgettable: white walls, dark tile floor, bare metal stairs. But the Greystones gazed around in awe.

"Natalie, does your mom's house have secret passages and stairways like this, too?" Emma asked in a whisper.

"Not as far as I know," Natalie muttered. Then she added: "And I *would* know. I'm certain my mom's house doesn't have anything like this."

"Wait—just your *mom's* house?" Other-Natalie asked. "Don't you live with your mom and dad both, like I do?" She clapped her hand over her mouth. "Your dad's not dead, is he?"

"No, only divorced," Natalie said, with an attempt at a carefree shrug.

"Oh," Other-Natalie said. She seemed to be struggling to absorb this information. "I thought your parents would be just like my parents, but . . . Isn't your mom pulling strings to make sure your dad's on a path to the presidency?"

"*Presidency?*" Finn asked, then looked proud that he'd managed to say all the syllables. "You mean, like, president?

Mr. Mayhew's not doing that! He sells—"

"I thought your dad was just running for governor, not president," Natalie interrupted, because she couldn't stand to have anyone talk about her real dad right now.

"One step at a time," Other-Natalie said, as if she were quoting someone. She rolled her eyes. "If Mom wants him to be president someday, he'll be president."

Had Other-Natalie ever seen how the Judge and the Mayor treated each other in private? Did she know how much her own parents hated each other?

I'm not going to be the one who tells her, Natalie thought.

"Now, shh," Other-Natalie said, placing a finger over her lips. "We have to be quiet once we're up the stairs."

All five of them began to climb the twisting stairs. Everything looked unfinished around them, the wall beams and floor joists completely exposed. Then, at the top, the kids crept through the narrow space carved between the walls of the rooms that had seemed so familiar to Natalie before.

Just something else about this house that seems like mine—but isn't, Natalie told herself.

Even without a blindfold on this time, Natalie still got turned around in the maze-like passageway. But when they reached a numbered keypad on the wall, she whispered a guess: "That's where you punched in the code to get into your mother's office before, right?"

"But that door's already open!" Finn pointed to the metal door right ahead of them, which was only *almost* fully closed.

Other-Natalie shrugged.

"Mom changes her codes a *lot*," she said. "She's really paranoid. I knew I'd be back soon, so I left it ajar. Now, shh. Even whispering might be too much once we're through that door."

She swung the door completely open, and they all crowded into the small space ahead. It looked no different from the secret passageway they'd been in before the keypad—except that a pile of backpacks lay in the middle of the dark floor. Emma dashed over to the computer hanging haphazardly from the top backpack and hugged it tight.

"It's here!" Emma exulted, clearly forgetting Other-Natalie's warning about the need for quiet.

Behind her, Chess and Finn snatched up their backpacks as well. Sheepishly, Natalie picked up the computer she'd borrowed from Other-Natalie's room.

"I was going to return this," she apologized, handing it to the other girl. "We weren't going to take it out of the house."

"Good thing, because you would have been caught immediately, anywhere on our grounds," Other-Natalie said grimly.

She's not joking, Natalie thought, her heart pounding. She wanted Other-Natalie to know how careful they'd been: "But we—" She broke off because suddenly there was a thud from the other side of the wall: a door slamming shut in the Judge's office. And then someone talking:

"I just confirmed it. The worst rumor of all."

This was Almost-Grandma's voice. Somehow, hearing the voice without seeing a face—or seeing some ridiculous costume or dress that Natalie's own grandmother never would have worn—made Natalie flip back to thinking once again of Real-Grandma. *Kind* Grandma. She put her hand over her mouth, as if that could hold back the pain. Or at least any audible sobs.

"Oh, you think there's a 'worst'?" This was the Judge, but without seeing her cold, cold eyes, Natalie could only picture her own mother. "Aren't all the rumors horrible?"

That was the tone Mom used when she was not just tired, but *weary*—worn out by the cruel injustices she tried to right.

But the Judge is all about being cruel, and creating injustices, not fixing them, Natalie reminded herself. *She's like . . . the mirror image of Mom. The evil version. The Judge is probably upset about something* good.

Emma clutched Natalie's arm and whispered, "Is she going to tell the Judge about *us*?"

Natalie looked around for somewhere to run, but of course there was nowhere else to go. And running would be noisy. Natalie crouched and put her arms around Emma and Finn, holding them still. She felt Chess's hand on her shoulder.

At least we're all in this together. . . .

She turned and saw Other-Natalie still standing, a clear gap between her and the other kids.

Natalie reached out and grabbed Other-Natalie's hand, too.

From the other side of the wall, Almost-Grandma let out a bitter laugh that was nothing like any sound Real-Grandma had ever made. Real-Grandma had never been bitter about anything.

"Yes, each rumor we hear is worse than the last," Almost-Grandma agreed with the Judge. "So is each truth we hunt down. But this . . . Susanna, your enemies have a woman in captivity who is said to look exactly like you. And now my sources have seen her and . . . it's true. She is your exact double."

It was all Natalie could do not to scream, "Mom! They've found Mom! She's alive!"

Emma tilted her head back and beamed at Natalie. She pointed toward the wall and mouthed what might have been the words "her enemies!" Then she pointed at Natalie and held two thumbs up.

Oh, she's saying that the Judge's enemies would be our friends? Natalie wondered. *So if the Judge's enemies have Mom, that means she's in good hands?*

She nodded at Emma but didn't return the grin. There was that word, "captivity."

Natalie leaned closer to the wall, listening more intently.

"If that's true, we don't have to guess where this woman came from," the Judge said, her bitter tone matching Almost-Grandma's. "Or what they plan to do with her. Is she cooperating?"

"Apparently she's injured," Almost-Grandma said. "Because she fought back when she was captured."

Of course, Natalie thought. Mom would have fought back. She would have fought as hard as she could to reach Natalie after the original tunnel between the worlds collapsed and all the kids made it to safety, but Mom . . . didn't. Natalie didn't like to think about it, but it was almost impossible that the police in this awful world *hadn't* caught Mom.

But wouldn't the police have been on the same side as the Judge? Wouldn't the Judge have known about Mom two weeks ago, as soon as we lost her?

Once again, Natalie was getting dizzy trying to sort out good and bad in this messed-up world. Or maybe it was just the worry over her mom that made her head spin.

"Would that woman's injuries prevent her from carrying out our enemies' plans?" the Judge asked. "Does she *want* to help them?"

"Our information is incomplete." Almost-Grandma sounded impatient, as if she hated not knowing things for sure. Grandma had been like that, too. "Either she had a head injury that's left her incapacitated or . . . she's being kept so sedated that she's not aware of anything."

Oh, Mom, Natalie thought, her heart aching all over again.

"Neither would prevent our enemies' plans," the Judge mused.

"So we kidnap this woman before our enemies can strike, right?" Almost-Grandma said, as casually as if she were talking about buying groceries.

"Exactly," the Judge said.

Natalie jerked her head back so quickly she barely managed to avoid hitting it against the wall. She tightened her grip on Finn and Emma. Chess tightened his grip on her shoulder, too. Emma began another pantomime, and though Natalie couldn't follow the wild gestures, she knew exactly what Emma was saying, because it was exactly what Natalie was already thinking:

We have to stop this.

"We will," Other-Natalie whispered. Clearly she understood Emma's charades, too. "I know what to do."

NATALIE

As soon as the kids heard the Judge and Almost-Grandma leave, Other-Natalie rushed through yet another secret door into her mother's office.

"I'll be right back—I need Mom's computer," she explained.

And then Natalie was alone with the Greystones.

"Guys," she whispered. "About Other-Natalie. She really is—"

"*I* like her," Finn said, snuggling close. "I can tell she's only pretending to be mean sometimes. Like you did when you first met us, Natalie." He giggled. "I know identical twins at school, Jamil and Ahmed, and they're not even as much alike as you and Other-Natalie!"

"I—"

But then Other-Natalie was back, holding the Judge's laptop under her arm while she typed in the code on yet another keypad, to close off the secret door into the office.

"Everything's on Mom's computer," she said, sinking to the floor alongside the other kids. "Her email, texts, transcribed audio . . . If she issues any commands from her phone to do something with your mom, we'll see it here." She flashed a confident grin. "And we can counter it."

She opened the laptop and turned it on.

Finn sniffed. "Did you stop for lunch in your mom's office?" he asked hopefully. "You smell like spaghetti now!"

Other-Natalie pressed her hands to her face. "No, I . . . It's my hands, okay? Because I touched the keypads. Mom puts . . . smelly stuff on them sometimes. To warn other people away."

Natalie gasped.

"Garlic, cilantro, and onion," she whispered. "Because I bet your dad's allergic to those things. Just like my dad is. They always make him cough."

Other-Natalie stared down at the laptop balanced on her knees, as if she didn't want to meet Natalie's gaze.

"Yes," she whispered.

"So the Judge is the only one who uses the secret passageways?" Chess asked. "And maybe your dad doesn't even know about them?"

Other-Natalie shook her head wildly.

"No, he has secret passageways, too," she said bitterly. "Just different ones." The corners of her mouth twitched up, but it didn't really seem like a smile. "The two sets of passageways only connect in a few places. Want to know what Dad smears on the keypads leading to *his* secret corridors and stairways? Cat pee."

All three of the Greystones looked stunned. Then Emma muttered, "Because your mom's allergic to cats. Whoa."

Just like my mom was allergic to the Greystones' cat, Rocket, Natalie thought. She remembered deciding that she didn't want to break the news to Other-Natalie that the Judge and the Mayor hated each other. Clearly Other-Natalie already knew.

"Your family has *two* sets of secret passageways, guarded by *smells*?" Finn began. "That's—" He clapped his hand over his mouth, as if he'd been planning to say "weird" or "crazy" and only realized at the last minute that it would be insulting. He finished weakly with ". . . different."

"What—do you have parents who get along?" Other-Natalie asked. "Is your world that perfect? No one I know has happy parents. They're always worried that one parent will inform on the other parent for criticizing the government or . . ." She shrugged. "You know. Maybe even that a kid will inform on *both* parents . . . Let me guess. Is this another case where everything is sunshine and roses in *your* perfect alternate world?"

Natalie waited for one of the Greystones to tell Other-Natalie that their father was dead, and it was the government in Other-Natalie's world that had killed him. But none of them said anything. Chess leaned his head weakly against the wall. Emma clutched her own laptop tighter. Finn squirmed a little closer to his siblings. All three of them looked as frightened as little bunnies watching a hawk swoop overhead.

Natalie felt oddly ashamed, as if the Judge and Mayor were her parents, not Other-Natalie's.

She cleared her throat. "Does anyone know the codes to both sets of secret passageways?" she asked.

Other-Natalie grinned—a real grin this time.

"Yeah," she said. "Me. I know everything about this house."

As if to prove it, she bent over the keyboard of the computer in her lap and began to type.

A second later, two words flashed on the screen: INCORRECT PASSWORD.

"Ugh," Other-Natalie muttered. "Mom did change that since yesterday."

"It's Friday, right?" Natalie said. "Try adding a three to any number in yesterday's code."

"But why?" Other-Natalie asked. "How would that—"

"Just try it," Natalie said. It was too much to explain: *Because that's what* my *mom does. It's because Grandma was born on a Friday, and her birthday was March 3—that's a three for both the month and the date. Mom has reasons for how she changes her password on any day of the week, and I know them all.*

Just thinking about it made her miss her mother. To cover for the tears pooling in her eyes, she jerked impatiently on the side of the laptop.

"Okay! Okay! I'll try it!" Other-Natalie whispered.

Her fingers moved more slowly over the keyboard this time—Natalie could tell she was adding numbers in her head as she went. But as soon as Other-Natalie pressed the last key, the forbidding message about the incorrect password vanished and the screen cleared.

"We're in!" Other-Natalie marveled, shooting a stunned look at Natalie. "I don't know how you knew that, but . . ."

"Because of my mom," Natalie explained impatiently. "Now, can we *please* find out how to save her?"

Other-Natalie whipped through her mother's email, texts, and other messaging systems so quickly Natalie could barely keep up. But then Other-Natalie put her hands down.

"Nothing yet," she reported. "We'll just have to wait and keep checking back. . . ."

"Wait?" Finn wailed. "I'm not good at waiting. Can't we look for *my* mom on there? And Joe?"

"We already searched the whole internet for Mom, remember?" Chess said gently.

"Did you search on my computer or my mother's?" Other-Natalie asked.

"Both," Natalie said. "But I only tried looking in your mom's personal folders on her computer. Are you saying her computer would have more access to the internet than yours?"

"Oh, because it doesn't have parental controls," Finn said, nodding wisely.

Other-Natalie snorted. "You think I couldn't shut those off? Nobody in this country has access to the full internet. Nobody . . . except the leaders."

Emma poked her head up from staring at her own laptop.

"You're talking deep web stuff here," she muttered. "You're saying there are secret passageways in the internet in this world, just like there are secret passageways in this house."

Natalie reached for the computer balanced on

Other-Natalie's knees. She typed "Kate Greystone," and started a search.

Instantly the screen flooded with hits, one site after another containing Kate Greystone's name. Natalie and Other-Natalie worked together, taking turns refining the search. It got to the point where Natalie had her right hand on the keyboard and Other-Natalie typed left-handedly, and they were so much in sync they could finish each other's words. Natalie hit Enter one last time.

And there it was—the information they needed most about the Greystones' mom.

"Chess, Emma, Finn—you won't believe this!" Natalie called out. "I know exactly where your mom is right now!"

FORTY-NINE

FINN

"You mean . . . she really is in prison?" Finn whispered forlornly, peering over Natalie's shoulder. He wasn't sure he'd read the word on the computer screen correctly. He leaned closer to reread the offending word, then glared at Natalie. "Why are you acting like that's good news?"

"Because now we *know*," Natalie said. "And we can start working on a plan to get her out."

"Okay . . . ," Finn said. "But what about Joe?"

"We'd have to know his last name to—" Natalie began.

"It's Deweese," Emma said, pointing to a lower entry on the screen. Finn saw the words ". . . was sentenced alongside fellow enemy of the people Joe Deweese, and both criminals were sent to the fates they deserved, which . . ." And then he squeezed his eyes shut because he couldn't stand to see such awful things written about Mom or Joe.

"They're both heroes, not enemies!" Finn complained. "Or criminals!"

Someone patted him on the back. Finn opened his eyes and looked up—it was Chess.

Finn frowned and went back to staring at the scary words on the screen.

"Is somebody going to write this down?" he asked. "Before it all disappears, like Mom's pictures did the last time?"

"He's right," Other-Natalie said. She pulled a phone from her pocket, positioned it in front of the computer screen, and took a photo.

"But you said this is the government's internet, not the regular one," Natalie protested.

"Yeah . . . but things disappear there sometimes, too," Other-Natalie said. "If the government decides they want someone to disappear, they can *really* make them vanish. Without a trace." She spread her hands wide, like a magician showing nothing left after a magic trick.

Finn shivered.

"But Mom's still alive," he said. "She didn't die. She didn't turn invisible. She's just . . . in prison."

"And we're going to rescue her," Chess said.

Finn *loved* Chess for saying that.

Other-Natalie leaned closer to the computer screen.

"So your mom's at Einber prison," she muttered. "And . . ." She scrolled down a little. "This Joe guy's at Handor? I've heard Mom and Dad talking; I'm sorry, but nobody gets out of those places."

"Mrs. Greystone and Joe will be the first," Natalie said. Which was just what Finn would have wanted to say, if he'd thought of it quickly enough.

He loved Natalie for saying this, too.

But Other-Natalie kept shaking her head.

"You don't understand," she said. "Things are so bad at Einber and Handor that the inmates, well, they *volunteer* to . . ."

"To what?" Emma asked.

"To be scapegoats," Other-Natalie said, twisting her face as if she'd smelled something disgusting all of a sudden.

"Scapegoats?" Finn repeated. "What's that? It sounds funny—I mean, goats are always funny. But the way you're acting—"

"It's not funny," Other-Natalie said. "Scapegoats stand in

cages at political events, and people yell things at them, mean things, and mock them, and . . . don't you have that in your world?"

"No," Finn said. "We don't."

Other-Natalie looked down at the floor.

"I guess . . . I guess we're just used to it here, but . . ."

"Why would anyone *volunteer* for that?" Emma asked.

"Because it's better than staying in Einber or Handor prisons?" Other-Natalie bit her lip.

Finn saw Chess dart his eyes toward Other-Natalie, then down at Finn, as if Chess didn't think the big kids should talk about this in front of him. Finn wanted to prove he could take it. Even though he wasn't sure he could.

"So it's like at Mom's trial, which your mom was in charge of. Everyone treated my mom like she was one of these skategoats—scraped goat? Scrap goats? You know what I mean," Finn said. His voice shook only a little. "People yelled mean things at her. She was handcuffed in a chair. That's almost as bad as a cage!"

"I didn't see that—Mom never lets me go watch trials with what she calls the riffraff, but . . . I guess you're right," Other-Natalie said. She bit down on her lip so hard this time that Finn was surprised her teeth didn't go straight through. "I never thought of it, but that is almost the same thing."

"That's not justice," Chess said. He seemed to be

breathing hard, as if he'd been running, not sitting still. "People are supposed to be treated as innocent until they're proven guilty. They should be allowed to defend themselves. They shouldn't be falsely accused. They should be allowed to tell the truth! They shouldn't be sent to prison and then just used as entertainment for people to mock when they aren't even guilty. When they were just trying to make your world a better place!"

Finn stared up at Chess. That was maybe the most Finn had ever heard Chess say all at once in his entire life.

"Your mom's a judge," Emma said to Other-Natalie. "Your dad's the mayor, and he's running for governor. Maybe even president someday. They're *in* the government! Can't they stop this?"

Other-Natalie wouldn't look at Emma. She let her hair fall forward over her face like Natalie used to do all the time. She seemed to be staring down at a bare spot on the floor.

"You don't understand," Other-Natalie whispered. "My parents *like* the world working this way. It helps them stay in power. My mother's the one who *started* having scapegoats at political rallies!"

Finn couldn't help himself: He pulled in a giant sniff, the kind that was supposed to hold back both snot and sobs, but never worked right. And this sniff was even more worthless than usual. In spite of his efforts, a tidal wave of tears filled his eyes, and he turned to bury his face against Chess's arm.

"Oh no," Natalie said, as fierce as ever. She slung an arm around Finn's shoulder, hugging him close. "This *is* still good news. Even with what Other-Natalie just told us. That makes this even better!"

"How—how do you figure that?" Chess asked.

One-handedly, Natalie started typing again.

"Because whoever's in charge of those two prisons is going to get an email in a few minutes from 'Judge Morales,'" she said. "And that email is going to demand that Kate Greystone and Joe Deweese be brought to the Morales-Mayhew house to be 'scapegoats' for the political fund-raiser being held here tonight," she said. "And then—"

"And then before anyone can do anything mean to them, we're going to kidnap them and take them back to our world!" Finn finished for her. He threw his arms around her shoulders, the snot, sobs, and tears forgotten. "Natalie, you're a genius!"

FIFTY

EMMA

Natalie's . . . not thinking clearly, Emma thought. *Neither is Finn.*

There were so many holes in their plan, even Emma couldn't count them all. But her brain started cataloguing them anyway.

Has Natalie forgotten our lever's gone and we don't have any way to get back to the other world? And anyway, how do Natalie and Finn think we're going to get Mom and Joe out of cages in front of five hundred people? Don't they remember how we failed just trying to get Mom out of a chair at the trial? And then there's Mom's code . . .

Emma's gaze drifted back to the laptop she still held in her own arms. While the Natalies were looking for Mom,

Ms. Morales, and Joe in the secret websites on the Judge's computer, Emma had focused on speeding ahead on her own mother's code.

I get another chance. There's got to be something here that'll help us, that'll make it so we really can rescue everybody. . . . I won't quit until I've translated it all!

But Mom's message was getting stranger and stranger. Emma had started feeling like her brain was divided, one part going forward with the decoding, the other part talking back to Mom.

Seriously, Mom? she thought, reaching the end of a particularly long phrase. *You made me decode that whole sentence about "making sustainable our very most earnest hopes and dreams and goals" when you could have just said, I don't know, "keep our hope going"? Why'd you take more than fifty letters to say what you could have said in sixteen?*

"Making sustainable our very most earnest hopes . . ."—that didn't even sound like Mom. Even if Mom thought she was writing the message for versions of Chess, Emma, and Finn who were years older—maybe even adults—this was crazy. It wasn't smart to use a lot of extra words in a code, because it created unnecessary work. And Mom was smart.

Then Emma came across the word "annihilate."

"Destroy," Mom. What's wrong with "destroy"? Why are you doing this, making me decode all these extra letters and words?

Suddenly Emma got chills. Mom *wouldn't* have done that without a reason. Mom *was* smart, and she loved Chess, Emma, and Finn, and she would have wanted this coded letter to help them, not just make them frustrated and mad.

Oh, oh, oh, oh, oh . . .

The chills ran up and down Emma's spine and turned into what felt like fireworks in her brain.

Mom had had a good reason for the weird, extra words, and Emma knew what it was. At least, she was pretty sure she knew. It had to be.

All the weird words embedded in the decoded message—"sustainable," "annihilate," maybe even "earnest," too—were a code of their own.

There were *two* secret codes embedded in this message.

At least two. Maybe even more?

And what if one of the extra codes tells us who to trust in the Morales-Mayhew house? What if this is what saves us, after all?

Emma raised her head, ready to shout out her idea to the other kids. But then she stopped herself. She'd messed up so badly before, showing the heart to Disguise Lady.

This time, she was going to figure everything out and be *sure* before she said anything.

It was all up to her.

FIFTY-ONE

CHESS

What if Other-Natalie's dad is the one Mom trusts in this house? Chess wondered.

If the Judge was the one who'd come up with the idea of mocking prisoners as "scapegoats" at political events, he knew *she* couldn't be the one to help them. And Other-Natalie's grandmother had already proved she was a horrible person.

So didn't that leave the Mayor just by process of elimination? Other-Natalie had been a little kid when Mom left the alternate world in the first place, so it wouldn't be her. And it probably wasn't a security guard or a cleaner or anyone else who just worked at the house, because with the Judge being so mean, Mom couldn't have been sure that any of them would stay in his or her job.

It was on the tip of Chess's tongue to tell Natalie, Emma, and Finn what he'd figured out and see what they thought. But what if he was wrong, and led them completely astray?

Other-Natalie's phone began ringing, and she scrambled to silence it.

"No, Dad, I do not want to talk to you right now," she muttered, muting it completely. "Leave a message."

"I could . . . ," Chess began. But he didn't say it loudly enough for the others to hear. Was he really going to volunteer to call the Mayor back, to talk to him on Other-Natalie's behalf?

He wouldn't be able to figure out over the phone whether it was safe to trust the Mayor. He needed to see the man in person. And then the Mayor would show the same heart symbol Joe had used, or maybe Chess would be brave enough to show the symbol himself. . . .

I have to be the one to try that, Chess thought. *I can't let anyone else take that risk.*

What if everything depended on Chess—and Chess was too much of a coward to do anything?

FIFTY-TWO

NATALIE

Natalie's fingers flew across the keyboard. Had the Judge sent other emails where Natalie could find names of people who arranged for prisoners to be scapegoats at political rallies? Were there even emails Natalie could use as a model for how the Judge would ask for certain prisoners?

"Just search for the term 'scapegoat,' in Mom's saved email," Other-Natalie breathed in Natalie's ear.

Natalie had already clicked the magnifying glass icon; she'd already begun typing *s-c-a . . .*

Finn hung over her shoulder, watching emails flood across the screen.

"People . . . people started *throwing* things at some of the prisoners who were scapegoats at other parties?" Finn asked, pointing toward a line in one of the emails. "Even hurting them?"

"Yeah, but look, my mom said that wasn't allowed," Other-Natalie said, reaching past Natalie to bring the whole message onto the screen.

Natalie's eyes zeroed in on one sentence in the Judge's scolding email: "When the scapegoats are hit by peach pits, apple cores, pebbles, or even more dangerous material, that limits the amount of time any of them can spend on display, and their cautionary effect is diminished." So the Judge didn't care about the prisoners being hurt; she just wanted to display them as long as possible. Natalie skimmed ahead—the Judge spent the rest of the email fretting about damage to party hosts' homes.

Evil, evil, evil woman, Natalie thought.

Finn nestled his head closer against her arm; she saw his lips moving, as if he was trying to sound out the long, bureaucratic words to himself. She was pretty sure he wouldn't make it through "cautionary" or "diminished," but she clicked out of the email anyway.

"Hey!" Other-Natalie complained. "I wasn't done showing—"

"Let me send these emails, then the computer's all

yours," Natalie mumbled.

Quickly, hoping she was too fast for Finn to follow much of anything, Natalie copied and pasted other email from the Judge's files. In minutes, she had emails ready to send to the heads of both Einber and Handor prisons.

"You'll help me with this, right?" she muttered to Other-Natalie. Her head swam with all the logistics she hadn't figured out yet—all the logistics she *couldn't* figure out, because she didn't know enough about this world. Natalie turned her head and peered straight into Other-Natalie's eye, and the feeling that she was looking into a mirror came back. Of course Other-Natalie would help. In spite of the world she lived in, Other-Natalie was a good person, just like Natalie was a good person.

In that moment, Natalie felt as certain of Other-Natalie's intentions as she was of her own.

Natalie hit Send.

"Okay," she said, tilting the laptop toward Other-Natalie. "Your turn. You scan again for anything you can find about my mom, and then let's finish arranging things for Mrs. Greystone and Joe."

"You're sure my mom and Joe will be okay?" Finn asked, his voice creaking with worry.

"Of course!" Natalie said, with more confidence than she actually felt. She held the computer with just one hand and put the other arm around Finn, pulling him close. "You've got *two* Natalie Mayhews working on this—what could go wrong?"

Just as she lifted the laptop toward Other-Natalie, she heard the little ding that meant a new email had arrived. A second ding followed quickly. Natalie lowered the laptop slightly to see the new messages. Both had identical subject lines: "Confirming prisoners slated for scapegoating display and elimination."

Wait—elimination? Panic coursed through Natalie. *Does elimination mean . . . death? If we don't manage to rescue Mrs. Greystone and Joe tonight, they won't just go back to prison? They'll be . . . killed?*

Natalie stared up accusingly at Other-Natalie—how could the other girl have left out that detail? But Other-Natalie was staring at the screen with a horrified expression that probably looked just like the one on Natalie's face.

"We've got to stop this," Natalie said, even as Other-Natalie said the same thing.

Natalie pulled the computer back toward her own lap, but at the same time she shot a glance toward Finn, hoping she could get him to look away. She couldn't bear to let him see the mess they'd almost made of things. She opened her mouth to say, "Oh, hey, don't you want to go help Emma with whatever she's working on?" or "Can you go make sure Chess is okay?"—she hadn't really decided *what* she could say.

But while Natalie was looking away and pulling down on the computer, Other-Natalie pulled the laptop up toward her. The more Other-Natalie lifted up, the harder Natalie tried to tug down.

The laptop slipped out of both of their grasps and went crashing to the floor.

FIFTY-THREE

FINN

"Did it break?" Finn asked, leaning forward with Natalie and Other-Natalie to gaze at the upside-down laptop on the floor before them.

Natalie snatched it up and turned it over. A spiderweb of cracks spread across the screen, which had gone totally black.

"I'm sure it just . . . needs a minute to reboot," she said in a wavery voice that didn't sound sure at all. She stabbed her finger at the button on the side. On, off. On, off. On.

The blank screen didn't change.

"But it didn't break until *after* you sent the emails, right?" Finn asked. "So Mom and Joe *will* be here tonight, won't they? So we can rescue them?"

"Right . . . ," Natalie said. Her tone made it sound more like she was saying, "No! We just lost your mom and Joe! We'll never be able to save them!"

Oh, because she thinks the computer is totally broken, and now she can't find her own mom to get her back, Finn realized.

He raised an arm to pat her shoulder comfortingly; he tried to decide what to say that might help. He settled on, "You didn't *mean* to break it, so nobody should get mad. And I bet the Judge has other laptops somewhere that Other-Natalie can find." He leaned close and whispered, "You've seen this house. These people are really rich. Of course they have lots of computers!"

"This . . . this was the only one that held all my mom's secret connections," Other-Natalie said. Her face, like Natalie's, was too pale. Neither of them looked like themselves right now. "It was the only one we could use to pretend to be her and send email. . . ."

"Well, then . . ." Finn really didn't know what to say to that. He swallowed hard. The walls of the tiny secret hallway seemed to squeeze closer together around him.

Suddenly Other-Natalie jumped up and pulled her phone from her back pocket again. Soundlessly, it lit up and vibrated in her hand.

"No, Mom, I don't want to talk to you, either," she

snarled, stabbing her finger at the screen.

The phone went still for only a moment before it began quivering again.

"Now it's Grandma," Other-Natalie complained, hitting the Ignore icon once more. "Leave me alone!"

"Maybe . . . maybe you should find out what they're all trying to tell you?" Chess suggested faintly.

"We don't even have a grandma," Finn said. "And our dad's dead."

Finn wouldn't have thought it was possible, but Other-Natalie's face seemed to turn even more sickly looking.

"Right," she muttered. "I'll listen to the voicemail." She tilted her head and put her phone to her ear. "Blah, blah, blah, yeah, this was nothing. Just Dad saying he's so glad I'm feeling better and I'll be able to join everyone celebrating his political achievements at the party. Now for Mom . . ." She listened again, and snorted. "Figures. Mom says it's regrettable I'm still feeling sick, but of course everyone at the party will understand why I can't be there. . . ."

"Don't they always say opposite things?" Natalie asked. "So you get caught in the middle?"

Other-Natalie lowered her phone.

"Um, not about public appearances," she said, squinting like she was totally confused. "Usually they agree on what they call 'the face we present to the public.' . . ."

The phone lit up again and began shaking in Other-Natalie's hand.

"Okay, okay!" Other-Natalie answered it. "Grandma?" She was quiet for a minute, listening. "Yeah, Mom already called to say I should stay in my room during the . . . Wait, what? But that's not . . . Grandma, explain. You can't just . . ." She dropped the phone and slumped against the wall. "She hung up on me." Now Other-Natalie looked like she might throw up. She looked like she might fall over.

"What else did she say?" Natalie demanded. "What happened?"

Other-Natalie winced. She clutched the wall.

"She said . . . there was a threat," she muttered. "Reports that . . . my parents' opponents might *attack* the party tonight."

"So they canceled it?" Finn wailed. "But that's how we were going to get Mom! That's how we were going to get Joe!"

Other-Natalie blinked. Now she looked like she was about to cry.

"They didn't cancel it," she said. "They changed the time. It starts in an hour."

FIFTY-FOUR

EMMA

“That’s not enough time!” Emma moaned.

Nobody answered. The others all looked like a bomb had gone off in their midst. Chess held on to Finn, but it was hard to tell who was propping up whom. Other-Natalie clutched her head, and . . . actually, Natalie was doing the exact same thing.

They all looked defeated.

Emma looked back at the list she’d been making of all the strange words from Mom’s coded message: *Annihilate. Sustainable. Earnest. Hope . . .*

“Hope” wasn’t actually an odd word, but Emma had

included it anyway. Because she *needed* it; she needed to remember that Mom would never have written the coded letter if she hadn't had hope that the kids could figure it out.

If Mom could hold on to hope, so could Emma.

She sprang up, stalked over to the others, and seized Other-Natalie's phone. She thrust the phone at the other girl.

"Call your grandma back," Emma demanded. "Get her to tell you everything she knows about levers and tunnels and how to get back to the other world. She wanted to get us out of here before—tell her we'll go and never come back if she lets us take Mom and Joe and, and Natalie's mom with us. If we're out of time, we'll just have to bargain. Even if it has to be with someone as mean as your grandma."

Other-Natalie recoiled as if the phone were a poisonous snake or a rabid dog.

"We can't do that," she muttered. "Not over the *phone*. Phone conversations can be intercepted. Anybody could be listening. There are always spies, always—"

"Fine," Emma said. "Then tell her you want to meet. In your room, maybe. That's safe, isn't it? You can use an excuse like, 'Hey, Grandma, come help me curl my hair for the party.' Or was she like your mom, saying you shouldn't go to the party? Then you can say, 'Grandma, I threw up again. Can I have some Gatorade and toast?'"

Gatorade and toast were what Mom gave Emma, Chess,

or Finn when they were sick. It made Emma's stomach hurt just talking about it. Or maybe it hurt because she was close to the numbered keypad by the nearest door, and the same food smells that made Finn think of spaghetti made Emma think of vomit.

Or maybe she just missed Mom.

Other-Natalie shoved Emma's hand away.

"You don't understand!" she said, suddenly frantic. "You don't know anything about this world. Or my family. We're always on display. We always have to pretend and deceive. Even when we can't be sure if anyone's watching or not. You think my room's safe? Look!"

She snatched the phone back from Emma, and began swiping her finger across the screen. Grainy security camera footage came up: the same view of Other-Natalie's bedroom closet that the kids had been able to see on the wall in the Judge's office.

"My own *mother* spies on me!" Other-Natalie complained. "I'm tapping into the footage that feeds into the security system for her office. But who knows who else can see it?"

Beside Emma, Natalie reeled back, looking aghast.

"Wait—I told you *everything* when we were in your room together," she groaned. "I knew the Greystone kids might see your closet from your mom's office, but . . . why didn't you warn me someone else could hear?"

"Well, I didn't know what you were going to say until you said it," Other-Natalie said ruefully. "And then . . . I just wanted to know. I was so sick of lies and pretending. And I'm pretty sure no one watches any part of my room but the area by that closet. But, Natalie, don't you see? When I tore that poster off my wall, that changed everything. Someone's going to see that, if they haven't already. Why do you think I've been hiding out in the secret passageways ever since? I'm in as much danger as all of you now!"

"It was just . . . a poster," Finn whispered. "It wasn't even a good picture of you."

"That poster was a symbol of the political party," Other-Natalie said. "Of our leaders. And the government. Ripping up that poster was like saying I hate the government. Nobody does that!" She gulped. "I'll call Grandma. She's not *always* mean. Maybe I can lie enough to get her to . . ."

She tapped the screen and put the phone to her ear. Emma was close enough that she could hear the recorded message that came in reply: "All phone circuits in this area are temporarily out of order. Please try your call later."

"That's weird," Other-Natalie muttered. Her thumbs sped across the screen, calling up one app after another. She groaned. "Texting doesn't work either. And I can't access the GPS trackers on Mom's and Dad's and Grandma's phones, to know where they are in the house—not that that's always accurate. . . . Oh, great. The security feed showing *my* closet does still work. . . ." Her voice turned completely bitter. "Because Mom can always spy, no matter what . . ."

Emma saw the view of Other-Natalie's closet spin across the screen again as Other-Natalie lowered the phone—as Other-Natalie gave up. But Emma also saw a flash of movement in the closet. The door was open now; it'd been shut before.

"Wait!" Emma cried, cradling her hand under Other-Natalie's and bringing the phone back to eye level. "Who's that?" A tall, shadowy figure in a dark uniform—brown, maybe?—stood just inside the closet doorway. The figure turned slightly, and Emma realized it wasn't a single person lurking in the shadows, but two. And maybe one of them was injured? Was that why the man (maybe?) in the brown uniform was carrying the woman (almost certainly) in the neon green shirt?

Neon green shirt, Emma thought. *And that woman's hair is so long and dark and streaming down. . . . Isn't that just like . . .*

Before Emma could say anything, Natalie began screaming behind her.

"Mom! That's my mom!"

And then she took off running.

FIFTY-FIVE

NATALIE

Natalie couldn't possibly run as fast as she wanted.

Mom Mom Mom Mom Mom pounded through her brain in time with her running feet. It *was* Mom she'd seen in the security footage, being carried either into or out of or just *through* Other-Natalie's closet. It had to be. Mom had been wearing her neon green workout shirt when she'd gotten trapped in this world; she'd thought she was just making a quick stop on her way to the gym on an ordinary Saturday morning. She hadn't even known the alternate world existed.

Natalie thought about how Mom's body drooped

helplessly over the brown sleeves of whoever was carrying her.

Was she injured or just sedated? Natalie wondered. *Injured or sedated?*

Either way, the sooner Natalie could get to her, the better.

The passageway light behind her clicked off a second before the one ahead of her clicked on, and in the instant of darkness, Natalie stumbled so badly she smashed her shoulder into the wall. Were the winding stairs ahead to the right or to the left? Why hadn't she made herself memorize the directions even when she was blindfolded?

"Turn here!" someone whispered behind her. And then hands shoved at her, too. Oh—Other-Natalie. Natalie saw that Chess, Emma, and Finn were running along behind her, too. Chess was even carrying all their backpacks. But she didn't slow down for any of them.

The light clicked back on, and the stairs were right ahead of her. Natalie sprinted toward them. At the top of the stairs, Other-Natalie whispered from behind her, "Now left! Right! Left! Left again!"

Natalie kept running. She reached what seemed to be a blank wall ahead of her. Other-Natalie dashed out in front of her and touched something down near the floor. The wall began to slide away. Natalie didn't even wait to see what was on the other side before she rushed forward.

Then she tripped over a pair of Nikes. She was back in Other-Natalie's closet. No—falling through the open closet door into the room.

Natalie scrambled up, taking in the entire room in one glance: the pieces of the ripped-up poster scattered across the floor, a dresser drawer left hanging open, the bed's comforter still holding a Natalie-shaped indentation on the corner.

The room was empty.

"Where is she?" Natalie moaned.

She peered into the other side of the closet; she looked under the bed. She raced around the corner to the door out to the hall, but it was still locked, just the way Natalie and Other-Natalie had left it. Or maybe it was locked again, after the man carrying Natalie's mom had run through it. . . .

Natalie whirled back around to face Other-Natalie, who was just now stepping past the jumble of shoes.

"We would have seen Mom and that guy if he went through the secret passageways, right?" Natalie asked.

"Depends on if he went through Dad's routes or Mom's," Other-Natalie said.

"Which one leads into or out of your closet?"

"Both," Other-Natalie began. "But—"

Natalie raced back to the closet and grabbed the other girl's arm.

"Then we have to go back. We have to search *all* the secret passageways. And someone should search the hall, too, just in case—"

"It won't do any good," Emma said. She was still several steps back, deep in the secret passageways. The fluorescent light from overhead made her face look sickly green.

Or maybe that wasn't from the bad lighting.

"How do you know?" Natalie asked, still gazing around wildly, as if there were some hiding place in Other-Natalie's room she'd missed. "They were just here! They couldn't have gotten far!"

"Uh, would you call the other world far?" Emma asked weakly.

"You're just guessing about that, right?" Chess asked. "We should still—"

"No, sorry," Emma said. "I'm sure." She held up Other-Natalie's phone even as she caught up with the other kids. "I kept watching the security footage of this room until it cut out."

"You could do that while running?" Finn asked, sounding awed.

Emma shrugged. "I did bash into walls a few times."

"What did you see? Where's the lever? Where's the tunnel?" Now Natalie couldn't ask questions fast enough.

"The man peeked out into this room," Emma said. "He

looked at his phone. He took a step back, and then I could see that there was another lever on the wall of the closet, and a tunnel beside it. And then he carried your mom into that tunnel. The tunnel closed—I guess from the other side—and then the lever was gone. Just like how Chess and Finn and I saw the lever disappear down in the basement closet."

Other-Natalie began feeling around on the walls inside her closet as she murmured, "There was a tunnel *here*? Can't we open it again?"

"Not without our own lever," Chess groaned. "The one the cleaner guy *stole*."

"But . . . but isn't it good that someone took Ms. Morales back to the right world?" Finn asked. He sounded so hopeful it made Natalie want to cry. "The police are looking for her *everywhere* back there. They'll catch the bad guy from this world, and they'll take her home, and . . ." His face fell. "She's probably right now wondering where we are."

"No," Emma said, her voice heavy. "The police in the other world won't find her. There isn't time."

"You don't know that," Natalie objected. "Back in our world, there could be police swarming all over Mom's house. Maybe the neighbors saw me making a scene in the yard this morning. Maybe . . ."

It was funny how Natalie now *hoped* that someone had witnessed her fury over the sign in Mom's front yard.

Emma only shook her head.

"No," she said. "I do know. Or . . . I'm pretty sure. Because I took screenshots of the security footage. In case we couldn't retrieve it later."

"That was smart," Other-Natalie said admiringly.

"Maybe, but . . . not good news," Emma said, her face turning even grimmer. She held up Other-Natalie's phone again. "I zoomed in on the view of the guy's phone when he held it out sideways. I saw the message he got."

She turned Other-Natalie's phone so the other kids could see the screen. Numbly, Natalie read the grainy, enlarged words:

PARTY MOVED UP BY SIX HOURS. GO OUT AND COME BACK AGAIN IN THE APPROVED SPOT FOR THE PARTY. MEET THERE ASAP. BRING THE WOMAN.

ALL PLANS ARE STILL A GO.

FIFTY-SIX

CHESS

"Something's still going to happen at the party," Chess moaned. "Even with the moved-up time." He waved his arms, trying to herd the other kids together, away from the secret passageway. "It's going to be dangerous. So . . . you all have to stay here. Where it's safe. I'll go down and find Ms. Morales and Mom and Joe. And . . ."

He wanted to add, *And get help from Other-Natalie's dad.* Because he couldn't do this alone. And he couldn't risk the other kids.

But Other-Natalie was already shaking her head.

"That'll never work," she said. "The way these parties

go—especially if there's been a threat of attack—the minute you show your face, you'd be arrested. Everybody knows everybody. And everybody would know you're an intruder."

"I could pretend to be . . . a waiter," Chess said. "One of those people who go around with food on a silver tray."

Even to his own ears, he sounded as young as Finn, suggesting playing dress-up.

"It's really brave that you want to do that," Other-Natalie said gently. "But all the workers are screened and vetted. They have ID cards they show to get their uniforms. They have to give their fingerprints. And that's just the start. During parties there are security cameras everywhere, and . . ."

"But *I* can go down there," Natalie said, turning to the other girl. "I can pretend to be you. That way you'll stay safe, and so will the Greystones."

Chess almost wanted to laugh. Natalie was doing the same thing as him: trying to protect everyone else.

Other-Natalie went over to her bed and began shoving the pieces of torn-up poster underneath it.

"Maybe the guy in the closet never saw this," she muttered. "And the door to the hall is locked, so nobody else saw it either. . . . Oh, why did I choose today for my grand gesture?"

She was practically shaking with fear.

That's how bad this world is, Chess thought. *If someone gets that worried about a poster . . .*

"Try calling your grandma again," Emma suggested, holding out the phone.

Other-Natalie took the phone, but she was only a few seconds into the call before she cut it off and dropped the phone to the bed.

"This never happens," she said. "I mean, I guess phone service goes down all the time for ordinary people, but not here. Not for my family or anyone like us."

"The bad guy got *his* message," Finn said.

Other-Natalie pressed her hands to her face.

"What if this is the big plot against the government that everyone's always afraid of?" she said. She darted her eyes side to side, as if seeing danger everywhere. "But I don't know who's on what side. That 'threat of attack' could mean anything. Are my parents plotting against someone? Is someone plotting against them? And, oh, both your moms could get caught in the middle. . . ."

Emma reached over and yanked down one of the backpacks Chess had been carrying, then dumped its contents onto the floor. For a moment Chess thought she was looking for her laptop but, no, she still had that clutched under her arm. She held up a round metal disk and slipped a cordless earbud under her hair.

"Hello?" she said into the metal disk. "Oh, good—*our* listening devices still work." She turned to Other-Natalie. "Do you think you could hide these in the clothes your parents and grandma are going to wear to the party, before it starts? We can each wear one of the earpieces, and then at least we'll know everything they hear."

"Just knowing stuff isn't enough," Chess said, and the hurt look Emma shot him made him regret opening his mouth. But her listening devices seemed just as childish as him imagining holding a silver tray.

We just need Finn to suggest something silly, and then . . .

Where was Finn?

Chess turned around. Finn had wandered over by Other-Natalie's desk. He'd plucked a red pen from an overflowing canister, and seemed to be drawing on a stack of white Post-it Notes.

"Here," Finn said, turning back to pass out the Post-it Notes. "Hearts for everyone."

Chess's eyes blurred so badly he could barely see what Finn handed him.

"Finn, these are great, but I messed up before," Emma said, and her tone was the most patient, kind one Chess had ever heard her use. "It's not really safe to show the heart symbol to anyone in this world. It's not a . . . heart kind of place."

Chess was blinking so hard, he couldn't tell if Emma cut her eyes over to Other-Natalie or not. He wasn't even sure how he felt about letting Other-Natalie hear about the heart symbol.

"I just wanted everyone to have one," Finn said, grinning crookedly. "It made me feel better to draw them. And, remember, we're from this world, and we're nice. And so's Other-Natalie. So couldn't this *be* a heart kind of place if people tried a little harder?"

Other-Natalie hugged Finn before anyone else had a chance to.

Everything could *work out,* Chess thought. *I'll figure out a way to get down to Other-Natalie's dad before anyone else has to be in danger. Maybe Emma's listening device idea could even help. . . .*

It seemed like Finn had energized the others, too, because Other-Natalie sprang up and said, "Natalie, we should *both* go down to that party, and stay at opposite ends, so we'll see and hear everything." And Emma rushed over to close the closet door as she muttered, "Let's make sure no one comes in and surprises us while we're sorting out our electronics and making plans. . . ."

But maybe Emma slammed the closet door too hard. An echoing thud seemed to come from below. Chess tilted his head to the side, listening, and then he scrambled over to the locked door out to the hallway and pressed his ear against the solid wood. Now he could hear an absolute roar of sound. But it wasn't from the echo of a single door hitting a wall. It was from a door downstairs being opened again and again. It was from voices and laughter, occasional booming cries or shrill shouts loud enough to stand out: "Thank you for inviting . . ." ". . . so glad to be . . ."

They'd run out of time for making plans or figuring out anything.

The party had already begun.

FIFTY-SEVEN

NATALIE

Natalie swayed a little dizzily at the top of the second-floor stairs. She and Other-Natalie had made probably the fastest change ever into party dresses and the best attempt at fancy hairstyles they could achieve in five minutes, while also working around the need for the earbuds and tiny microphones of their listening devices. But what had seemed possible in Other-Natalie's familiar room felt head-spinningly risky out here in the open, perched above the bright lights and swirling colors of the party below.

Find Grandma, Natalie told herself, taking a cautious first step down the stairs. *That's all you have to do. Find Grandma and . . .*

She'd forgotten the "Almost" again, forgotten that Other-Natalie's grandma wasn't hers. Because as Natalie kept descending into the glitter and chatter of the party below—a party that she saw as a snake pit, no matter how many tuxedos and ball gowns gleamed around her—she wanted to trick herself into imagining Real-Grandma's arms hugging her, Real-Grandma whispering as she had when Mom and Dad fought, "This isn't your problem. You're going to be okay, no matter what. . . ."

But losing Mom in this awful world *was* Natalie's problem. And it was both Natalie's problem and her fault that the Greystones' mom and Joe were going to show up at this awful party to be caged and mocked.

And . . . eliminated?

Natalie gulped. There had never been a moment in the past year when she hadn't longed for Grandma to come back—when she hadn't been certain that that would have helped. But even if she'd been alive again and here now, Natalie's grandmother couldn't have done anything.

Maybe there were all sorts of things that were comforting for little kids that didn't work anymore once you grew up a little.

Maybe thirteen was just the age when you had to start relying on yourself.

But I'm not alone. I can count on the Greystones to help as much as possible. And Other-Natalie, too.

The real question was, what was possible? Even working together, how could they save their moms and Joe and get out of this awful world together?

As she reached the bottom of the steps, she paused for a second and pretended to need the balustrade for support. She felt the two earbuds she wore in her ears shift, tugged by her hair. The right earbud was linked to a tiny wireless microphone Chess carried in his shirt pocket, and the left earbud was linked to the microphone Other-Natalie had duct-taped inside the bodice of her orange dress, just as Natalie had taped a matching one into *her* orange dress. (Natalie had been impressed that Other-Natalie had two party dresses that looked so much alike—until Other-Natalie opened a backup closet in a nearby room to reveal that she had dozens of them.) But Natalie heard nothing from either earbud, so maybe it had all been for nothing.

"Hello?" she whispered, dipping her head so nobody at the party would see and think she was talking to herself. "I'm downstairs now. Won't talk for a while except, you know. To other people."

"Got it," Other-Natalie whispered back. The two of them had decided Natalie should enter the party first and go all the way down to the basement. Or "the party headquarters," as Other-Natalie called the transformed space that now included an add-on with a soaring glass ceiling and tiers of even lower levels. Other-Natalie would wait and then come down herself but stay on the first floor until Natalie found a good lookout post below. They figured that if anyone questioned seeing the "same" girl twice, Other-Natalie would know better how to respond.

Other-Natalie would look for her mom and dad, even though she had very little hope that she could get them to tell her anything.

"We won't talk much now either." Chess's voice came out even fainter than Other-Natalie's.

But somehow just hearing his voice gave Natalie the courage to look up and peer directly out into the crowded party.

"Ooo, is that the latest hairstyle?" someone asked eagerly off to her left. "One of those fashions that's going to catch on like wildfire because *you* started it?"

If any of Natalie's friends had asked that back in the real world, both Natalie and the friend would have fallen over on the floor laughing. Natalie's hair was hideous. Because she needed to hide her earbuds—and needed her hair to match Other-Natalie's, even though Natalie's was sweaty and gross, and Other-Natalie's wasn't—the two girls had settled on a severe, pulled-back bun arrangement that they'd described to each other as "what someone from the 1700s would do . . . if she's trying to become a nun . . . and thinks it's sinful to show her ears." Had Natalie finished Other-Natalie's sentence, or had it been the other way around?

Now Natalie turned to the left, to see another teenaged girl. It wasn't the double of anyone Natalie knew in her own world, but somehow the girl's turned-up nose, chilly blue eyes, and ingratiating expression seemed familiar.

Oh yeah. From the poster in Other-Natalie's room . . .

The girl had to be secretly making fun of her. Natalie flashed her most dazzling smile and pretended to believe the girl had paid her an actual compliment.

"Thanks! I'm not sure this style will catch on, though, because you need thick hair to make it work right—it's not good on every face shape, either."

The girl recoiled and put a hand up to her head as if to hide her thin, wispy blond hair.

Natalie could imagine her real grandmother spinning in her grave. She could practically hear her grandmother's voice in her head: *Never be mean to another female about her appearance. Especially if it's something she has no control over . . .*

Natalie wanted to argue with Grandma's imagined voice: *Yeah, but Grandma, you never imagined a world like this one. I'm fighting back any way I can. And I don't want this girl asking questions I can't answer, and then figuring out I don't belong here. . . .*

What was it about this world that made everyone mean? Even Natalie?

Natalie sighed, and offered in a kinder voice, "Hey, want to come downstairs with me? I'm starving, and I think that's where the food is."

"You mean, into the headquarters? Sure!" the other girl said, as if delighted to be asked. And . . . as if it was a big deal. The girl leaned her head close and whispered, "Why *did* your parents change the time for this party? My mother says it shows how powerful your parents are, that they can get everyone to show up in *evening* attire on an hour's notice for a *luncheon*. . . ."

Was she making fun of Other-Natalie's parents or truly admiring them? It was hard to tell.

"Oh, you know, my parents like to keep people guessing," Natalie said, flashing another dazzling smile. This one was even more fake.

She turned her head and pretended to not quite recognize someone off in the distance: "Oh, who *is* that? Anyone you know?"

She hoped that Other-Natalie, listening from upstairs,

would understand that Natalie was really asking for background info on the girl standing beside her.

"Lana Devins," came through Natalie's left earbud. "Wants to be my best friend, but, unh-uh. I'm sure she secretly hates me. Get away from her as soon as you can."

Meanwhile, the girl—Lana—was turning her head side to side and asking, "Who?"

"Oh, never mind, just someone I thought I knew," Natalie said with a shrug. "You haven't seen my grandma anywhere, have you?"

"Who cares about *grandmas*?" Lana asked mockingly.

You are now officially dead to me, Natalie thought.

But she kept smiling as they went toward the stairs to the basement—smiling and nodding at the other partygoers and staring around every chance she got, searching for a glimpse of an elderly woman in an orange dress.

Almost-Grandma was nowhere in sight. Plenty of other women in orange dresses were—everything from pale sherbet colors to slightly brighter gingers to eye-jarring carroty sheaths. The women and girls who weren't wearing orange had navy blue dresses instead.

"Wish I'd worn green, just to see what happened," Natalie muttered.

She meant it only for Other-Natalie's and Chess's ears

through the listening device, but Lana gasped.

"Natalie!" she exclaimed, horror spreading over her face. "I know you think you're protected because your mom is Judge Morales and your dad is the mayor, but . . . don't make jokes like that! Being in the party—you know that's like, sacred!"

It took Natalie a moment to realize that Lana meant a political party. And that she was completely serious.

The orange and blue dresses—and the sparkling champagne flutes, the gleaming diamonds on women's necks and the precisely folded ties peeking out from men's tuxedo jackets—seemed more menacing than ever now. Somehow this scene felt scarier than the poorer-looking mob at Mrs. Greystone's trial, with their orange-and-navy ballcaps and windbreakers and sweatshirts.

Is it just because I know more about the evil of this world now? Natalie wondered. *Or is it because these are the people with power—without being forced to act a certain way because of some chemical in the air?*

It seemed more like these people *wanted* to be awful.

Natalie got turned around in the crush of partygoers; the crowd carried her and Lana not toward the basement stairs Natalie knew, but to an open, grand stairway leading down into the part of the basement that took up a full two stories, with the soaring glass ceiling overhead. Nothing in this part of the house looked familiar. It was too big, too showy—too scary. Soldiers stood at the top of the stairs, checking names and scanning fingerprints, but they waved Natalie through. Lana held out what looked like an engraved invitation with a shaking hand.

Perversely, Natalie found herself arguing, "She's with me. You don't need to check *her* identity."

Lana shot her such a grateful look Natalie almost admitted, *Really, I just think I might need your help figuring out how to behave down there. . . .*

They descended the stairs together. Natalie had to hold back a gasp when she took in the full transformation of the "basement." The heavy velvet curtain that had once hidden the fancier half of the room was now at the completely opposite side, blocking off everything even vaguely familiar. The whole room sparkled and glowed; all the carpet had been pulled back to reveal shimmering marble floors below. Even the heavy, twisting pillars were embedded now with lights that threw off eerie shadows.

Just look for Grandma, Natalie reminded herself.

"I'm heading down the stairs now into the first-floor section of the party," Other-Natalie said through the earbud in Natalie's left ear. Natalie nodded, even though Other-Natalie couldn't see her, of course.

Natalie heard footsteps—amazingly, the listening device worked well enough that she could hear the *tap-tap-tap* of Other-Natalie's heels on the stairs. Then the footsteps stopped.

"Um, Natalie, Chess—somebody," Other-Natalie whispered. "What exactly do Mrs. Greystone and Joe look like?"

Natalie waited for Chess to answer, but he didn't. So she turned to Lana and pointed at the gleaming gold cages centered at the front of the basement, before the velvet curtain.

"I bet I can predict what the scapegoats will look like tonight," she said, trying to sound as if she liked seeing people mocked, as if she were excited about the scapegoats arriving. "It'll be a white woman with dark hair, and a really tall, dark-skinned man."

"Your parents told you that ahead of time?" Lana gasped. "You are so lucky! Did they tell you what the scapegoats' crimes were and how long they'll be on display? Or how many things we'll be allowed to throw at them?"

"You'll see," Natalie said, trying to smile mysteriously even as her stomach dropped and she fought the urge to retch.

How horrible did people have to be to enjoy mocking other people? Even criminals?

"Oh no!" Other-Natalie whispered in Natalie's ear. "That's what I was afraid of! The prison guards just brought two people who look like that through the front door.

Something's happening! They don't usually bring in the scapegoats until later in a party, after people have had more to drink. . . . Where are you, Natalie? And—"

Natalie missed the rest of Other-Natalie's words. Because just then someone tugged on her arm—a man in a dark suit with an earpiece of his own. He had close-cropped hair, bulging muscles, and a look in his eye as though he were constantly scanning the room looking for threats.

"Yes." He spoke into his collar, even as he shoved Lana aside. "I've just located the daughter, and I'm taking her to the front of the room so she'll be with her parents for the announcement." Then he lifted his chin and spoke directly to Natalie. "Miss, come with me."

"I'm supposed to stand up front?" Automatically, Natalie recoiled. Then she tried to think of a way to explain her behavior. "You mean, close to the *scapegoats*?"

"Don't worry," the man said. "The rest of the security detail and I will protect you. So will the soldiers here tonight. And you'll be in plain sight of everyone in the room, everyone at the party. Nothing's going to happen to you."

Except I'll be in plain sight of everyone in the room. So if Other-Natalie does come downstairs, everyone will know that one of us is an impostor. . . .

Had Other-Natalie heard what the security guard said? Would she know to stay on the first floor—or, even better, to dart back up to her room or into a secret passageway?

Natalie wanted to lean down and scream into the microphone hidden in her dress, "Hide! Now!" But she couldn't do that with the guard watching her so carefully—or with everyone at the party now watching her progress up to the front of the room.

The Judge and Mayor emerged from behind the curtain at the front of the room—the curtain that now hid the furnace and the closet and everything else Natalie might have recognized. The Mayor had his arm around the Judge's shoulder; both beamed out at the crowd as if they were the happiest couple ever. It did something to Natalie's heart to see them like that, even though she knew it was only an act.

"Liars!" she wanted to yell at them. "Fakes! Deceivers!"

She wanted to yell at the crowd, too: "Nothing you see is real!"

But all she could do was let the guard keep tugging her toward the front of the room, past even more soldiers and toward Other-Natalie's parents.

The Judge and Mayor stepped up to a microphone located between the two scapegoat cages. A second later, Almost-Grandma came from behind the curtain and joined her daughter and son-in-law. The guard gave Natalie a shove, and she found herself beside the microphone, too.

Almost-Grandma's eyes widened at the sight of Natalie—was she that distressed to see her? But she draped her arm around Natalie's shoulder and steered her around to face the crowd. And the microphone.

Natalie had found Almost-Grandma, after all.

But there wasn't a single word she could say to her without everyone at the party hearing.

FIFTY-EIGHT

FINN

Finn stood in front of a keypad deep in the heart of the secret passageways. He rose on his tiptoes and sniffed.

"Are we sure this is the right one?" he asked. "It smells more like cat pee than spaghetti."

While the two Natalies went down to the party, the Greystones had grabbed all the backpacks to cover their tracks, and were now headed for the Judge's office. That way, they could watch the security camera footage and make sure the Natalies stayed safe. Other-Natalie had said about a million times, "Make sure the office is empty before you go in there." And she'd drawn them a quick map showing routes through the secret passageways, along with the keypad codes they'd need along the way.

Finn was really glad Emma and Chess were good at reading maps. The least he could do was help by using his nose. But all the secret passageways and hidden keypads seemed to smell bad.

"It's probably just because my hands stink from touching so many keypads," Chess said, reaching past Finn to punch in a string of numbers. The door clicked open.

"Everything in this house stinks now," Emma said. "Everything in this world stinks."

"You don't think anyone's using a smell again to try to change how people think and feel, do you?" Finn asked. "Like the leaders did at Mom's trial?"

Emma sniffed thoughtfully, then shook her head.

"No—that was all fake," she said. "This seems more real. And I can still *think* while I smell it. It's real cat pee, real garlic, real . . . evil."

Chess pulled a tiny microphone out of his T-shirt pocket, muttered, "We won't talk much now either," and seemed to be switching it off.

"Did you just cut off contact with the Natalies?" Emma gasped.

"I can still hear them, and I'll turn this back on when we have something important to say," Chess said, gesturing at the earbuds in both of his ears. "Natalie's in the middle of the party now, and I don't want to distract her talking about cat pee." He reached over and ruffled Finn's hair. "But it kind of helps me to think about other things besides . . ."

Besides danger, Finn thought.

He felt proud that he could still think and talk about cat pee. He could still draw hearts. But, really, that was mostly to keep *himself* from thinking about danger.

"We should be quiet anyhow now, until we're sure the Judge's office is empty," Emma whispered, pointing toward the open door before them.

Chess nodded. All three kids tiptoed back into the narrow space they'd hidden in before. The Judge's broken laptop still lay on the floor where they'd left it.

Finn picked up the laptop, because shouldn't they put it back on the Judge's desk?

Or maybe he could use it as a weapon, to swing at any bad guys who might be hiding in the Judge's office. . . .

Chess stepped up to yet another keypad and opened another door. Now the three Greystones found themselves at the back of the Judge's office closet, where Finn had seen election flyers that morning. It felt like an eternity ago.

"Shh," Chess breathed, pushing the closet door open a crack, to peer out. Then he said, a little too loudly, "What?"

Finn pushed the door farther open so he could see, too.

He could tell right away that no one was in the office. But the office was completely destroyed. The pillows of the couch were ripped and tossed all over the place, shedding their stuffing. The desk drawers were overturned and spilling out onto the floor. The desk itself, which had seemed as huge and solid as a rock before, had been split in half, and sagged all the way down to the floor.

Only the giant election signs had been left intact.

No, they're different, too, Finn realized.

On every one of them, the outer layer calling for Judge Morales's reelection had been peeled off. Now all of the enormous signs showed the Mayor's confident grin and the instructions VOTE FOR ROGER MAYHEW!

Chess fumbled for the microphone in his T-shirt pocket.

"I've got to tell the Natalies," he said.

Emma grabbed his hand and stopped him.

"It'll only scare them," she said. "They're already afraid. Let's figure out what this means, first."

"Is this how someone is fighting the evil Judge?" Chess asked dazedly. He pointed toward the row of Roger Mayhew signs. "Does this mean for sure that *he's* the good guy in the house?"

"If this is what the Judge's office looks like, what's going on in the rest of the house?" Emma asked.

"Oh no, Natalie—" Chess wailed.

Finn ran over to the broken desk. He reached under it, and . . . yes! He could still feel an angel's wing; he could still feel the button hidden in the carved wood. He gazed around for the security camera projection on the wall, but it wasn't there.

"Up," Emma said, pointing toward the ceiling.

Finn craned his neck.

Above them, he could see a scene of dozens—maybe hundreds—of people in fancy dresses and tuxedos. It made Finn dizzy that he had to look up but the camera was looking down; he could mostly just see the tops of people's heads. Everything felt topsy-turvy. But the people were laughing and talking and drinking from shimmery goblets. They stood on shiny floors under glowing chandeliers; they all looked like they believed everything was fine. No—everything was wonderful. They were having the time of their lives.

"That's the wrong scene," Chess gasped. "We need the basement, where Natalie went."

"That *is* the basement," Emma said. "Or what used to be the basement. Look."

She reached under the broken desk to guide the camera. The viewpoint flowed backward, past the party scene into shadows. A glaring light appeared—maybe because someone had swept a curtain aside? The curtain fell back into place, except for a thin crack where it didn't meet the wall completely. That left just enough light so Finn could see: Now the security camera showed the area of the basement by the furnace and the closet where Chess, Emma, and Finn had hidden. The whole area was now closed off from the rest of the room by a navy blue, floor-to-ceiling velvet curtain. Finn could still hear the hum of chatter and the clink of glasses from beyond the curtain, but he couldn't actually see the party.

"Okay, Emma, you're right," Finn said. "Now, back to the party—"

Just then someone stepped out of the basement closet: a man carrying an unconscious woman. A very *familiar* unconscious woman.

"There's the bad guy again with Ms. Morales!" Finn exclaimed. "Yay! Now we can rescue everyone and find his lever and escape! We're going home!"

FIFTY-NINE

EMMA

But I don't understand, Emma thought.

How could they rescue anyone when there was still so much they didn't know?

Beside her, Chess muttered, "We've got to tell both Natalies." He yanked the tiny microphone from his pocket, but then he dropped it to the floor. Were his hands shaking that badly?

The man in the basement laid Ms. Morales on the floor and reached back into the closet. He pulled out something that looked like a bunch of orange frills and began wrapping it around Ms. Morales.

"Is that a dress?" Emma asked. "Why would he put a dress over her exercise clothes?"

Maybe there was an unusual sound out in the party-room part of the basement that was too faint for the Greystone kids to hear. Something made the man crouched over Ms. Morales raise his head and peer toward the crack in the curtain. Now, for the first time, his face was visible.

Emma gasped. Chess froze, even as he reached for the fallen microphone.

"That's the cleaner guy who stole our lever!" Finn exploded. "Ace Two!"

Emma's brain began running a million miles a minute.

That dress . . . That cleaner returning now, *and hiding with Ms. Morales right by the party . . . Who's planning to meet them? And why? And where's our lever? Maybe someone will hide Mom and Joe behind that curtain, too. . . . How do we get to* them*?*

What if Chess was right, and Mayor Mayhew was the one they could trust? The one who might help them escape?

Emma's brain might have been racing faster than usual, but it was like a rat in a maze, running down one dead-end path after another, then constantly having to backtrack.

"I don't like that dress he's making Ms. Morales wear," Finn said. "She's not even awake!"

"No, I don't like it either," Emma agreed. Why couldn't she understand anything?

"I—" Chess began.

But before he could say another word, Finn jumped back from the desk and cried, "What?"

Emma whipped her gaze back to the scene on the ceiling. A muscular man in dark clothes stepped out from the closet behind the cleaner. The man seemed to be trying to tiptoe, but the cleaner turned his head, starting to look back. Muscle Man swung something that looked a little like a shorter, oddly shaped baseball bat. He knocked the cleaner to the side, then slid an arm around Ms. Morales's shoulders and began dragging her back toward the closet. But maybe she was more alert than she'd seemed, because suddenly she reached up and grabbed the bat, trying to yank it from the muscular man's grip.

"No, no, stop!" the muscular man whispered. "You don't understand! Don't you see—"

He glanced around frantically. Was he worried the cleaner would spring back up and attack them both? Was he afraid someone from beyond the curtain would hear them?

Emma couldn't make sense of anything. The man swinging his head around gave her the best view yet of his face, and . . . was she seeing double? The muscular man's face looked exactly like the cleaner's.

"Oh!" she squealed. "That guy's from the other world! He's . . . he's the security guard *our* Mr. Mayhew hired to watch over our house!"

From the floor, Ms. Morales struggled to get control of the bat, but the security guard jerked it away from her. No—it wasn't a bat.

"And that's our lever!" Finn cried.

A split second later, Emma heard gunfire.

SIXTY

CHESS

For a nightmarish moment, Chess thought the gunfire was from the guard shooting the cleaner or the cleaner shooting the guard—or, even worse, one of them shooting Ms. Morales. Then he saw the guard, the cleaner, and Ms. Morales all lift their heads toward the curtain, and he understood: The gunfire was on the other side of the curtain, out in the party.

And that was even more nightmarish.

"Natalie's down there!" Chess cried. He crashed past Emma and Finn and ran back into the office closet, dashing toward the secret passageway.

"Chess, wait!" Emma cried behind him. But he barely heard her.

"Come with me!" he shouted back over his shoulder. But he didn't turn around to make sure Emma and Finn followed. Or maybe it was safer for them to stay in the Judge's office?

Nowhere in this house is safe. That's why we've all got to leave. . . .

As he sped through the secret passageways—past where they'd lingered before, toward the spiral staircase down to the basement—Chess heard screams through both of the earbuds stuffed into his ears.

"Natalie?" he called urgently. "Tell me you didn't get shot. Tell me you're hiding somewhere and you're safe. . . ."

Then he remembered that his microphone was still on the floor in the Judge's office—in his panic, he'd forgotten he dropped it.

"Natalie, are you all right?" he heard one girl call to the other, but he couldn't tell which one it was. He was too rattled to remember which ear held which girl's earbud.

"Natalie? Answer!"

Left earbud, Chess thought. *Right earbud, please answer. Please, please, please, please . . .*

Then he heard a crunch through one of the earbuds—the exact sound a tiny microphone might make if it fell and someone crushed it underfoot.

He ran faster.

A new voice emerged from the agonizing screams coming through his earbud: Mayor Mayhew on a PA system commanding, "Everyone. Please remain calm. We have the gunman in custody now. Stay flat on the ground, facedown, while we search for any accomplices. . . ."

See? Chess told himself. *This Mr. Mayhew can handle even a gunman and stay calm. If he's the person in this house who can help us, he'll get us out of here safely.*

Chess reached the spiral staircase and sped down. But the route before him split, one door and keypad to the right, another set to the left.

I'll go with whichever door the Mayor's code opens, Chess decided.

It was the door to the left. Chess raced down a long, narrow passageway and turned a corner.

This isn't how we came before, is it? Chess wondered. He reached a sliding panel left half-open, and understood: *No, Natalie was leading us through her mom's passageway. This route leads to the closet Emma, Finn, and I hid in, the same closet the cleaner walked through after he stole our lever.*

Did that mean that the lever thief was connected with Mayor Mayhew?

But Other-Natalie's grandma knew about that closet and its lever, too. . . .

Chess stepped past the sliding panel. The closet door before him was open only a crack, and he peeked out. He was indeed facing the area behind the velvet curtain, not the party room where the gunfire had sounded.

And where Natalie would be . . .

Chess tried to make out the dim shapes on the floor before him. Three people were still struggling to gain control of the lever: Ms. Morales, the cleaner in the brown uniform, and the Ace Private Security guard Mr. Mayhew had hired in the other world. The security guard was whispering, "Susanna Morales, I'm here to help you! I followed this other man who trespassed at the Greystones' house—your ex-husband hired me to guard it, and—"

"Where am I?" Ms. Morales moaned.

"She doesn't need to know," the cleaner hissed. "She needs to go back to sleep." Something gleamed in his hand—a needle, maybe? Was it attached to a syringe?

"Watch out!" Chess cried.

He meant to warn Ms. Morales, but she was so groggy that the Ace Security guard reacted first. He reached out and punched the cleaner. The cleaner fell forward, his head clunking against Ms. Morales's.

Silence. Both Ms. Morales and the cleaner stopped moving.

"Oh no—I knocked them *both* out?" the guard muttered. He felt for a pulse on both Ms. Morales's neck and the cleaner's. He nodded approvingly—clearly they were both still alive. He scooped Ms. Morales's body into his arms and kicked the syringe out of the hand of the unconscious cleaner.

Between them, the lever slid to the ground as if the guard had completely forgotten it.

I've got to grab that, Chess told himself. *Before the guard sees it . . .*

But the guard was already turning back toward the closet. Did he know Chess was there? Had he heard Chess's warning?

Before Chess could decide what to do, someone stepped past the curtain blocking off the party room, and the guard whirled in that direction.

"Excellent work. You're right on time."

It was the Mayor.

Chess saw the guard's body sag with relief, even as he held on to Ms. Morales.

"Roger, you would not believe how happy I am to see you right now," the guard began babbling. "I don't have a clue what's going on, but I can tell you exactly what happened. After . . . what are all those people screaming about? Where did they come from? I thought this house was completely empty when I arrived, but—"

"You do *not* address me as 'Roger,'" Mayor Mayhew snapped. "It's 'Mayor.' Or, very soon, 'Governor.' And, always, 'sir.'"

Of course the Mayor would have to act like that. Neither he nor the guard knew they were from opposite worlds. The Mayor undoubtedly thought he was talking to a rogue cleaner guy; Ace Security undoubtedly thought he was talking to Natalie's dad. The *real* Mr. Mayhew.

If only I could know for sure that the Mayor is the trustworthy person in this house, Chess thought. *Then I could explain everything to both of them. And they could both help. . . .*

Chess wished so badly for someone older and wiser and more experienced than him to help. He fingered the crookedly drawn heart Finn had given him, which Chess had tucked into his jeans pocket like a talisman. Emma had said it wasn't safe to show a heart like this to anyone, not after what had happened with Other-Natalie's grandma. But Chess was so tired of acting cowardly, so tired of not knowing what to do.

The paper rustled in Chess's hand. The Mayor glanced up.

Only then did the Mayor's first words fully register: *Excellent work. You're right on time.* If the Mayor thought the guard was the cleaner, that meant he approved of what the cleaner had been doing; he wanted Ms. Morales unconscious. Why?

And the Mayor sounded so calm after we heard gunfire. . . . What if that doesn't mean he's just a good leader? What if it means he knew the gunfire was coming? Or . . . that he was the one who planned it?

It was too late for Chess to ask these questions. It was too late for him to have these doubts.

Because Chess wasn't hidden anymore.

The Mayor was looking right at him.

SIXTY-ONE

NATALIE, A FEW MOMENTS EARLIER, BEFORE THE GUNFIRE

Just as Natalie turned to stand with the Judge, the Mayor, and Almost-Grandma, she heard the clank of chains. Out of the corner of her eye, she saw guards shoving Mrs. Greystone and Joe into the scapegoat cages on either side of the front of the room, right by a huge velvet curtain.

Natalie had to pretend not to know them. She couldn't even turn her head and look at them directly, because if she did, she might start wailing, *I'm so sorry! I thought I was helping—I was trying to! But it's my fault you're here; it's my fault if we can't stop everything and rescue you from being eliminated. . . .*

She knew how much the Greystone kids loved their mother; she knew how much they'd risked trying to save her. How could Natalie be the person sending Mrs. Greystone to her death?

And Joe . . . Oh, Joe, you saved all of us kids the last time we were in this world, and I didn't even know your last name. . . .

The Mayor tucked an arm around Natalie's shoulders, pulling her closer to him and farther from Almost-Grandma and the Judge.

"Stand by me, sweetie—you'll guarantee me the teenage-boy vote!" he whispered.

Natalie pushed him away.

"Ugh, Dad—that's just gross!" she complained.

The Mayor wrapped his arms completely around Natalie and leaned his face even closer to her ear to warn in a more threatening tone, "No scenes."

Natalie knew the exact moment he realized she was wearing earbuds. His lips must have brushed the hard plastic. His hug turned stiff, and under the cover of gripping her head lovingly and leaning his forehead against hers, he yanked out both earbuds and slid them into his tuxedo pocket.

"We'll deal with this later," he muttered under his breath. "Earbuds at a political rally? That's so disrespectful, so . . ."

"Whatever," Natalie whispered back. Wasn't that what Other-Natalie would say?

But her heart thudded with panic, because now she couldn't hear anything from Chess, Emma, Finn, or Other-Natalie. And what was the deal with the Mayor and his weird hug? It felt like the most fake thing in this messed-up world. Almost-Grandma's hug had felt real. So had the Judge's, even with all her scoldings. (Mom scolded Natalie a lot, too.)

Why was the Mayor's hug so different?

The Mayor spun her around to face the crowd again. Natalie made herself focus on plastering a fake smile on her face. Her vision blurred. Beneath the shimmering crystal peaks of the additional section, the crowd in its silks and satins seemed less like people and more like another type of carpet, spilling down across all the tiered levels below. And dotted throughout the crowd were soldiers in darker uniforms, looking grim and ready.

Natalie barely managed to hold back a shiver.

"Welcome to all of my supporters!" the Mayor crowed into the microphone. "Together, we will defeat our enemies!"

The crowd cheered so loudly that Natalie barely heard an odd crackling noise—what was that? But she saw the Judge jerk her head suddenly to the side, and then Almost-Grandma was diving toward the floor, dragging the Judge and Natalie with her.

"Get down!" Almost-Grandma screamed. "Let me . . ."

Were her last words ". . . protect you"? Natalie couldn't be sure. But she finally made sense of the sound she'd heard before: gunfire. She heard more gunshots and screams, but she didn't feel scared; she had Grandma holding her and Mom together, keeping them safe.

Almost-Grandma, Natalie reminded herself. *Other-Mom* . . . But that wasn't how it felt.

And then Mayor Mayhew's voice echoed above her: "Everyone. Please remain calm. We have the gunman in custody now. Stay flat on the ground, facedown, while we search for any accomplices. . . ."

Natalie turned her face to the side, peeking up and out. Mayor Mayhew stood at the microphone, seeming completely unharmed, completely unruffled. A line of soldiers now stood between him and the still-shrieking crowd; the soldiers faced outward and stood with their shoulders so close together that Natalie couldn't see past them.

"Mom? Grandma?" Natalie whispered, pushing back on both of them so she could lift her head. A lock of her hair swung down into her face and she brushed it away. It was so sticky. . . . Natalie pulled her hand away from her face and looked at it.

Her hand was covered in blood.

SIXTY-TWO

FINN, RIGHT AFTER THE GUNFIRE

Finn scooped up the tiny microphone Chess had dropped and took off running behind his brother. Emma raced alongside him, her backpack thudding up and down. But Finn had barely wedged himself back into the Judge's closet before Chess was out of sight, far ahead around the next corner in the secret passageway.

"Chess is really worried about Natalie," Finn whispered.

"Aren't we all?" Emma muttered back. She grabbed the hand where Finn clutched the microphone, flicked it on, and called into it: "Natalie! Other-Natalie! We're coming to help!"

Finn stuffed the device into his shirt pocket to keep it safe. He swung his arms to run faster—it was hard just keeping up with Emma, let alone catching up with Chess. He couldn't even outrun his own thoughts. He wanted to ask Emma, "Who do you think was shooting a gun? And why?" But maybe she didn't know.

Maybe Finn didn't actually want to know the answer, either.

So ask her something she does know, so I don't have to keep thinking those questions, Finn told himself.

Other questions he'd been avoiding flooded back into his mind now, too.

"Do you know what a limb nation is?" he asked.

"A *what*?" Emma asked, panting a little because she was still running. "Limbs are on trees or, like, arms and legs on people. And you know what a nation is. A country."

"Maybe I'm not saying it right," Finn said. "Maybe it's e-limb-nation?"

"You mean, elimination?" Emma asked. She slowed down, almost stopping. "That's getting rid of something. Finn, where did you see that word?"

Suddenly Finn didn't want to talk about this either. Especially not when they were both running toward gunfire.

"Never mind," Finn said. He faked a smile and tried to turn it into a joke. "It's too big a word for me. Maybe I didn't read it right. Like I told Mom the last time she helped me read—there shouldn't even *be* words longer than three syllables. I said, 'Maybe Emma and Chess want to read four-syllable words, but *I* don't!'"

"Four syllables . . . ," Emma repeated in a strange voice. "Finn, that's the key! You had the answer to Mom's second code all along! I should have asked for your help from the very beginning!"

And then, to Finn's surprise, she stopped running completely, dropped her backpack to the floor, and yanked out her computer.

"Sustainable," she muttered. "Usually. Substantially. Annihilate . . ."

"Emma, what are you doing?" Finn asked, tugging on her arm. "We've got to save Natalie! And Ms. Morales and Mom and Joe . . ."

"And this is how we're going to get enough help to do it," Emma murmured.

Finn angled his body so he could see the laptop screen—Emma was deleting shorter words from a long list and lining up other words, then highlighting the first letter of each word that remained. All of the remaining words had four syllables. It took Emma only a few minutes before she snapped the laptop shut, stuffed it back in her backpack, and grabbed Finn's arm to take off running again.

"You're done now?" Finn asked.

Emma seemed to be running faster than ever.

"It was an easy code, once you gave me the key," Emma said, huffing and puffing a little. "It said, 'Susanna Will Help in M-M House. Just Tell Her the Truth.' Finn, it's not Mayor Mayhew who's secretly on our side. It's the Judge!"

SIXTY-THREE

EMMA

Emma wanted to shout into the secret passageway ahead of her, “Chess! Don’t trust the Mayor! Wait for us so we can tell you who you can trust!”

But she didn’t know who else might be listening, who else might be hiding in the passageways. Instead, she leaned toward Finn’s shirt pocket and called, “Natalie! Other-Natalie! We can trust the Judge! Could you . . . could you pass that on to Chess? He’ll know what you mean!”

But Chess was the only Greystone wearing earbuds connected to the two Natalies’ microphones. So she had no way of knowing if they’d gotten the message.

She and Finn would just have to run as fast as they could.

They reached the secret stairs to the lower level, sped down them, then raced through an open doorway.

We're close enough behind Chess that it must have been him *who left it open, right?* Emma thought. *Not anyone we don't want to see?*

Through the walls, she could hear the crowd noise outside, the screams dwindling, replaced by a still-anxious buzz, people trying to reassure themselves: "Mayor Mayhew says we're safe. . . ." "They already captured the gunman. . . ." "The Mayor has everything under control. . . ."

It's all the Mayor? Emma thought. *Nothing about the Judge?*

She and Finn sprinted down a seemingly endless passageway, then turned a corner into another one. As they came to the next turn, she suddenly realized where they were.

"Finn! This is leading back to the basement closet!" she hissed, whipping around the corner.

"And there's Chess!" Finn whispered back.

Chess was on the other side of the wooden panel, with the closet door open. And he was facing Mayor Mayhew.

Emma had no choice.

"Chess! Don't trust him!" she called. Would Chess believe her? Would he believe her quickly enough to act?

Chess turned toward Emma. The Mayor reached into the closet and grabbed Chess by his backpack straps. It looked like he planned to pull Chess out and punch him.

"Stop!" Emma cried. Her foot struck something hard and she almost fell. Oh—it was the flashlight she'd dropped the last time she'd stood in this closet.

Emma picked up the flashlight and swung it at the Mayor.

SIXTY-FOUR

CHESS

Emma kept slamming the flashlight against the Mayor's arm, and Finn used his fists. Chess joined in by shoving the Mayor's chest.

But the Mayor only laughed.

"You're just kids!" he said, stepping back to dodge the blows. "You really think you can hurt me? *Me?*" He turned toward the Ace Security guard still clutching the unconscious Ms. Morales. "Why aren't you helping? Tie these kids up and get rid of them. Then we'll continue our plan."

Bafflement spread over the guard's face. He looked down at Ms. Morales's unconscious form, over at the cleaner knocked out on the ground, then back to the Mayor.

"But—" the guard began.

The Mayor puffed out his chest and squared his shoulders in his tuxedo jacket. He seemed calm and in control again. He put his hand on the guard's shoulder.

"Do I need to remind you who hired you?" the Mayor asked.

Why would the guard believe us over him? Chess thought, his heart sinking. Mr. Ace Security was from the better world, but he still believed that this was Natalie's dad, the man who'd hired him. And as long as the Mayor was there, the three Greystones wouldn't be able to convince the guard otherwise. They *were* just kids, and flashlights and an eight-year-old's fists were no match for a rich man in a tuxedo, who could hire anyone he wanted. He could even get people to run around with syringes and . . .

Syringes, Chess thought.

Chess stepped forward and snatched up the syringe that the guard had kicked away when the cleaner fell. It could be a weapon, too.

But instantly the Mayor grabbed it from Chess's hands.

"Give. Up," the Mayor roared. "Nobody who challenges me survives!"

He held the syringe high in the air like a trophy, like a taunt that he had power and the Greystone kids didn't.

But then he began to cough.

"Is he allergic to *syringes*?" Finn whispered.

"No, garlic and onions, which . . . were all over Chess's hands," Emma said. "Chess! Could you—"

There wasn't time for Emma to tell her idea. There wasn't time for Chess to think and ponder and agonize about what would or wouldn't work.

There was only time for the Mayor to swipe the paper with Finn's crookedly drawn heart from Chess's hands.

And Chess let him.

Wait for it, Chess told himself. *Wait* . . .

Chess was good at waiting. He waited until the Mayor lifted the paper toward his face, then Chess grabbed it back, sending a swirl of garlicky stench through the air. Chess's hands had sweated all over the paper. He hadn't meant to sweat. He didn't have any brilliant plans. But he had a little hope now.

Maybe one of the things I thought made me weak and useless can actually help. Maybe the Mayor will go into a coughing fit, and then . . .

Chess didn't have the "and then" part completely figured out, but he didn't need to. Not yet.

"We never give up!" he yelled at the Mayor.

"Neither"—*cough*—"do—I . . . ," the Mayor replied.

But then the Mayor slumped forward, coughing and

coughing and coughing.

Chess joined hands with Emma, and Emma with Finn. Chess scooped up the lever still lying on the floor, and all three of them took off running for the velvet curtain.

SIXTY-FIVE

NATALIE, A FEW MINUTES EARLIER, IMMEDIATELY AFTER THE GUNFIRE

"My girls are injured!" Mayor Mayhew wailed, peering down at Natalie, half buried under the Judge and Almost-Grandma. "*All* my girls are injured! Soldiers! Move them where they'll be safe!"

Natalie felt hands sliding under her shoulders and grabbing her ankles. Hadn't she learned in first aid in sixth grade that you *weren't* supposed to move injured people until you knew where they were hurt? She was still confused by the blood she'd felt on her face. Where had it come from? Was it hers—or Almost-Grandma's or the Judge's?

"Mom? Grandma?" she moaned as whoever was carrying her laid her down on the floor again, back by the velvet curtain. Her ears rang from all the shouts still echoing through the room, the hundreds of people in the crowd screaming in fear and confusion. She couldn't hear her mother or grandmother answer.

"Shh, shh." A woman's face hovered over Natalie, haloed by the ceiling lights. "I'm a doctor. They called us right away. You've been badly hurt. Lie still."

"You came . . . fast," Natalie said.

But she felt her face again. Nothing hurt there or anywhere else.

"You're in shock," the doctor said, gently pressing Natalie's arm down again. "But the pain's going to hit with a vengeance later on if we don't give you something to deal with it now." Someone handed the doctor a syringe, and she lifted it toward the light to tap out the air bubbles. Natalie pretended to lie still and calm and trusting, but her mind was racing.

This doctor was already here, ready and waiting, and she hasn't even looked for any wound. . . . I don't think she's really a doctor.

The doctor angled the needle toward Natalie's arm. But Natalie rolled away. She knocked the syringe out of the doctor's hand, then sprang to her feet, shouting, "Mom! Grandma! Don't let them give you anything!"

SIXTY-SIX

EMMA

Emma whipped past the curtain to come upon an odd scene. Natalie seemed to be fighting with a woman wearing scrubs and a large badge that said "Dr. Smith." Beside them, other medical personnel were bent over the Judge and Other-Natalie's grandma, both prone on the floor. The grandma, the Judge, and Natalie all seemed to have blood splattered down their orange dresses.

Even as Emma watched, the Judge rose from the floor and shoved away the nearest medical personnel.

"Don't touch me!" the Judge screamed. "Or my mother or daughter!"

"Chess, Emma, Finn—help us!" Natalie screamed.

"Wait—who are *they*?" the Judge asked, whipping her head back and forth as if ready to fight off everyone at once.

"I know you're good!" Emma shouted at her. "I know, because my mom—"

She couldn't say everything out loud, because the medical personnel were all around. And beyond them, Emma got a quick glimpse of chandeliers, uniformed soldiers, a glittering glass ceiling—and partygoers in tuxedoes and ball gowns cowering on what looked like a marble floor. Emma had to settle for hissing at Chess, "Finn and me, we solved the rest of Mom's code, and it's the Judge. . . . You have to trust me on this. . . ."

She looked back at the Judge, and the woman's face had changed somehow. Even in a torn ball gown, with blood streaked across her forehead, she looked more like the real Ms. Morales—the kind one—than she ever had before.

Emma raced to the Judge's side. The Judge made no move to fend her off. Emma reached into her pocket and touched the heart drawing Finn had given her, but she didn't pull it out. She didn't need to. Mom's second coded message had said, "Just Tell Her the Truth," so Emma stood on her tiptoes and whispered in the Judge's ear, "We're Kate Greystone's kids. We've come to rescue her and Joe."

It was such a relief to say those words, even in a whisper.

It was such a relief not to need codes or symbols, lies or pretense. It was such a relief to reveal what Emma wanted most, what had been driving her all along.

No matter what happened next, no matter what else she still didn't understand, Emma knew that truth.

Emma touched her heels to the floor again. The Judge tilted her head, considering. Then she reached into a slash in the side of her dress—a pocket?—and pulled out a single key.

"For the cages," she whispered. "And—"

"Watch out!" Natalie screamed.

The Judge threw an elbow to the side, knocking away a man in scrubs who'd been reaching for her arm and the key. He stumbled backward.

"Take my daughter with you," the Judge whispered, locking her gaze back on Emma's face. "And my mother. She . . . she's hurt. And I don't know what they're trying to give her. I think Natalie and I are fine, but—"

"Isn't there anyone here you trust?" Emma asked.

"My mother. My daughter. A handful of soldiers and guards and two or three other employees . . . ," the Judge murmured, her face a mask of sorrow. Or maybe the sorrow was real, and the change in her face that came next was the mask. She looked cruel again, and totally in control. "Jorge! Alain! Sherise! Break ranks and come to my aid!"

Emma lifted her head and saw her mother and Joe in the

two scapegoat cages. Mom was screaming, "Kids! Run! Save yourselves!"

Beyond the scapegoat cages, a line of soldiers stood in solidarity, their backs turned so they were facing the crowd—and blocking the crowd from seeing whatever the medical personnel had been doing to the Judge, Natalie, and the grandmother. Now three of the soldiers broke away and ran back toward the Judge.

"Take these 'medical personnel' away," the Judge commanded.

Emma stopped watching the soldiers. She took the key and ran to Mom's cage.

"Mom! Mom! Mom!" Emma cried.

Mom was still wearing her old familiar jeans and a sweatshirt, but the clothes only hung on her. Her face looked hollow and haunted. Her hand trembled as she reached through the bars to touch Emma's face.

"Am I dreaming?" Mom whispered. "Emma? You found me? You figured out how to set me free?"

"We're real," Emma assured her, working the key into the padlock on the cage. The door creaked open. "And we worked together. Chess, Finn, Natalie, and me. It took all four of us, and . . ."

She wanted to say, "Other-Natalie and the Judge helped, too," but maybe that wasn't safe with the soldiers so close by.

Emma couldn't stop staring at Mom's face, but she slipped the key into Chess's hand so he could unlock Joe's cage, too.

Mom stumbled out of the cage and threw her arms around Emma and Finn. Emma could have gotten lost in that hug. It could have lasted forever and that would have been fine with her. But in no time at all, the Judge was there, tugging on Mom's arm and whispering, "I only have a minute or two before I'll have to yell that you're escaping. I'll have to pretend again that you're my enemy, or someone will be arresting *me*. . . ."

"Susanna, I—" Mom began, her eyes flooding with tears. "You come, too. Where you'll be safe."

"If I stay here, I can keep you and your kids safe," the Judge whispered back. "And Mother. And Natalie."

"But not any of the citizens of this regime," Mom countered. And it wasn't quite as though she and the Judge were arguing—it was more as though they were both very sad.

But the Judge had stopped looking at Mom. She seemed not to even hear Mom's words. She had her gaze locked on one man in the line of soldiers standing over the crowd—a soldier who'd turned his head to peer back at the Judge and Mom.

"You!" the Judge screamed, making all the soldiers flinch. "Are you the traitor in our midst?"

She stormed toward the soldiers even as she held a hand

behind her back gesturing toward Emma, Mom, and Finn as if to say, *Go! Go! Go!*

Emma, Mom, and Finn all turned to run, catching up to Chess, Joe, and Natalie, who were huddled over Other-Natalie's grandma. Joe reached down and scooped her into his arms. The whole pack of them had barely made it to the velvet curtain when Emma heard the Judge scream, "Soldiers! The prisoners are escaping!"

SIXTY-SEVEN

CHESS

"I've got the lever!" Chess screamed, racing away from the soldiers and the crowd. "We just need to grab Ms. Morales, and then—" Would Ms. Morales still be lying on the floor behind the curtain? "Natalie, we tried . . . but the Mayor . . ."

There wasn't time to explain. There wasn't time to peek past the curtain and see if the Mayor had stopped coughing and would block them from getting away. Chess could only run as fast as he could away from the soldiers, toward the nearest wall. He smashed through the curtain, and the security guard from the other world was still standing there, stunned.

The cleaner, Ms. Morales, and—yes!—the Mayor were all on the floor, barely moving.

"Miss Natalie!" the guard cried, as if she were the one he needed to report to. "Your dad is having an allergic reaction. But I helped him and . . . look! We found your mom! I've been trying to call 9-1-1, but my phone won't work—"

"This is a dead zone. You have to come with us," Chess snapped as he ran past.

Behind him, he heard Natalie cry, "Mom! It's Mom! Pick her up and come along! Hurry! We're in danger!" He knew she'd make sure her mother escaped this time.

"Emma!" Chess screamed. "How far do we have to go to find a place this lever will work?"

"I don't know!" Emma screamed back. "We never figured that out! Maybe another building, maybe another room, maybe just not in the exact same spot as before . . ."

"Just two feet," Mom panted from beside Emma. "You have to hit a place on the wall that's at least the length of the lever away from the last spot anyone used . . ."

Chess hadn't even thought to ask Mom, even though she was right there with them.

"But go into that closet first, so we don't take the whole roomful of partygoers back with us . . . ," Mom gasped.

Chess dashed through the closet door and swung the lever. He must have hit a lucky spot: The lever settled into the wall as though it had always been there.

"It worked! It worked!" Finn crowed.

"Get everyone in, and then you can turn it!" Emma screamed.

Chess reached out and grabbed Mom's arm—strangely, it felt like he needed to hold her up. Finn and Emma were right behind her.

"Natalie!" Chess shouted back over his shoulder. "Joe!"

"Coming!" Natalie yelled behind him.

Shoving Mom, Emma, and Finn deeper into the closet, Chess reached back for Natalie's hand, too. But his hand only brushed dead air. He turned to look.

Natalie was right there, alongside the Ace Security guard carrying Ms. Morales, and Joe, who still held the grandmother in his arms.

But right behind them the soldiers from this world had trampled down the curtain. And behind them, an angry mob of partygoers were screaming, "Catch the traitors! Kill them all!"

SIXTY-EIGHT

NATALIE

Natalie leaned down as she ran, so she could keep an eye on the security guard carrying Mom. And she kept shouting into the microphone hidden in her dress, "Other-Natalie! We're leaving! You come, too!" She put her hand to the seam where the electronic device should be—and all she felt were shards of plastic and metal stuck in the tape. The microphone had been smashed to bits, probably when Almost-Grandma tackled her.

Then she saw the soldiers and the mob behind her.

"Joe, hurry!" she screamed, because he was the one struggling to keep up. Almost-Grandma couldn't weigh that much. But Joe seemed overcome by the burden of carrying her. He'd seemed so tall and strong before—maybe he'd shrunk? He might even be weaker than Natalie herself now.

"We'll carry her together!" Natalie yelled, cradling Almost-Grandma's torso in her arms as Joe carried her legs. Almost-Grandma's dress was blood-soaked, and she seemed barely conscious, murmuring, ". . . love . . . I always loved you, Natalie . . . But it was so hard to show when . . . we had so much evil to fight . . . and we couldn't tell you . . . truth . . ."

"I know, Grandma," Natalie murmured back. Was Almost-Grandma dying? Natalie wanted to say everything she hadn't been able to say at the end with her own grandmother. "I love you too. And . . . we're not going to let anything happen to you, not if I have any choice. . . ."

With Joe, and just behind the Ace Security guard carrying Mom, Natalie rushed toward the closet where the Greystone kids were screaming for her.

Then she felt a hand on her shoulder.

"Stop!"

It was a soldier. A big, burly soldier who could probably pick up Natalie and Almost-Grandma with just one hand. Maybe Joe, the Ace Security guard, and Mom, too. Natalie had no hope of fighting him off—especially not with dozens of other soldiers and an angry mob behind him.

Then someone slapped him. A girl's voice rang out: "Soldiers should know their place!"

Natalie twisted her gaze farther back: Other-Natalie's non-best-friend Lana was standing there pulling a hand back from the soldier's face. She put both hands on her hips. "That's *Natalie Mayhew*! You can't disrespect the daughter of Judge Morales and Mayor Mayhew like that!"

Lana winked at Natalie. And that was all the time Natalie needed to cram into the closet alongside Joe and Almost-Grandma and the security guard carrying Mom. She would have liked a moment to whisper, "Thank you"; she would have liked a chance to tell Other-Natalie that Lana might be best friend material after all. But Chess was already yanking the lever sideways.

The whole closet began to spin.

Oh, right—we're opening a new tunnel, instead of going back into one left from before. So we'll spin a lot, instead of having to run and run. . . .

Natalie couldn't tell if any of the soldiers or partygoers followed her through the door. Was that even possible while the tunnel spun? But she could see Chess, Emma, and Finn huddled with their mother through all the whirling; even as she held on to Almost-Grandma, she reached out and took Mom's hand, too.

And then the spinning stopped, and Natalie had to blink

her way back to seeing clearly again.

Her hearing must have come back too, because someone was shouting directly in her ear as she sagged out of the closet, "Natalie! Natalie! What's going on? Why are you here, instead of at school? And . . . wait—Natalie! You found your mom?"

It was Dad. She knew it was her dad, rather than Mayor Mayhew, because there was no cruelty in his gaze, only confusion—and love and relief.

And he wasn't wearing a tuxedo.

She didn't know if Mom's neighbors had called him or if it'd been the security guard. She was just glad he was there. "Chess, Emma, Finn—you found your mom, too?" Dad called.

None of the Greystones answered, but Chess scrambled up, jerked the lever to the right, then ripped it completely away from the wall. Instantly the haze around them vanished. The other world—with its soldiers, partygoers, soaring glass ceiling, marble floors, and scapegoat cages—was gone, totally sealed off from the ordinary basement of Mom's house.

For a second, Natalie's heart ached, thinking about Other-Natalie being left behind. Natalie hadn't even had a chance to say goodbye.

But Dad was still asking questions as everyone else spilled out of the closet too.

"Wait, Natalie—is that blood on your dress? And who are these people you're holding on to?"

Joe moved away and began to explain weakly, "It's a long story. . . ."

Natalie rolled to the side because she was afraid of crushing Almost-Grandma beneath her.

Dad's face turned pale, and he clearly stopped listening to Joe.

"Natalie! That woman looks so much like your grandmother. . . . And there's so much blood. . . . Just like . . . like . . ."

"Dad, I can explain everything, but we need help first," Natalie said firmly. She turned to the security guard her dad had hired. "Call 9-1-1. I'm sure it will work now."

Dazedly, the guard pulled out his phone and began hitting the numbers. He had to ease Mom down to the floor to do that. But as she slipped down, her eyelids fluttered.

"Roger?" Mom moaned. "Is that you? I never thought I'd be so happy to hear your voice again. . . ."

Dad scrambled over and gave Mom a big hug, lifting her off the floor.

"I thought you were dead!" he groaned. "I thought I'd never see you again!"

Natalie blinked again watching her parents embrace, just

as she'd watched Other-Natalie's parents embrace back in the other world. No—it wasn't like that at all. This hug was *real.* It didn't mean her parents were getting back together. It didn't mean either of them had changed enough that they would fit together as a married couple again. But this was still them caring about each other—and her. This was having Mom back; this was Natalie knowing exactly where she belonged.

She dived in to join the hug.

Finn tapped her on the shoulder.

"We did it, didn't we?" he crowed. "We rescued our moms and Joe! All the danger's over!"

Natalie saw Chess behind Finn, still clutching the lever even as he hugged Emma and his mother. She saw how pale and gaunt Mrs. Greystone looked, how nervously Joe watched the Ace Security guard and kept glancing back at the closet. She saw Almost-Grandma lying still on the carpet, still bleeding on her orange dress.

And Natalie heard Emma tell Finn the truth.

"We really did rescue our moms and Joe," Emma whispered. "And all the danger really should be over . . . for us. But only if we never go back."

EPILOGUE

FINN, EMMA, CHESS, AND NATALIE, ONE WEEK LATER

Finn clutched his mother's hand as they walked toward the hospital door.

"I didn't like it when you had to stay in the hospital and be away from us even *longer*," he complained.

"Neither did I," Mom agreed, mussing his hair. For a moment, Finn thought she was going to grab him into her arms and swing him around like she used to when he was a really little kid. For a moment, that was what Finn wanted. But *he'd* been grown-up enough to rescue *her*—he really didn't need her hugging him constantly.

"They just had to make sure Mom and Joe weren't malnourished," Chess said reassuringly. "There's no danger that the hospital will make her stay today."

"Oh, right," Finn said.

It was great how Chess could understand what Finn was afraid of even before he'd figured it out himself.

Finn grabbed Chess's hand. He noticed that Emma took Mom's hand, too, as all four of them walked together into the huge, glass-enclosed lobby of the hospital.

Emma poked her head out to call over to Chess, "Are you going to be embarrassed if Natalie sees you like this now? Holding hands with your entire family?"

"Nope," Chess said.

Mom gazed back and forth between Chess and Emma, a baffled look on her face.

"Is this something else I missed while I was away?" she asked.

"Chess might as well be a teenager now," Finn explained. "He's in *love*."

"Finn, Emma, you really shouldn't tease—" Mom began.

"It's okay," Chess said, as calm as ever. "After what we've been through, do you think a little teasing is going to bother me?"

The elevator was open when they reached it, and they all got in. Finn pushed the button for the top floor. When they stepped out a few minutes later, Mom stopped at a wide window that looked out on the entire town.

Emma was mostly just glad not to see any blue or orange banners hanging from any of the buildings off in the distance. But Mom's thoughts seemed to be elsewhere as she peered down at the city hall.

"Maybe I shouldn't have brought the three of you for this visit today," Mom murmured. "Maybe I should have just handled this on my own. . . ."

"Mom, we know what the other world's like," Chess said quietly.

"And we know Other-Natalie's grandma better than you do!" Finn argued.

"Just don't hand her any paper." Emma tried to make her words sound like a joke, but nobody laughed.

They went down the hall and turned the corner into a room that Natalie and her mom had turned into the friendliest-looking hospital room ever. Vases of flowers covered every table, and they'd added comfortable pillows and color-coordinated quilts and afghans to every chair.

And no item in the entire room was navy blue or orange.

"Kate!" Ms. Morales cried, springing up from one of the chairs to hug Mom.

"Susanna, I'm so sorry for bringing your family into this whole mess," Mom said. "I—"

"Stop," Ms. Morales said firmly. "I'm fully recovered, Roger is being nicer to me than he was even when we were supposedly happily married, and Natalie . . . well, look. It's almost like Natalie has her grandmother back again."

Natalie was curled up by Other-Natalie's grandma on the hospital bed, hugging her close.

"This girl has barely left my side the past week—she's driving me crazy," Almost-Grandma complained. But everyone could see she didn't mean it.

"And our family was already involved," Natalie said. "We just didn't know it."

Mom tilted her head and squinted, a habit Emma didn't remember her having before.

"I'm afraid I don't understand," Mom said. "You'll have to explain."

"You mean, just because everyone in your family and Other-Natalie's family were genetic doubles?" Emma asked Almost-Grandma.

"But not doubles otherwise," Finn said, with a shiver. "*Our* Natalie's dad is a nice guy, and Other-Natalie's dad was *awful.*"

Chess shot a glance toward Finn, but then he said what he was thinking, anyway.

"Did Mayor Mayhew want the Judge to die?" Chess asked.

Almost-Grandma frowned and stared down at the gauzy bandages on both her legs. She was still healing from being shot protecting the Judge and Natalie.

All the Greystone kids had already heard Natalie's description of how Almost-Grandma had seen a man with a gun out in the crowd the afternoon of the party, and then thrown herself in front of the gunshots, so she was the only one injured.

But she'd bled so much that it had looked like the Judge and Natalie were hurt, too.

The longer Almost-Grandma went without answering, the more the Greystone kids wondered if they'd ever hear her side of the story. But then she lifted her head.

"I can only tell you what my daughter and I guessed and heard," Almost-Grandma said. "I don't think the Mayor would have *minded* if my daughter died. But he mostly just wanted to take away her power, while gaining more for himself."

"That's not very nice!" Finn protested.

"I don't see how hiring someone to shoot the Judge makes the Mayor more powerful," Emma complained. "That doesn't make sense."

"It *shouldn't* make sense," Almost-Grandma agreed. "But the twisted way we thought inside that house, inside that world . . . Everyone was so busy lying and deceiving, we lost logic along with truth. My daughter and I had spies among my son-in-law's loyalists, just as he had spies who'd infiltrated our circles. We knew he'd hired a gunman, but Susanna and I thought changing the party time would foil that plan. We also knew my son-in-law had captured this world's Susanna. We believed he was going to bring her in as a double to replace his own wife. He planned to mostly keep this world's Susanna sedated, and if she asked questions, she would just seem crazy. He figured she would lose her job as a judge, she would be totally discredited. . . . After that happened, maybe he would have brought the real Judge Morales back and made her suffer through being out of power, while he had total control. Or maybe he would have kept this world's Susanna and my world's Susanna both imprisoned and miserable."

Natalie reached back and grabbed her mother's hand as though she never intended to let go.

Emma bit her lip.

"You and the Judge were always on the same side, right?" she asked. "I asked Mom why she didn't say in her letter that we could trust *both* of you, why it didn't say, 'Just Tell Susanna or *Estrella* the Truth'—Estrella's your first name, right? That would have been *so* much easier. But Mom said that answer should come from you."

Almost-Grandma winced, and Mom put her hand gently on Emma's shoulder.

"Emma, really, maybe we should talk about that some other time. . . ."

"No, Kate, the girl asks a fair question," Almost-Grandma said. "Truth is not always comfortable." Her eyes bored into Emma's. "When . . . when my world first became a tangled web of deceptions, Susanna was already a judge. And I was so proud of her, so impressed by what she'd achieved. I told her not to sacrifice herself. I told her to do whatever she had to, to stay in power and keep her status. That was what I believed eight years ago, the last time your mother saw me. She had good reason not to trust me then. It took me a while to see that I was wrong. Or to see that both Susanna and I had to work against the others in power, the ones who wanted to keep ordinary people ignorant and afraid. By then, the only way we could do that was behind the scenes, in secret."

"But you wanted the *Mayor* to become governor? Even president?" Finn asked. "Why didn't the Judge just take over by herself?"

"Because governors, presidents—they're always in the public eye," Almost-Grandma said. "Susanna needs access to those offices, to get the information she needs to force the government to change. But the way my world works, she'll never succeed if she tries to do that out in the open. She needs to be in the background, and to work privately with other people who wouldn't trust her if she were governor or president. People like . . . your mother."

Now it was Finn who grabbed his mother's hand and held on tight.

"So you and the Judge had to pretend all the time, in your world," Chess said. "But you knew Natalie and Emma didn't belong there. Why were you so mean to them? Why were you mean to *Other*-Natalie?"

Almost-Grandma peered at each of the Greystone kids, one after the other. "I've already apologized to Natalie here, but I wanted to apologize to the three of you as well. You came to my attention just as my daughter and I learned of her husband's plans, and we were desperately trying to stop him. We'd already been betrayed. There wasn't time to explain; I wasn't even sure there was time to avoid the impending disaster. I used the only tactic I knew well: fear. I thought if I kept the four of you—and my granddaughter—out of the way, and too frightened to come out of hiding, I could keep you safe until my daughter and I stymied her husband's plot." Then she grinned, almost merrily. "Little did we know we needed *you* to stop him!"

"Why didn't you have him arrested?" Finn asked. "Why didn't you just tell everyone the truth?"

"We didn't have the kind of proof that anyone else would believe," Almost-Grandma said. "And to keep our smuggling project going—"

"*Smuggling?*" Finn repeated. "Like what pirates do?"

"Better," Natalie said, beaming proudly, as if Almost-Grandma truly belonged to her.

"*We* thought so." Almost-Grandma smiled, too, but her eyes stayed sad. "With our colleagues, we'd been working to smuggle endangered people to safety in your world. We just did it under the cover of claiming to show off 'scapegoats' at political parties and then pretending to, uh, 'eliminate' them afterward. Without having them be injured by people throwing things. And we worked through cleaning crews. . . ."

Chess thought of the cleaner they'd seen slipping into Natalie's closet, and of the odd conversation between Almost-Grandma and the cleaner the kids began thinking of as Ace Two.

"Were all the cleaners on your side?" Chess asked. "Like the guy we saw you with in the basement—was he helping you? Or was he just pretending, but really working for the Mayor?"

It didn't seem possible, but Almost-Grandma's eyes took on an even more troubled sheen.

"I . . . don't know," she said, pressing a trembling hand to her face. "I thought he was trustworthy, but . . . that's the problem with so many double agents, so much deception. Who was he ultimately double-crossing? Us or the Mayor? What would he have done if his doppelgänger and you children hadn't interfered?"

"Not knowing is the *worst*," Emma agreed.

"No," Almost-Grandma said. She dropped her hand so emphatically it seemed like she was punching her own bed. "Losing faith, losing hope, seeing no way out—that's the worst. And that's what my daughter and I grappled with. . . . That's how we felt as the party began that afternoon."

For a moment, everyone was silent. Chess knew all of them could remember moments from that day when they'd felt hopeless, too. Then Finn chirped, "*We* didn't see a way out when that cleaner guy stole our lever! But he came back!"

"Yes . . ." Almost-Grandma didn't look any less troubled.

"We've pieced together what happened," Natalie said. "The cleaner guy who stole your lever took it back to your house in this world. He crossed back and forth there—because my mom was being held prisoner in the *other*-world version of your house, and he thought he could bring her in and out through our world. He didn't know that my dad had hired the Ace Security guard to watch your house here."

"Good thing our buddy Ace One followed Ace Two,"

Emma said. "And that he picked up *our* lever as evidence."

"I think that makes it sound like Ace Two was a bad guy," Finn said.

Nobody argued with him.

"But Other-Natalie and the Judge . . . they'll be okay back in their world, won't they?" Chess asked, and his voice cracked, making him sound as young as Finn.

Almost-Grandma snorted.

"It looked like the Judge had the upper hand again when we left," she said. "Once you kids incapacitated the Mayor."

"He was a lot more allergic than our Mr. Mayhew, wasn't he?" Chess asked. "I didn't know that. I wasn't trying to poison him or anything."

"Chess, *he* grabbed the paper from you—" Emma began.

"And he'd probably made his allergy worse by sneaking in and out of the Judge's office through the secret passageways so many times," Natalie said. "Almost-Grandma thinks he's the one who destroyed that office. Just to terrify the Judge."

Chess gulped. "I just wanted to stop him from overpowering us. When he said no one could stop him."

"No one human, by himself, is unstoppable," Almost-Grandma said, gazing off into the distance. "Sometimes when good people face down evil, it starts to feel like an impossibility. Or as though you yourself have to become evil, too. But that's not true."

"You're saying the Judge won!" Finn crowed.

"Not the whole war, but . . . that battle," Almost-Grandma corrected. "It was possible for her to win once she wasn't worried about me dying." She patted Natalie's leg. "And . . . once she thought her daughter was safe."

"But her real daughter isn't actually safe," Chess muttered.

"You want someone to go back for Other-Natalie, don't you?" Emma blurted.

"It's not just that," Natalie whispered. She glanced at Almost-Grandma before going on. "I didn't like to talk about it, but now you know *my* grandmother died a year ago, and we all thought it was cancer. We thought she'd ignored her own health to take care of me. But . . ."

"After hearing about the timing, and doing some research—and hearing how Natalie felt so connected to my granddaughter—well . . ." Almost-Grandma's voice trailed off.

"Tell us!" Finn begged. "No more hiding and secrets and lies!"

Almost-Grandma still took a deep breath before continuing.

"None of us believe now that Natalie's grandmother had cancer," she said. "It was agents from *my* world who killed her. They poisoned her—and then faked the autopsy—because they thought it would weaken me. They believe the connections between the worlds are that strong. The more that the evil and lies of the other world seep into this one, the more powerful our enemies become."

Mom stumbled backward. She might have fallen to the floor if Finn and Emma hadn't been holding on to her.

"It's not fair that I ever came to this world," Mom moaned. "I thought I was just protecting my children; Joe thought he was protecting his. But we brought evil with us. We opened the door to evil coming through. . . ."

"The other side found their way into this world on their own," Almost-Grandma corrected gently. "There was other meddling that looked minor but really wasn't—I also believe it was the other world's agents who made it look like this world's Morales house was going up for sale, and *they* were going to buy it. So they could have another staging area. Just like they were using your house, Kate, and moving the lever around in the basement to taunt us. . . ."

"No," Mom wailed.

"I can only conclude that our enemies were behind both of those actions," Almost-Grandma said. "But, Kate, if it hadn't been for you and Joe, they would have controlled all the levers, all the routes back and forth from the very beginning."

"We have to move," Mom gasped. "We can't stay another night in that house. . . ."

Once that news would have devastated Emma. But she didn't even care right now.

"You're saying we have to go back to the other world," Emma whispered. "You're saying it takes good to fight evil. And . . . no one in this world is safe, either, until we fix the other one."

Almost-Grandma didn't answer. But Natalie surprised everyone by springing up from the bed.

"*I'm* going back," she said. "I couldn't live with myself if I didn't. Who's with me?"

For a moment, no one spoke. Chess and his mother gritted their teeth in exactly the same way. Ms. Morales reached over to clutch Almost-Grandma's hands with both of hers. Finn sat up straighter and taller, and put his arm around Mom as though he believed he needed to comfort her.

Code, Emma thought. *This is all like a code, too. And I know exactly what it means.*

"All of us," she said, staring steadily back at Natalie. "You know we're all going. Because we're all in this together."

ACKNOWLEDGMENTS

Second books in a series are always challenging to write, so I am particularly grateful to everyone who helped me with *The Deceivers*. My editor, Katherine Tegen, kept me from getting lost in my own plot twists, and I am in awe of the support she and everyone else on the team at HarperCollins have given to Greystone Secrets. Special thanks not just to Katherine, but also to Sara Schonfeld, Kathryn Silsand, Mark Rifkin, Christina MacDonald, Allison Brown, Molly Fehr, Joel Tippie, Ann Dye, Maggie Searcy, and Aubrey Churchward. And thank you as well to Anne Lambelet for the beautiful cover and other artwork.

Several friends and relatives graciously answered some very specific and detailed questions I asked them while working on this book: My friend Dr. Andreas Schuster gave me medical information (and kindly said, "Oh, that's *possible,* even if it's not likely" when I suggested truly outlandish ideas). My friend and fellow writer Christy Esmahan and her son-in-law, Arturo Almazan, gave me advice about regionally accurate Spanish terms. And my sister and niece, Janet and Meg Terrell, helped me get into the right mind-set for thinking like the Greystone kids.

Thanks as well to the people who have helped me through many years of writing books: my agent, Tracey Adams, and my family, especially my husband, Doug. And I am always grateful for the support of the friends in my two Columbus-area writers groups: Jody Casella, Julia DeVillers, Linda Gerber, Lisa Klein, Erin McCahan, Jenny Patton, Edith Pattou, Nancy Roe Pimm, Amjed Qamar, Natalie D. Richards, and Linda Stanek.

TURN THE PAGE FOR A SNEAK PEEK OF

GREYSTONE SECRETS #3: THE MESSENGERS!

ONE

FINN

Mom inched the car into the garage. The Greystones were finally home.

But nobody moved until Mom said, "Quick. Grab whatever you need from the house, and let's get out of here."

Finn's older sister and brother, Emma and Chess, sprang out of the car and dashed for the door into the kitchen. But Finn shook his head.

"I don't need anything." He dived into the front seat of the car, grabbed Mom's hand, and held on tight. "I'll help *you*."

"Oh, Finn," Mom said. She drew up the corners of her

mouth into a shaky smile. "You can take your favorite toys. Or games. There's room. It might be a while before we come back here again. Or . . ." She looked down at Finn's hand in hers and whispered, "It might be forever."

A month ago, Mom wouldn't have said that. She would have pretended everything was fine. She *had* pretended everything was fine, actually—back then, she hadn't told Finn or Emma or even Chess how much danger she was in. She'd just left, and pretended it was an ordinary "business trip."

A month ago, she'd probably treated Finn and Emma and Chess as though they were younger than eight and ten and twelve.

Now it felt like they'd all grown up.

And *Mom* was the one *they* needed to protect.

"Toys and games?" Finn said, like those were unfamiliar words. The corners of Mom's mouth quivered. He tried again. "We're going to stay at Ms. Morales's house for now, right? She's got all the old toys and games Natalie outgrew. We could probably play forever and never get to them all." He leaned close and whispered, "They're really rich. You know?"

Mom's smile almost looked real now.

"And generous," she murmured.

"Come on," Finn said.

He reached past her to open Mom's car door. Together,

they walked into the house. Chess was coming up from the basement.

"All clear," he reported. "Emma checked upstairs and I checked downstairs. There's nobody here."

Mom put her hand over her mouth. Her already-pale face turned completely white.

"*I* should have checked," she said. "I should have left you three kids in the car until I knew for sure it was safe. . . ."

Chess might as well have had his thoughts written on his face: *Nowhere's safe.* But he patted Mom on the arm and repeated, "Nobody's here."

Chess was at that age when it seemed like he could grow three inches taller overnight. That must have happened last night, because he towered over Mom now. His arms and legs looked even spindlier and more stretched out than ever, as though his whole body were made of Silly Putty and someone had pulled it too far.

"But anybody could show up, anytime," Mom muttered. "If they've been using our house as a crossing point . . ."

She meant the bad guys. Finn, Emma, and Chess had known nothing about it until a month ago, but all four of the Greystones had escaped from a bad place when Finn was only a baby. The bad place was a completely different world—Finn had started thinking of it as almost a mirror image of the world he'd known most of his life. Duplicated versions of lots of people existed in both worlds, but they were sadder and meaner—or at least more desperate—in the other world.

Even some of the people who were actually nice in the other world had to *pretend* to be mean, just to survive.

Finn liked to think of it as though his entire family had escaped from the bad world when he was only a baby, but he knew that wasn't completely true.

His father had died in the other world. He'd been *killed*.

And could you really say that his family had escaped, when the bad people had found a way to follow them?

And when Finn, Emma, and Chess—and their friend Natalie—had had to go back to the other world again and again, and they still hadn't ended all the danger?

"We're going to fix everything," Finn said now. "We're going to make it so the bad guys never bother us again. We'll make it so they never bother anyone again! Even in the other world!"

Mom ruffled Finn's hair. She always did that. If he'd wanted to, Finn could have closed his eyes and imagined that the last month of his life hadn't happened, and he was still just a goofy little kid whose worst problems were that his hair stuck up whether anyone mussed it or not, and he had trouble remembering not to talk all the time in class.

But Finn kept his eyes open, and fixed on Mom's face.

"You're . . . so brave," she whispered. "My little Finn. Who knew?" She turned to Chess. "And you and Emma . . ."

"Mom, we really shouldn't stay here long," Chess said gently. "I just need one box from upstairs, and then I'll be ready. I don't think Emma wanted much more than that."

Mom squared her shoulders.

"Then Finn and I will get everything I need from the Boring Room," she said.

The Boring Room was what the Greystone kids had always called their mother's basement office. It had turned out not to be so boring, after all. Finn hoped neither Mom nor Chess noticed how hard he had to work to quell a shiver of fear as he started walking toward the stairs.

Halfway down the steps, Mom sniffed, made a face, and laughed.

"I guess you were all too busy rescuing me to clean Rocket's kitty litter, huh?" she asked.

"It wasn't my turn," Finn said. "Honest!"

And just for a moment, this felt normal and right, to argue over chores. But the Greystones' pet cat, Rocket, was still at Natalie's dad's house, and there was no telling when they'd be reunited.

And when Finn reached the bottom of the stairs, the first thing he saw was a pile of Hot Wheels cars. Emma had dumped them on the floor a week ago when she and Chess had received an unpleasant surprise.

We won't have any surprises today, Finn told himself. *See? This is just our normal basement rec room, and that's just Mom's normal Boring Room over there. . . .*

He trailed Mom into the Boring Room with its empty desk and vacant bookshelves. And then Finn couldn't pretend anything was normal, because the secret door to the hidden space behind the Boring Room hung wide open. Mom turned on the light and ducked through the secret doorway to peer around at the shelves holding canned food and boxes of cash. The shelves at the back of the secret room were cracked and sagging. But that was the only sign that a tunnel had once lain behind those shelves, leading into the other world.

Mom picked up a can of tuna fish and absentmindedly rolled it back and forth in her hands.

"I thought I was so well prepared," she muttered.

Finn grabbed one of the boxes.

"We should take the cash," he said, because anybody could have figured *that* out.

He opened the box—it was empty.

"The police already took it as evidence," Mom said. "Mr. Mayhew explained all about that." Mr. Mayhew was Natalie's dad. "I'll have to go down to the police station and claim it and . . . I just haven't felt up to doing that yet. You know. I may have to lie."

"Because the police don't know about the other world," Finn said. "They don't know you were trapped there. Because they *can't* know about the other world."

This made Mom snort and nearly giggle, and it was like having Normal-Mom back, Before-Everything-Happened-Mom back.

"Can you imagine telling them the truth?" she asked. "They'd never believe me!"

"Honest, Officer!" Finn said, as though she'd asked him to act it out. "You *really* don't want to meet your evil twin!"

Mom's smile faded.

"Finn . . . remember, *we're* from the other world," she murmured, still rolling the tuna can back and forth in her hands. "You can't assume one world's all good and the other's all evil. I have to believe that everyone in the other world still has the capacity to—"

She broke off as chimes pealed through the house. It was the doorbell.

"Mom?" Chess called from above. "I don't know who . . ."

Mom took off running for the stairs. Finn was right on her heels.

Then Finn heard Emma cry from even farther away: "No, Mom, I see who it is! Stay hidden!"

TWO

EMMA, A FEW MINUTES EARLIER

Emma had just picked up the book *Codes and Ciphers for Kids* when she heard a car drive by outside. Her heart thumping, she raced to her bedroom window.

A rust-colored SUV was pulling into the driveway next door.

And . . . it was just their neighbors, the Hans, bringing their son Ian home from a soccer game. He had a smear of mud across his face, and his green uniform looked sweaty.

Perfectly normal, Emma thought. *Nothing out of the ordinary.*

She was pretty sure Ian had soccer games every Saturday. Still, it took a moment for her heart rate to return to normal.

This is . . . not very scientific of me, Emma thought.

If she made a pie chart showing her entire life, she could label almost all of it "Normal" or "Ordinary." Or maybe "Happy and Fun." Maybe that was the label she really wanted. Only a tiny sliver—the past month—would need the label "Weird and Scary."

So didn't it stand to reason that most of what she saw around her now would continue to be ordinary and normal?

Oops, she thought. *I forgot about the first two years of my life, when we all lived in the other world. That was weird and scary, too. I just didn't know it.*

And, really, hadn't her entire ten years of life always had weird stuff going on in the background? She'd just *thought* everything was ordinary and normal because she didn't know about the other world or the secrets Mom had been keeping until about a month ago.

Anyhow, the labels shouldn't be "Happy and Fun" vs. "Weird and Scary," she told herself. *Those aren't opposites.*

The happiest moment of her life had been rescuing her mom from the other world. And even though she'd been worried and scared, she'd had fun figuring out the codes that Mom had left behind. On their trips to the other world, those codes had helped the Greystone kids and their friend Natalie to rescue not only Mom, but also Natalie's mom, a man named Joe Deweese, and three kids who were the closest thing this world had to doubles of Emma, Chess, and Finn. Those three—the Gustano kids—had been kidnapped by people from the other world who thought the Gustano kids belonged to Mom. The Gustanos' mom *was* this world's version of Mom, but their father wasn't like the Greystones' dad. So the kids weren't exact duplicates like their mothers were.

And the Gustanos belonged in this world, where everything was normal and ordinary and sane. While the Greystones were . . . were . . .

Caught in between?

Emma decided it was too messy to try to figure out the right description—or a pie chart of her life. She liked it better when math and science gave her clear-cut, logical answers.

She liked it when life made sense.

She looked down at the book in her hand, *Codes and Ciphers for Kids*. She'd had the idea that maybe she should take the book with her to Ms. Morales's house. Just in case there were more codes to crack as the Greystones and Natalie's family decided what to do next. But after everything Emma had been through, the book looked babyish now. Nobody was going to slip her a message written in lemon juice. Nobody was going to send her codes as easy to decipher as pig Latin.

She put the book back on her shelf. There really wasn't

anything she needed from her room. During the past month, the three Greystone kids had been living with first Natalie's mom and then Natalie's dad, so Emma already had all the clothes she wanted.

But Emma still slid open her closet door and dug past boxes of Legos and crumpled-up diagrams of inventions she might make someday. At the back of the closet, she found a little plastic safe that she'd begged for at Christmas one year. She spun the combination lock forward and back and forward again, and the door swung open.

The only things she kept inside were an old-fashioned calculator that had belonged to Mom when she was a little girl, and a piece of paper with columns of numbers scrawled from top to bottom. As far as Emma knew, the numbers were just scribblings, a scratch pad of notes. Gibberish. But her father had written those numbers. And even though Emma had been only two when he died, she could remember clutching this paper and saying to Mom, "Daddy did? Daddy did?"

And Mom would always say, "Yes, that's your father's math."

Was that the only nudge Emma needed to fall in love with math, even as a two-year-old?

Emma heard another car puttering a little too slowly

down the street. She tensed, listening hard.

Stop it! she told herself. *It's a public street. All sorts of vehicles drive by all the time. This has nothing to do with my family. Or the other world . . .*

She shoved her thick, dark, curly hair away from her face and forced herself to go back to staring at the page full of numbers. With everything else they had to worry about, wasn't it just silly and sentimental to want to take this paper with her?

Outside, the car shut off its engine. It sounded . . . close.

Emma stomped her feet with impatience, because she *couldn't* stop straining to listen to what was happening outdoors. She tried to force herself to study her shoes instead: her favorite red sneakers. Emma could remember her joy at finding these shoes on a shopping trip with Mom a few months ago. It felt like Emma had been a totally different person then—someone who had no trouble concentrating on numbers. Someone who knew nothing about other worlds or danger.

Someone who thought happiness was as simple as a pair of red shoes.

Thud. Thud. Those were definitely car doors closing outside. Emma couldn't help analyzing the sounds. Had a third or fourth door shut at the same time? Was each *thud* doubled?

Emma gave up and went back to the window.

A tan car sat in the Greystones' driveway. It wasn't one Emma recognized. But that didn't mean anything, because ever since Mom had gotten back from the other world, people kept calling and stopping by to bring them casseroles and congratulations, celebratory cards and gifts. The Greystones' friends didn't even know the whole story, but they were so relieved that everything had turned out okay and the family's long ordeal was over.

(At least, most of their friends thought the ordeal was over. Natalie's family and Joe Deweese knew better.)

Emma heard footsteps. The tan car was close to the garage, and Emma had taken too long getting to the window. So whoever had been in the car was already on the sidewalk leading to the front porch. And Emma couldn't see that sidewalk because the porch roof blocked her view. She had to yank her window open and poke her head out.

And she'd delayed a little too long doing that, too. She caught only a quick glimpse of the last person to step onto the porch.

No, it was too fast even to be called a glimpse. It was more like an impression—the *idea* of the person, not the actual view.

And still Emma recognized the person exactly: her stance, her bearing, the way she swung her arms when she walked, the way she clenched her jaw to brace herself for some unpleasant task or chore. Emma had never met this person before in her life, but she knew exactly who it was: Mom's double from this world. Mrs. Gustano.

Oh no. Oh no . . .

They'd all been so worried about dangerous people from the other world showing up again. Why hadn't any of them thought about how certain people from this world were huge threats, too?

Emma jerked her head back into the house, slammed the window shut, and took off racing for the stairs.

BOOKS BY BESTSELLING AUTHOR

MARGARET PETERSON HADDIX

GREYSTONE SECRETS SERIES

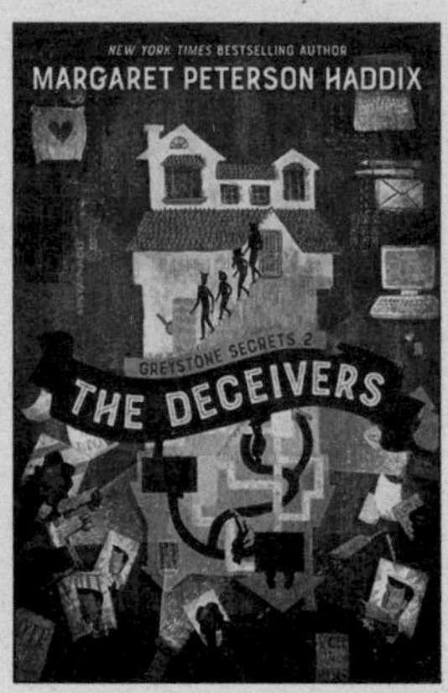

"A satisfying narrative that portrays the complex anxieties and internal lives of close, caring family members grappling with a single set of extraordinary circumstances."

—*Publishers Weekly* (starred review)

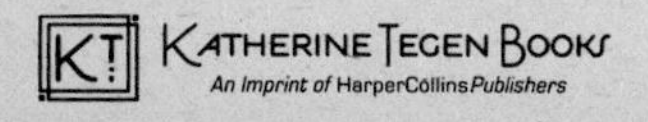

harpercollinschildrens.com